"Well?" he said, his voice low, but insistent. He put his glass on the table and turned to her.

"I don't know what you're talking about," she said.

"Kiss me, sweethcart."

He had never addressed her with such an endearment. Did he mean it? She gazed into his eyes, exposing her vulnerability. His fingers, warm, strong and masculine, worked their magic on her bare back and arms, sending tremors through her. They set her on fire wherever he touched.

She knew she was out of her league, and that he would expect more than she knew how to give. Her lips trembled when she said, "I'm not sophisticated, Brock. I only look as if I am. You...you can teach me what every woman longs to know and feel, because it's never been mine."

She tensed when he sucked in his breath, but he tightened his hold on her and whispered, "Do you want me to teach you?"

"Yes. Oh, yes. I do. I do."

Books by Gwynne Forster

Kimani Romance

Her Secret Life
One Night With You
Forbidden Temptation
Drive Me Wild
Private Lives

GWYNNE FORSTER

is a national bestselling author of twenty-three romance novels and novellas. She has also written four novels and a novella of general fiction. Gwynne has worked as a journalist, a university professor and as a senior officer for the United Nations. She holds B.A. and M.A. degrees in sociology, and an M.A. in economics/demography.

Gwynne sings in her church choir, loves to entertain at dinner parties, is a gourmet cook and an avid gardener. She enjoys jazz, opera, classical music and the blues. A devoted museum and art-gallery visitor, Gwynne lives in New York with her husband.

PRIVATE LIVES

ESSENCE BESTSELLING AUTHOR

GWYNNE FORSTER

KIMANI ROMANCE

KIMANI PRESS™

Recycling programs
for this product may
not exist in your area.

ISBN-13: 978-0-373-86104-0
ISBN-10:   0-373-86104-4

PRIVATE LIVES

www.kimanipress.com

Printed in U.S.A.

Dear Reader,

I hope you've enjoyed this short period in the lives of Allison Sawyer and Brock Lightner. A woman and a man who, having tired of misplaced affection and ill-conceived perceptions of themselves, had decided to go it alone in the belief that having no relationship was better than the kinds of relationships they had in the past. Their struggles to deal with the possibility of true love are impeded by their unwillingness to take a chance, stubbornness and fear of the unknown—until the tide of love becomes so powerful that they haven't the strength to resist it. I hope I've dealt well with these characters. I developed a particular affection for Brock, because I thought he knew how to support a woman in her endeavors without trying to make her dependent upon him—something Allison would not have tolerated.

Time was when the strong, harsh and hard hero was all the rage, but my taste is for men who have human frailties, but overcome them; who can hurt all the way to their souls and still stand strong for themselves, for their women and for their families; and who love their women above and beyond all else. I believe my hero is such a man. Let me know whether you agree.

Kimani Press is reissuing several of my early bestselling titles. *Obsession, Beyond Desire* and *Secret Desire,* all-time favorites with my readers, were the reissues for the year 2008. *Swept Away, Fools Rush In* and *Scarlet Woman* will be reissued in 2009. All of these are Kimani Arabesque titles, so keep a sharp lookout.

I love to receive mail, so don't forget to keep my mailbox full. If you send me a self-addressed and stamped legal-size envelope, I'll send you an autographed bookplate and information about my next release and my book-signing tours. You may write to me at P.O. Box 45, New York, New York 100044-0045. You can visit me online at www.gwynneforster.com.

My thanks for your continued support.

With best wishes,

Gwynne Forster

To my husband, whose strength and courage in the face of personal difficulties is admirable beyond words, and for his unswerving support and the joy, the love with which he fills my life. And to my stepson, a distinguished engineer, who always finds time to install/explain/repair his parents' computers, printers, phones and other gadgets, to brighten our lives in other ways and to travel several hundred miles in order to do it. No woman has a more loving and supportive husband and son. As always, I thank God for my talents and for the opportunities to use them.

Chapter 1

So this was it! Allison Sawyer parked in front of the rustic-looking log cabin, turned off the engine and rested her head on the steering wheel of her blue Audi.

"What's the matter, Mom?"

She put on her brightest smile and looked back at five year-old Dudley. "Everything's fine, son. Just fine." She'd come to the right place. He'd never find them there. With the help of her older sister, Ellen, she hadn't left any tracks to follow, or at least she'd hoped so. She got out, looked around and breathed deeply the Adirondack mountain air. She unlatched Dudley's car seat, and he jumped out of the car, grabbed her hand and gazed up at her with a broad smile on his face. He loved the outdoors, and woods were all around them. She felt as if she was about to burst.

After a lifetime of trying to please first her father, whom she adored, and then her much older ex-husband, now she had to please only herself.

"I don't really have any idea who I am," she said under her

breath as she unlocked the cabin door. "I guess I'm in for a surprise." She walked into the cabin, which for the foreseeable future, would be her home. She looked around. *Not bad,* she thought. It could have been far worse, and the chances of Lawrence Sawyer finding her were remote.

Alexandria, Virginia's muggy summer heat did not appeal to Brock Lightner any more than the garden parties and formal shindigs of his fancy friends and neighbors. He had no intention of trussing himself into a summer, white tuxedo like a turkey stuffed for Thanksgiving, just to escort his unattached female friends, society matrons and politicians' wives to the round of Beltway receptions and parties. When he told them that he was a private investigator, their gazes would sometimes move from his face to his crotch. He had tried to let them know that just because his occupation was sometimes dangerous, it didn't necessarily indicate sexual prowess. Now he was sick of it, and vowed that there'd be some changes made.

That morning Brock locked the back door of his Alexandria town house, got into his SUV with his German shepherd, Jack, and headed for the cabin he'd had custom-built to his specifications in the Adirondack Mountains. The one thing he hated about his mountain retreat was that he'd be without his piano for nearly a year. From now on, when he got the urge to make music, his guitar would have to suffice. As he drove, he envisioned the changes he'd make in his life. For starters, his days as a private investigator were behind him. When he returned to Alexandria, it would be to resume his career as a lawyer. For the next twelve months, though, he planned to write a memoir about his adventures as a private detective.

After the seven-hour trip, Brock arrived at Indian Lake shortly before sundown. He found his cabin just as he'd left it the previous September and settled in. At dusk, he noticed a light coming from the only other cabin within miles and decided that he'd better check it out. As far as he knew, the cabin had not been occupied for the past two years.

"Come on, boy," he said, patting Jack on his haunches. "Let's go." He jogged up the hill wondering what and who he'd find. He rubbed Jack's back, his signal that the dog should be gentle, and knocked on the door. Brock heard someone slip the door chain into place before cracking the door ever so slightly to take a look at him.

From what he could tell, the woman peering out at him was tall. He smiled at her and the door opened a tiny bit more. Shock waves coursed through him as he got a good look at her beautiful, oval-shaped brown face with its flawless skin. He'd never seen such eyes, large, light brown almond-shaped orbs beneath long black lashes. He wondered if he was seeing a mirage. The slight wrinkle that flashed across her forehead gave her a look of vulnerability. He immediately felt the urge to protect her. But why would he want to protect a woman he hadn't even gotten a good look at?

He inhaled deeply and heard himself say, "I'm your neighbor down the hill. I just arrived today and was surprised to see anyone up here. This place isn't usually occupied, so when I saw a light, I thought I'd check it out. My name's Brock Lightner."

The woman closed the door, appeared to test the strength of the security chain and opened the door a little wider than before. "Glad to meet you," she said in a soft, refined voice. This time he got a good look at the beauty before him. *Just the woman to take his mind off his work,* he thought.

It struck him that she wasn't particularly friendly, or maybe ·she was just being careful. After all, a smart woman wouldn't open her door to a strange man in such an isolated place, especially not at night. "Nice to meet you," he said. "I hope we'll be good neighbors." There was an awkward silence between them. Then he tightened his hold on Jack's leash and said, "Well, I'll be headed home."

He'd never felt anything like that before. And he knew if

she wasn't married, he'd be back there, and not just once. He sensed that she was there alone. If a man had been with her, he would have been the one to open the door, because darkness had already set in.

Allison quickly closed the door after Brock Lightner left so abruptly. His visit raised concerns, but they revolved around her fear that he was someone her ex-husband had hired to follow her. She had remained in Washington, D.C., after the divorce, but avoiding her rich and powerful ex-husband had been a full-time job. After living for short periods of time in North Carolina, Louisiana, Tennessee and Nevada to throw him off her trail, she decided to settle in this remote cabin near Indian Lake, off Route 28 in the Adirondack Mountains.

Allison's marriage to Lawrence Sawyer had been rocky. When they divorced, she was given sole custody of their son after her husband was charged with child abuse, a decision that Lawrence regarded as a personal insult and for which he swore revenge. Being a single parent barely thirty years old might have tested some women. But Allison's relationships had convinced her that it was probably for the best.

"Who was that man, Mommie?"

"He lives down the hill. But I want you to remember that you're not to talk to strangers. And if anyone tries to grab you, remember what I taught you to do?"

"Yes, Mommie."

Allison was startled when the phone suddenly rang. She twirled around and rushed to answer it. "Hi," she said, recognizing the voice of her older sister, Ellen. She sat down. "My God, you won't believe it but there's someone else nearby."

"Who?"

"I've never seen anyone like him. That man smiled and my blood turned red hot."

"You're kidding me," Ellen said with a note of disbelief.

"Well, you won't find anyone like that here in the nation's capital. Be careful."

"I plan to. It would be just like Lawrence to try to trick me with a good-looking man."

"You always said you had the strength of Hercules. Now you can prove it to yourself by resisting this guy."

Allison slumped in the chair. "I am not looking forward to it." She hung up the phone and turned to see her son, Dudley, staring at her with a quizzical expression on his face.

"Is the man coming back to see us, Mommie?" Dudley asked after Allison had read him a bedtime story and tucked him in.

"I don't know. We don't know him, so we have to be careful. Close your eyes and imagine you're on a nice sunny beach while I read another story about the little boy who loved to build sand castles." She read until he went to sleep, turned out the light and went to her room.

Why am I suddenly so awfully lonely? This isn't like me, Allison thought as she lay in bed. She gazed out of her window at the moon, cold and distant, shining through the trees. "He's tantalizing, all right," she said aloud, "but I'm not falling into that trap."

As they usually did on Saturdays, Allison and Dudley got into her car the next day and drove to the only supermarket within twenty miles. When she approached the butcher's counter, she saw Brock and spun around, hoping to get out of his way before he saw her. But apparently she did not move fast enough.

"Well, how nice to see you again," Brock said. "Maybe you can give me a few tips about cooking beef. I'm not familiar with this cut."

When he stood at her door the night before, she had glimpsed very little of him other than his remarkable face and impressive height. Now her breath shortened at the sight of his lean, muscular thighs and beautifully shaped legs protruding from Bermuda shorts that covered one of the nicest, tightest butts she'd ever seen on a man. She wasn't quite sure of her facial expression, but she was certain that a gaping mouth didn't flatter her.

"I, uh…I beg your pardon," she said.

He repeated the request and stepped closer. "This is a lot for a guy to figure out. Which steak is tender?" A grin floated across his face. "Maybe it isn't steak. I want something to grill in a hurry that will be tender."

"Try that filet mignon," she said, pointing to the cut of beef. He stood in front of her and she couldn't move away. "Would you mind…?"

His gaze was on her and he didn't smile. Her hand went to her chest as if she could stop the racing of her heart, and still he stared. His eyes seemed to draw her to him. Trembling, she must have swayed toward him because his hand reached out to steady her. He didn't release her and he kept his gaze locked on hers, holding her captive.

"Mommie, Mr. Wood showed me a big dog out there."

Dudley's voice brought her to her senses. "I…I have to go," she said, though she wasn't obliged to give the man an explanation. "Come back here. I don't want you near that dog."

"He won't hurt him," Brock said.

"Is he your dog, mister?" Dudley asked.

"Yes, he is. His name is Jack and he won't hurt anybody unless that person hurts him or threatens me."

"Gee, can I play with him?"

Brock glanced at Allison before answering Dudley. "Ask your mother. We'll do whatever she says."

"Come on, son," she said and left without saying goodbye.

By the time Brock finished his shopping and stood outside, he saw no trace of the woman he'd met in the nearby cabin. She still hadn't introduced herself or divulged her name and she avoided calling her child by name. Clearly she had something to hide. *Hmm. He'd have to think about that.* One thing was certain: she was just as attracted to him as he was to her.

Facing one another in the grocery store, he realized that he'd stirred something in her that made her tremble and almost lose her balance. She had a child, and probably a husband, so he'd better get a grip. He doubted that he had fooled her into thinking he didn't know one cut of beef from another. He'd just needed an excuse to talk to her, and she was probably smart enough to figure that out.

Using his cell phone, he called the telephone company Monday morning and asked that his house phone be connected. "So you're back!" the customer rep said. "For you, anything. It's been pretty dull around here ever since you left last September. You coming to the harvest fest this year?"

"That's months off, Marge. We'll see. How are you?"

"Same old, same old. Only difference is now we got a TV here in the office and a couple of chairs for people to sit in. Did some lucky gal marry you since you left here?"

He couldn't help laughing. Marge asked him that question every year when he returned to his cabin and called to have his phone reconnected. "I'm over the hill, Marge," he said, which was his usual reply.

"Shucks, Brock. Ain't a woman under ninety who wouldn't marry you if she got the chance. Those over ninety would, too, if they could see what you looked like. I'm making biscuits when I get home. Drop by around five-thirty if you want some."

"You didn't have to add that last part. I'll be there. Thanks, Marge, for the welcome." To his mind, Marge offered just enough mothering to make him feel at home, and although she was naturally friendly, she didn't pry. She was probably around sixty, he imagined, and that was part of her charm. That plus the fact that she adored a man she'd lived with for over thirty years and who would have married her if she'd been willing.

He put Jack in his SUV and drove to Marge's house. "Well, don't you look good," Marge said, opening the back screen door and coming out to greet him.

He hugged her. "You're the one. Where's Bob?"

"Come on in. Bob just brought in some pike he caught in the big lake over in Sabael. I cleaned a couple for you. Sit down. Bob's in the shower."

"Have you met my neighbor?" he asked Marge, getting around to the real reason for his agreeing to come to her house.

"Allison? We've met, but she stays to herself. The only reason I know her name is because I work for the telephone company. She'll go up there to the office and pay her bill, but she's yet to introduce anybody to her child. That little boy of hers must be suffering for somebody to play with. He ought to have playmates. I suggested to her that he'd meet some children in Sunday school, but I coulda been talking to the wind."

"Is her husband with her?"

"If he is, nobody up here's seen him. Be careful where you step, son. She's a real looker and she's got good manners, but she's as tight as a drum."

"Why do you think I'm interested?"

Marge threw back her head and released a guffaw. "'Cause you're a young, healthy man with plenty of testosterone. That's why. Here. Try these." She put three hot biscuits on a plate along with butter and homemade jam.

He bit into a biscuit. "You're still rockin', Marge. I could make a meal of these. Why do you think my neighbor shies away from people?"

"You asking me? Why would a young, attractive woman move up here and hide away in the woods with a five-year-old? Every man in Indian Lake has asked me about her."

"How long has she been up here?"

"Since late April. It was still snowing when she got here. Nobody moves here that time of year. People come in the summer."

"I know. Thanks for the goodies and for my fish. Come over and pick some raspberries. They're ready to fall off the bushes."

"I'll send Bob over. Thanks." He bade her goodbye and

headed home. Something told him he'd better stop thinking about that woman. He slowed his SUV as he passed her cabin, saw a light and shook his head. Maybe when he got to know her, and he would, he'd discover that she wasn't an enigma at all.

On Sunday morning he jumped out of bed, startled by Jack's barking, and ran to the back door. He looked out and saw a long-antlered deer at his back fence. He dressed, went outside, tossed a few pebbles at the deer and chased it away. Deciding to go for a walk, he put a leash on Jack and headed up a trail leading to a small lake about a mile from the highway. *What on earth?* He reached down and rubbed Jack's back. What was this kid doing alone on a trail in the woods?

"Hi. Are you lost?" he asked as the boy got nearer.

"I don't know. I was looking for your dog. I wanted to play with him."

He didn't like the sound of that. "Did you ask your mother?"

"No, sir. She'd say no. But you said he wouldn't hurt me."

"That's right. I did. What's your name?"

"Dudley."

"Well, Dudley, I'd better introduce you to Jack properly. Give me your hands." He let Jack smell the boy's hands. "Now pat him gently on the head. You see. He's wagging his tail and that means he's friendly. Whenever a dog's tail is sticking straight up and not moving, that means the dog is probably dangerous and you shouldn't go near him. Do you understand?"

"Yes, sir. Jack isn't dangerous 'cause he's wagging his tail."

"Dudley, what are you doing here? Where have you been?"

If he'd ever heard the sound of panic, that was it. The woman charged toward them, with tears streaming down her face, and grabbed her son. Jack's growl startled her and she jumped back.

"Easy, boy." He rubbed Jack's back. "I'm sorry, ma'am, but my dog just made friends with Dudley and he's trying to protect the boy from you. The dog doesn't know you. Would you mind holding out your hands?"

She stared at him. "It's all right, Mommie. Jack wants to be friends. His tail isn't sticking up, so he won't hurt you." She allowed the dog to sniff her hands and then patted him on the head as Brock suggested. Then Brock lifted Dudley and placed the boy in her arms. She hugged him, but put him down at once because of his weight.

"I thought I'd go crazy. I didn't know where he was."

"I was looking for Jack," Dudley said. "I wanted to play with him."

"Don't do this again," Brock said to the boy, now convinced that the woman was a single mother. "Jack just chased a big deer away from my back fence. All kinds of wild animals live in these woods, Dudley, and they'll hurt you." He looked at her, frightened and vulnerable, and it took a lot of willpower to resist taking her in his arms and comforting her. "You've never told me your name." He sounded so cool that he almost laughed at himself.

"It's Allison Sawyer," Dudley said, "and we live in that red house up there."

Allison didn't have to be told that the expression on her face when she looked at Dudley was not what anyone would describe as motherly. "How are you, Mr. Lightner? Thank you for intercepting Dudley." She wanted to kick herself. She had inadvertently let him know that she'd remembered his name.

"How did he get out of the house without your knowing it? And if I may say so, you ought to keep your fence locked. Some of the animals around here, bears included, will come right up to your door if they smell food."

Dudley took a few steps closer to Brock and looked up at him. "I turned the lock and opened the door."

Allison could see that Dudley had jettisoned her plan to avoid Brock Lightner and she didn't know what she could do about it. The man gazed down at her intently, as if he were testing the water before diving into it.

"Don't you think you should change the lock on that door? If he can get out so easily, someone may get in just as easily."

The man's eyes seemed to suck her in like quicksand. What was wrong with her that she couldn't stop looking at him? "That's... I'll see if someone up at the general store can fix it for me," she said in a voice that didn't sound like hers. "Thanks for your kindness. Come along, Dudley."

"But, Mommie!"

"Did you hear me? I said come on." She didn't look at Brock Lightner because she knew he was judging her, and unfairly, too. But she had to protect her son and she didn't know the man or his reason for being in Indian Lake. Dudley poked out his bottom lip and prepared to cry. But she ignored that, grabbed his hand with more force that she'd intended and turned to head up the road. She noticed that Brock tightened his hold on the dog's leash and stopped.

"I thought you said he isn't dangerous."

"He isn't right now, but he's agitated because Dudley's crying and you pulled him a little roughly. Jack has established a bond with Dudley."

"Believe me, Dudley can test a saint when he puts himself to it. Goodbye."

"Can we pick some raspberries, Mommie?"

"No, Dudley. We are going home. I have a lot of work to do."

Later she put Dudley on a stool in her kitchen and looked him in the eye. "You did a very bad and very dangerous thing when you sneaked out and wandered into those woods. You heard what Mr. Lightner said about the wild animals. They can hurt you very badly. If you ever do that again, I am going to lock you in your room. Do you understand?"

The boy reached up and pinched her chin. "You ate some ginger snaps, Mommie. There's a little piece right there."

She stared at him for a second. He giggled, having learned how to charm his way out of trouble and, even though sh knew he was trying to snow her, she laughed and hugged him. She couldn't help it. He was the delight of her life. The ringing of the telephone saved her from further disciplining him.

"Hello." She never identified herself when answering the telephone.

"Allison? This is Layla. How's that rewrite coming?"

"Kicking and screaming. It's like pulling hens' teeth and they don't have any teeth. There isn't a whole lot you can say about white icing, Layla. But with so many people allergic to chocolate, cooks are going to have to learn how to make creamy white icing."

"That's why you're doing this cookbook. The sales force is on my back, Allison," Layla continued.

"It's not due until next week."

"I know, but you said you could have it in early. Oh, well. How's Dudley?"

"Holding up my work, as usual. Otherwise, I'm happy to say he's fine."

"Good. I'm looking forward to receiving your precious manuscript in my hands next Wednesday."

"Don't worry. It will be there." She hung up and hurried back to the kitchen where Dudley remained on the stool.

"Mommie, why can't I play with Jack? If I can't play with Jack, can I have a dog?"

"I don't know anything about taking care of dogs. Now if you'll let me work for a couple of hours, I promise to find you a guitar teacher. You did really well in your math and reading this morning. Why don't you work on that map?"

"I'm going to start on a new map." He jumped down and went to his room.

Maybe moving to such an isolated place had been a bad decision. Dudley needed playmates and he didn't have access to libraries, museums or other activities. But what could she do? If Lawrence kidnapped Dudley and whisked him out of the country, as he'd threatened to do, she'd never see her child again. She made a pot of coffee and forced herself to focus on her work. Looking at the computer screen, her mind's eye conjured up Brock Lightner's sleepy, light brown eyes and the dimple in his left cheek that had seduced her into believing he was harmless.

Maybe the man wasn't all that interesting and the problem wasn't him but her loneliness. Maybe she should pack up and head west. She rubbed her hands as if in despair and closed her eyes. *Snap out of it, Allison. You have to finish this book!*

Brock decided to go back home and get to work. He couldn't understand Allison Sawyer's skittishness around him, although he could understand why an intelligent woman would not allow her child to go off with a stranger. As soon as he managed to find out where she'd lived before, he'd have all the information he needed to know. He hadn't spent ten years as a successful private investigator for no reason. She was on the lam, either from the law or someone, and nothing would make him believe otherwise.

He remembered that he hadn't talked with his mother for a couple of days and phoned her. "It's great to be back up here," he told her. "First chance I get, I'm going over to the big Indian Lake and try to catch some striped bass. At this small lake over here, people fish for pike and sunfish."

"Don't try talking around me, Brock. I want to know if you've definitely given up being a private investigator. I worry every minute. It's so dangerous."

"Good grief! Well, you can put that behind you. I'm writing an account of my experiences and that's a good way to get it out of my system."

"I don't suppose there're any nice girls up there."

The chuckle that began deep in his throat exploded into a laugh. "Mom, the village probably doesn't have more than two hundred and fifty people, if that many. The post office and the bank are three miles up the road. One supermarket nearby serves everyone in a ten-mile radius. How's Dad?"

"Reginald's playing golf. One day last week, he shot a seventy-two and there's no living with him."

It sounded like a complaint, but he heard the pride in her voice. "Good for him. I'll be in touch."

Now, if I can get one page written, I can say I've started. But do I write it as fiction or nonfiction? He'd thought about that question for weeks and hadn't come to a conclusion. He called his brother, Justin.

"You want to sound clever or you want to make some money?" Justin said—always the practical one—when Brock put the question to him.

"I want to make some money and I want to get investigating out of my system."

"Then you can figure out the answer," Justin said. "I know what I'd do."

"Write a fictionalized first-person account. That's exactly what I'm going to do."

He opened his laptop and started typing, attacking the story as if it were an enemy. After two hours, he printed out eight double-spaced pages, got a cup of coffee, went out on his deck and sat down to read what he'd written and decide whether he liked it or not. Jack settled beside his chair. He'd read for only a few minutes when Jack jumped up and growled. He'd never seen a wild boar up there, but there was no mistaking the tusks protruding from its mouth. He didn't like shooting animals, but if he saw it again, he'd have to eat a lot of roast pig. He didn't want Jack near the animal because it posed a danger even for bears. He walked out to the gate, threw a few sticks and drove the boar away.

The following morning, shortly after seven, he put Jack on a leash and jogged down a trail toward the Adirondack Lake, exercising himself and his dog. He saw Dudley at about the same time as Jack barked and stopped.

"Dudley, where is your mother?"

"She's asleep, I think."

He hunkered beside the boy. "How many times have you wandered out of the house without letting your mother know about it?"

Dudley looked him straight in the face, then he patted Jack on the back. "Lots of times."

"Why do you disobey your mother?"

Dudley looked down at his feet and then gazed up at him with the saddest eyes that he'd seen in a child's face. "The house is so small and I like it outside. I already did my lessons this morning."

"Where is your father, Dudley?"

"He doesn't live with us."

"Then you have to learn to obey your mother. Come on." He took the boy's hand and started for Allison Sawyer's house. To his amazement, Dudley didn't resist going home. Indeed he seemed happy to hold Brock's hand. He knocked on Allison's front door.

"She's asleep, Mr. Lightner, and I think she's going to send me to my room."

After a few minutes, the door opened and Allison stared up at him with a questioning expression on her face. For an answer, he looked down at Dudley.

"Oh, my Lord. Don't tell me he was out there again," she said in a voice laced with fear.

"You didn't repair that lock, did you?"

She seemed defeated. "I have a deadline to meet and when he promised not to sneak out again, I decided to wait to change the locks."

Better to shock her now than to cry with her later. He didn't spare her. "Yesterday afternoon, I chased a wild boar from my gate. Those animals will attack a bear. If Dudley encountered one, I doubt you'd see him alive again."

Her almost-plaintive expression opened a hole inside of him and he grasped her shoulder. "You don't have to replace the locks. I'll do it for you. Now. Today. You can't watch him every minute. If it's the money…"

She shook her head. "No, it isn't that and I thank you for bringing him home. I'd die if anything happened to my child."

"I know you would. I'll be glad to run up to the store and get the locks and a chain for that fence, but I suspect you'd feel safer knowing you were the only one with the keys. I take it your windows lock. Right?"

"Yes, they do. Thank you," she said. "I'll drive to the store and get the locks, and I should have them around noon. Thanks. I…I appreciate your help, Mr. Lightner."

She had a way of looking at him that made him feel as if he could twist iron with his bare hands. His breath shortened and he forced himself to look away from her. "It seems as if Jack is taken with Dudley. I suppose even dogs need playmates. I'll see you later."

"Can I go stay with Jack and Mr. Lightner, Mommie?"

"No, darling. We shouldn't impose on our neighbor." She wanted to move, but Brock wouldn't let her. His gaze was like fingers stroking and caressing her body, warm and seductively.

He took a small notepad from his pocket, made a step toward her and said, "Call me when you get home. This is my cell-phone number." He wrote the number on the pad, tore it off and handed it to her. A smile played around his mouth, making his full, bottom lip even more inviting. "The sooner we do this, the better."

He said it softly, but there was no mistaking his meaning. She knew he was talking about the locks, but his words sent jolts of excitement through her, upping the sexual tension between them as well.

When Dudley began to pout, Brock patted the boy's shoulder. "Good boys always obey their mothers. See you soon."

Dudley reached toward Allison and took her hand. "Come on, Mommie. Let's go get the locks now so he can fix the door." She stared at him. In all his five years, that was the first time he'd given in without creating a scene. She realized it was also the first time he had received a gentle reprimand from a man. When Allison had left his father, Dudley had only known abuse. Lawrence had responded to Dudley's stubbornness by slapping him, which was particularly abusive punishment for a toddler less than three.

Maybe she was doing the wrong thing. But she knew she'd been fooling herself if she thought that Dudley wouldn't sneak out again and she couldn't risk that. She strapped him in the backseat of her car, got in and drove up Route 28. At the general store she bought locks and a length of heavy chain to secure the wire fence.

"Buy some hot dogs, Mommie, and let's have a picnic."

She didn't have time for a picnic, but Dudley needed a diversion, so she went next door to the supermarket and bought what she needed for an outdoor picnic. She'd told Brock that she'd be back home in an hour, but when he neither called nor came, her temper began to rise.

"He gave you his cell-phone number, Mommie," Dudley said when she grumbled about it.

She hadn't intended to use that number, but what choice did she have now if she didn't want to risk Dudley sneaking out the next morning before she got up. She dialed his number.

"Mr. Lightner, this is Allison Sawyer," she said when he answered. "I'm back home with the locks and the chain."

"Good. I'll be there in about twenty minutes."

When his voice seemed to trail off, she realized that he didn't know how to terminate the conversation, at least not to his satisfaction. *This is terrible,* she thought. *I do not like where we seem to be headed and I am not going there.*

"Mommie, I'm hungry. Can we have the picnic now?"

"Mr. Lightner is coming to change the locks, so we'll have to wait."

He agreed without protest and she thought nothing of it. However, when Brock arrived with Jack, Dudley ran to embrace the big German shepherd and said to the dog, "We're going to have a picnic, Jack. Do you like hot dogs?" Jack wagged his tail.

Stunned by the child's deviousness, she threw up her hands and looked at Brock. "He's five years old. How am I going to manage when he's fifteen?"

"It'll probably be a lot easier then," Brock said. She gave him the locks and chain and walked toward the kitchen, intent upon leaving Brock alone with the job.

"This'll go much faster and smoother if you hold this lock in place while I get this screw started," he said. "These Segal dead-bolt locks are almost tamper-proof. I'm glad you got one for the front door as well. Here, hold this for me."

She stood inches from him, watching his biceps flex as he forced the screws into the door's hard wood. She looked at his fingers, long, lean and tapered, capable of giving a woman pleasure after pleasure, and her attention strayed from the task at hand as her gaze traveled over his long, lean frame. She sucked in her breath and his head whipped around. With one hand on the screwdriver and the other on the screw, he stood motionless, gazing into her eyes. She swallowed hard and tried without success to shift her gaze, for he held her spellbound.

"Are you going to invite me to your picnic?" he asked in words so soft that she barely heard him. "Are you?"

She managed to break contact with his eyes, but her gaze caught the chest hairs exposed by the open placket of his T-shirt and traveled to his bare arms, so muscular and strong.

"Well?" he said.

"Uh. Yes, of course," she replied, shaking herself out of the trance. "As soon as… Can you fix the back gate today, too?"

"I'll do that and anything else you need done," he said in a tone that told her to take it any way she wanted to.

Chapter 2

Brock tested the locks. Satisfied that to enter the house, an intruder either had to use a key or take the door off its hinges, he headed out to the seven-foot-high fence that protected the back deck. If Allison Sawyer was living in a state of denial, he definitely was not. It took him only a couple of minutes to loop the chain through the welded-wire fence and hook it with a heavy-duty padlock. He brushed something from his shorts and went back into the house without knocking.

Allison looked up at him. "Mind if I clean my hands somewhere?" he asked, barely able to control his urge to laugh. "Oh, yeah, and if we're going to have a picnic, please fix a couple of extra hot dogs. I'm starving," he said over his shoulder, aware that he'd unsettled her.

"Thanks for replacing the locks and fixing that fence," she said, when he came out of the bathroom. "I feel a lot safer."

"My pleasure. If I were you, I wouldn't leave food scraps in that trash can back there. It's a good idea to put it on the road around nine in the morning. The garbage collector passes here at ten. You'll attract fewer wild animals, although that's hardly avoidable in the cold months."

"How long have you been coming up here?" she asked Brock.

"This will be my sixth summer, but it's the first time I planned to spend the winter here as well."

Her eyebrows shot up in surprise. "Why?"

Brock explained that he was trying to finish a book, but didn't tell Allison what it was about.

"If you need peace and quiet while you write, this is definitely the place for it," she said.

He hated small talk and he could see that she was comfortable with it. "Want me to help you prepare the food? I'm handy in the kitchen."

"It's about ready. I suspect you're handy with a lot of things," she said and winced, apparently realizing the embarrassing double entendre.

He rewarded her with a grin and a wicked wink. "Like I said. I'm real handy around the house." He would stop meddling with her if she'd come down off her high horse, but he had a feeling she didn't plan to do that, so he said, "Are you going to make me call you Mrs. Sawyer forever? I'd be a lot more comfortable eating your hot dogs if you'd call me Brock." He looked around. "Where's Dudley?"

"Out back on the deck with Jack. I'd better check. I don't want Dudley near that fire."

"If he went too close to it, Jack would bark. My dog knows the danger of fire." And he could feel a different kind of fire circling around them, hemming them behind an emotional barrier from which they might never escape.

"Are you married?" he blurted out, even though he knew it wasn't the time for that question.

"Not any longer." She looked up at him, open and vulnerable. "Are you?"

"I've never been married."

"But you must be—"

He interrupted her. "I'm thirty-four, and we'd better get to that picnic before things change here."

"Yeah." She handed him a plastic tablecloth and napkins. "There's a table on the deck," she said, and headed for the kitchen. *At least she hadn't denied the heat between them.*

As he set the table, he marveled at Dudley's affection for Jack and the gentleness with which the dog played with the child. "Don't ever get rough with him, Dudley. Treat him the way you want him to treat you."

"Oh, I won't hurt him, Mr. Lightner. He's my friend."

Allison put strips of carrots, sliced tomatoes, warm hot dog rolls, potato salad and sliced hard-boiled eggs on the table, and removed the hot dogs and toasted marshmallows from the grill and put them on the table. She looked at him. "I don't have any beer. Would you like some white wine?"

"Thanks, but I don't drink anything alcoholic midday. Lemonade or something like that will do the trick." He didn't say that he rarely drank anything, other than wine at dinner; for the time being, she'd learned enough about him. She brought iced tea for them and ginger ale for Dudley.

"What can I give Jack?" Dudley asked them.

He didn't allow anyone to feed his dog, because he didn't want Jack to obey anyone but him. "He's not hungry. I fed him a short while before we left home." He beckoned to Jack. "Sit here." Jack settled on the floor beside Brock and closed his eyes.

"We have raspberries for dessert," she said and served them with a dollop of whipped cream. "I bought them yesterday morning, so they're still fresh."

As he ate the berries, he looked at her, hoping for a hint as to the direction she wanted their relationship to take, but she looked everywhere except at him. He wished she wouldn't be so nervous, that she'd feel comfortable with him. He figured that because she'd been married, at least long enough to produce a child, she should know how to hold her own with a man. He'd get to the bottom of that, but he sensed that she was not a worldly woman and he'd better tread with care. He took his plate to the kitchen, rinsed it and put it in the dishwasher. As he turned to leave the kitchen, he saw that Dudley had followed him.

"Can I clean my plate, too, Mr. Lightner?"

"Absolutely. Little boys should do everything they can to help their mother, and that includes obeying her."

"Yes, sir." He stood on tiptoe to rinse the plate and then put it in the dishwasher. "Will you come to see us again, Mr. Lightner?"

"If it pleases your mother, I will." At that moment, he saw from his peripheral vision that she stood just behind him and made a snap decision to go home. He didn't crowd women, especially if they weren't on equal footing with him. He was in her house and he wanted her to know that he knew he didn't belong there.

"Thanks for your hospitality, Allison. If you need me for anything at all, you have my cell-phone number." To Dudley, he said, "Be a good boy and obey your mother. Don't go out of this house unless she's with you. Got that?"

"Yes, sir. I got that." The boy hugged Jack and then looked up at him. He hunkered in front of the child and put his arms around him. "Thanks for inviting me to your picnic. I enjoyed it. Bye for now." He stood, looked down at Allison, winked at her and left.

Brock left Allison in a dilemma. If he'd moved to Indian Lake at the behest of her ex-husband, would he make it impossible for him to get into her house without her permission, and would he have to remain in that tiny hamlet for eight or ten months in order to accomplish his mission? It didn't seem likely, but she had learned that Lawrence Sawyer would go to great lengths to get what he wanted. Brock Lightner had a worldly, almost jaded, demeanor that fascinated and excited her. Young, strong, muscular and sensitive, too. What was it like to have that kind of man make love to you?

She'd married a man twenty-two years her senior. In her youthful innocence, their long and romantic walks in Washington, D.C's Rock Creek Park had seemed idyllic. And his delight in reading to her beside her parents' fireplace on cold evenings had seemed to her like domestic bliss. It had not occurred to her that his willingness to postpone sexual intimacy until after their marriage wasn't necessarily a good thing; her married girlfriends didn't discuss their sexual experiences with her. But once married, she learned that Lawrence considered sex his right no matter how she felt about it, and that in their bed, he took selfishness to the extreme. She bought some books on the subject and confirmed her belief that she wasn't getting her due. He didn't want children, and after she had Dudley, he showed no interest in her, other than to parade her at his social and business affairs. He had no patience with their son, and when Dudley should have been reprimanded or corrected, Lawrence abused him with physical punishment. Although she had long since stopped loving Lawrence and realized after little more than a year that their marriage could not last, it was for his treatment of Dudley that she divorced him.

"Mommie, can Mr. Lightner come to see us again?" Dudley asked her, interrupting her reverie of the past. "I like Mr. Lightner."

"We'll see," she said. "Right now, I want you to take a nap. After you wake up, you must read for an hour and then we'll go to the post office."

"All right, Mommie. Can you get me a book about dogs and puppies?"

She told him she would and watched in awe as he pulled off his shoes and clothes and started to his room. "Can I have a kiss?" she asked him. He turned back, kissed her quickly and said, "I have to hurry and finish my nap, so I can read."

Was this her Dudley? Normally, he had a fit when she told him to take a nap. "Is Providence playing a joke on me?" she asked aloud. "Brock told him to obey me and look at him."

She threw up her hands and went back to her computer. Revising that book had become a chore, one that she wanted to finish as quickly as possible. The telephone rang. She saw her editor's phone number on the caller ID screen and lifted the receiver.

"Hi, Layla."

"Hi. You're not going to like what I have to say, but it will make your book a top seller."

Allison blew out a long breath and pounded her right fist on her desk. "What is it?"

"Best Bet Publishers just released a dessert cookbook almost identical to yours. We won't be able to sell yours unless you include pictures of the finished products."

"What? You're suggesting that I make all the desserts again just to photograph them? I'm not even using the same oven and that means—"

"I know. I know. And it isn't in the contract, but if you want the book to sell, this is what you have to do. Go along with us on this and we'll advertise it and support it to the hilt."

What choice did she have? "All right, but you'll have to push back the publication date."

"We'll give you three more months."

She hung up and would have screamed in frustration if screaming would have helped. She put the manuscript aside. Who was going to eat the desserts she had to make? Previously she sent them to the church for their Sunday morning coffee hour, but she hadn't been to church in Indian Lake. She made a list of her immediate needs and when Dudley awoke, she told him that their afternoon plans had changed and took him to the supermarket.

"This is a surprise. I wasn't expecting to see you again so soon," the deep masculine voice said. She turned around knowing she'd see Brock. "Say, why so glum?" he asked before she could greet him.

"That's not the half of it. You're a writer. How'd you like being asked to redo your book before your editor even saw it?"

"Don't you have a contract?" She told him about her editor's request and her reasoning. "I can see her point, but that's rough."

"I don't have a photographer, my oven's just so-so and who's going to eat all the desserts I make?"

"I can get you a first-class photographer and I sure can eat whatever you cook that's got chocolate in it."

"I can, too, Mr. Lightner," Dudley said and went to stand beside Brock, who smiled at the boy and patted his shoulder. "I don't think Mommie is happy, but I love chocolate."

She tried to keep her eyes away from his long, muscular legs. Her eyes disobeyed her and roamed up his body until her gaze settled on his face.

His knowing expression did not match his words. "Why don't you make this easy on yourself and get a decent stove."

"Where? The general store carries two woodstoves. I need a gas stove."

"Why don't I take my SUV and drive us down to Lake George. You'll definitely find one there." She asked him how far it was and when he questioned her, he realized that she hadn't left Indian Lake since she arrived there in late April. When she hesitated to accept his suggestion, he said, "All right, you go without me, but how are you going to bring the stove back in that Audi of yours?"

If she let him drive her and Dudley to a big town where she didn't know her way around and could easily become confused, how much of a risk would she be taking? At her hesitation, his shrug said she could do as she pleased. Sorry for what may have appeared to him as her discourtesy, she put a hand on his bare arm and jerked it back when she felt the electricity emanating from their contact. He grabbed her hand.

"You and I had better get used to this," he said. She looked beyond him to a safe object.

"Let's go get in the SUV. I can sit in the back with Jack," Dudley said.

Brock gazed steadily at her until his expression changed from accusing to awareness and bored into her like a hot dart. Without thinking, her right hand rubbed her breast and he took a step closer to her. She realized what she did and, embarrassed, she swung around, putting her back to him. For the first time, then, she felt his hands on her, strong and possessive, kneading her shoulders.

"Brock. Please!"

He released her at once. "I'm not sorry, Allison. I had to touch you. Shall we go to Lake George or not?"

"All right," she said, hating to give in but wanting to accept his offer. "I'll leave the Audi at my place."

Later, as he strapped Dudley in the backseat, Jack jumped into the front passenger seat. "Look here, buddy," Brock said to the dog, "You can't deprive a guy of an opportunity to sit with the object of his affection."

"I'll be comfortable back here with Dudley," Allison said.

"At least you acknowledge one fact," he said, grinning at her. "Move over, Jack." He motioned for the dog to move and he did.

"Come on and get in," he said to Allison, holding the front passenger door open. "No way are you sitting back there behind me."

During the one-hour trip to the city of Lake George, he noticed that she didn't object to the occasional pressure of his leg against hers—he didn't do it intentionally—but seemed comfortable with him. So he was taken aback when she asked him, "Why are you being so nice to me?"

If he had been a man to show his hand at every opportunity for one-upmanship, he wouldn't have been so successful as a private detective, so he opted not to give her a straight answer. "Dudley couldn't possibly love chocolate as much as I do and he can't eat as much of it either."

"Well, you're certainly going to have to eat a lot of it. Half the recipes in my book use chocolate." She didn't pursue the question and he'd known she wouldn't.

He let a grin float over his face. "How good a cook are

you? My dad and my brother are certified chocaholics, so not to worry."

"How big is your brother, Mr. Lightner? Can he come to play with me?"

As he'd thought, the boy was lonely. "I'm sorry, Dudley, but my brother is older than I am."

"What does he do? Is he also a writer?" she asked.

"No. Jason's a lawyer and a good one. Here we are," he said as he passed the Lake George sign. "If you don't find a stove here, we can drive up to Rutland tomorrow morning. It's a bigger town."

"Don't spend so much of your time helping me out when you should be working," she said with a note of concern in her voice.

He was still driving when she made the statement, so he had to settle for a reassuring glance at her. "Every minute I spend in your company is time well spent." When he reached the shopping mall, she still hadn't responded to his efforts to draw her out. He parked and turned to her. "I do not play games with women, children or animals, Allison. Life's too short for that kind of nonsense."

She looked him in the eye and said, "I'm glad to know it. It's comforting to know that you're a man of your word."

"I see you know how to play hardball. Good. It's my style as well."

"All right, Brock. Let's stop it before it gets out of hand."

He wished she hadn't backed down, but perhaps she was right. If they continued, they would definitely get into a fight, and even though he wanted to get a rise out of her, he didn't want to annoy her.

"Sorry. I'll take my cue from you." He'd put his hand on the door, but now he withdrew it, turned and looked at her. "I mean that in every way. Stay there." He got out, walked around to the passenger door and opened it. Jack looked at him for instruction and he let him out. "Sit, Jack." He reached across Allison, unbuckled her seat belt—surprising her when he did it—and held out his hand to her. His jaw almost dropped when she took his hand without a word and got out of the car.

"Which store do you recommend?"

He told her, opened the back door, lifted Dudley from his car seat and walked along with her, holding Dudley's hand and Jack's leash.

"We'll sit out here while you shop."

"I…uh…I'd hoped you would go in with me."

He was waiting to be asked. "Wait here." He tied Jack to a canine hitching post, told the dog to sit and went back to Allison.

"I hope somebody at the general store will be able to hook up this stove," she said as they headed back to Indian Lake. "If I touch it, I'll probably blow up the house."

He took that as a cue that she didn't want to ask him to do it and he decided not to offer. He was getting fed up with their cat-and-mouse foolishness. But he wished she'd lighten up and accept that he would gladly do whatever he could to make her life easier.

He saw a fast-food restaurant off the highway and drove into its parking lot. "Will a scoop of ice cream ruin Dudley's dinner?"

"Probably, but he seldom gets out… Why not? He'll love it."

He put the car in Park and turned toward the backseat. "Say, buddy, I'll buy you some ice cream, but you have to promise your mother that you'll eat all of your dinner."

Dudley clapped his hands with glee. "I will, won't I, Mommie? I'll eat everything."

"If your mother tells me that you broke your promise, I'll be very disappointed in you."

"Oh, no, you won't," Dudley said. "I'll eat all of my dinner. Can I have chocolate?"

"You may, indeed." He tried to imagine the expression on Allison's face as she gazed at him. If he were egotistical, he'd swear that she admired him. He shook it off. "You want to stretch your legs?" They got out of the car and Dudley surprised him when he grabbed his hand and said, "Can you go with me to the bathroom before we get the ice cream?"

He glanced at Allison, realized that Dudley's request had surprised her as well, and said, "Sure," as casually as he could. The boy had already become attached to him, which could become difficult the longer he was around Dudley.

As they walked away from the car, he said to the child, "I'm glad to go with you, but why didn't you ask your mother?"

"'Cause she has to take me to the ladies' room and I don't like going there. I want to go to the men's room."

"You'll soon be old enough to go to the men's room by yourself." What else could he say? He remembered how much he'd hated it when his mother took him to the ladies' room. They found Allison leaning against a bubble gum machine in the front of the restaurant.

"It's different, Mommie," Dudley said as they approached her. "You oughta go see it."

"He wants chocolate ice cream," Brock said, changing the subject to one certain to engage the child's attention.

Allison wasn't talkative by any means, but as they ate their ice cream, he noted her unusually quiet manner. Distant. He'd almost call it standoffish. "What's the matter, Allison? I'm not trying to undermine your authority or to make a place in his life. But I love children, and when they turn to me, I'm not ever going to push them aside."

"I don't think that. It's… This is moving so fast, as if it's going to have a life of its own and as if I have no control over it. I had a life that I didn't control, and I don't want that again."

He could see that something ate at her constantly and if she said otherwise, he wouldn't believe her. He'd thought that she could be hiding out in Indian Lake. What other reason would she have for secreting herself and her son away from civilization?

"I don't want to control you or anyone else, Allison. I assume you're familiar with the words *no, don't, stop* and *leave.* You can use any of those words with me and I'll understand."

"That's not what I'm talking about. You can control a

Private Lives

person in many ways, including by being nice, all the while using subtle means to keep that person in line. Some people are skilled at it." She stopped eating and leaned back in the chair. "Did you see Alfred Hitchcock's *Gaslight?*"

He nodded. "I saw it. Did you experience something similar?"

"Not similar, but just as vicious."

"Mr. Lightner, shouldn't we go check on Jack? Suppose somebody steals him?" the worried little boy said.

"I pity the person who's stupid enough to try that. Jack can definitely hold his own. All the same, we'd better go." He reached over and stroked the back of Allison's hand. "I'd like you and me to have an understanding. As far as I'm concerned, a casual friendship between us is unlikely. Are you ready to go?"

She nodded. "I hope someone at the store can install my stove this evening. Otherwise, what will Dudley and I eat?"

"Use the one you have tonight, and tomorrow we'll get a guy who installs appliances. I'll get a dolly from the hardware store and put the stove in the corner of your kitchen."

Later that evening Brock defrosted a Swanson TV dinner for his supper. Alone, he thought about Allison's reluctance to accept his friendship, even when he offered help that she sorely needed. It wasn't as if she had the option of calling a handyman. There was no one for maybe miles around who could help her if the man in the hardware store didn't come to work. He'd install the stove, but only if she asked him.

Early the next morning, the birds chirped and a soft cool breeze energized him. He sat on his back deck with Jack at his feet thinking of Dudley and of how easily he developed affection for the child. He didn't need further proof that he would enjoy fatherhood. The raspberry bushes rustled in the breeze and he remembered a white wicker basket that he'd put in his pantry the previous summer. He went inside and got it. He was looking at what seemed like a bushel of raspberries and because Allison liked raspberries, he figured he'd pick some for her that were really fresh. In less than half an hour, he had filled the basket with large, plump, sweet berries. After forcing himself to wait until ten o'clock, he put the leash on Jack and patted the dog's rump. "Come on, boy."

A seemingly harassed and frazzled Allison answered his knock at the door. When she saw him, she put her finger to her lips for quiet.

"Hi," she said. "Dudley's in his room doing his math assignment and if he hears your voice, that will be the end of it. Come on in."

"You didn't call someone to install your stove," he said, sensing the reason for her frustration. She shook her head. He handed her the basket piled high with raspberries. Her eyes sparkled.

"I picked these for you a few minutes ago and my fingers are all scratched up. Don't I deserve a kiss?" She clutched the basket as if it held diamonds. He took it from her and put it on the table beside them.

"Look at my fingers," he said, pretending to beg for sympathy. "Don't I deserve a kiss?"

A smile crawled over her face. "You do, but I think it's best that you and I avoid playful kissing."

He sobered at once. "Let me tell you, Allison, when I kiss you, there will be nothing playful about it." A gasp escaped her lips as she sucked in her breath. "That's right, and it's what I want to do to you right here and right now."

She stared at him and moved her lips, but not a word escaped her mouth. "Come here to me, Allison."

Her trembling lips parted. "Brock. Brock, I…"

Her arms seemed to rise of their own volition as he stood gazing down at her with desire ablaze in his eyes. She couldn't stand it. She needed him and had from the first time she saw him.

"Come here, sweetheart," he said, the soft words barely audible.

Her only thought was that he was tantalizing, all man, and

she wanted him. Somehow, he had her in his arms, his fingers pressed into her flesh, and he continued to stare down at her. Why didn't he do something?

"Open your mouth and let me in," he said and plunged his tongue into her eager lips. She felt his hand at the back of her head as he possessed her and then his other hand fastened her hips to his aroused body. Heat spiraled through her. Tremors shook her and he tightened his grip on her buttocks. She wanted… She needed… Moans spilled from her throat as he let the wall take his weight and gripped her to him, possessing her as if he owned her, and in that minute she knew he did. Her hips moved against his, seeking, practically begging for friction, for anything that would soothe the burning inside her. He didn't spare her when she pulled his tongue deeper into her mouth, but let his hand stroke her left breast until, besotted and weakened by desire, she slumped against him.

He looked at her for a long minute, kissed her forehead and her eyelids and said, "Don't be upset, Allison. Some people live a lifetime without experiencing what just happened between you and me."

"I know."

He gazed steadily at her, almost as if he tried to read her thoughts. "If you need me for anything, even if you only want to say hello, you have my cell number. Be seeing you." He patted Jack, picked up the dog's leash and headed toward the road.

Allison watched him go, all the while wishing she had the courage to tell him to stay there with her. She carried the basket of fresh raspberries to the kitchen, placed them on the table and sat down. She had to get a hold on herself; falling for Brock Lightner could be dangerous. Who was he? He had the manners of a gentleman, the charm of a rascal and the bearing of a stud. And she had a feeling that when he wanted to, he could be honey sweet. He was trouble, all right.

In the darkest days of her marriage, she had fantasized about having a man like Brock in her life. But as she mulled over the past few days, she admitted that her daydreams fell far short of Brock the man. She'd never imagined what she had felt while he had her in his arms. Now that she had tasted him, felt his masculine strength and experienced his heat, she knew he'd give her what she had wanted and longed for all these years. But if she opened herself to him, would she risk her life and that of her child?

Her sister, Ellen, said that her willpower, for which Allison was famous, was about to be tested. Ellen didn't know the half of it. When Brock Lightner held her in his arms, she'd had no willpower. She took a shower, not realizing that in doing so, she tried to wash away all that had happened to her that morning.

"He's still in me," she said to herself, as she sat down to work. But work held no interest, so she phoned the hardware store hoping to speak to the man who installed stoves.

"He doesn't work here on a regular basis, miss," the young male voice said. "He just comes when we tell him there's an order. Did you call before?" She told him that she had and asked for the repairman's telephone number. "I don't have it," he said. "We don't have that many calls to install stoves. I'll put a note on the board telling him to get in touch with you. You ought to hear from him sometime this week."

She did not want to call Brock and ask him to install her stove. But what choice did she have? She had three months in which to test two hundred recipes, and every minute that passed was a loss of precious time. She remembered Brock's offer to find a photographer for her, and used that as an excuse and called him.

"Lightner."

"Brock, this is Allison."

"Hi."

He said nothing and the silence made her more annoyed. He could at least make it easy for her. "You said you knew a good photographer. Would you please give me his name and phone number?"

He immediately gave it to her. She realized that he'd memorized the number and reasoned that the man was probably a friend. The thought comforted her. She jotted down the number and weighed the idea of asking him to install the stove.

"Did you get someone to install your stove?"

"Not yet. They don't know when he'll be in town and no one knows his telephone number. It seems that installing a stove is a rarity here."

"I don't see the point in contacting the photographer until you know when you'll have something for him to photograph. I was going to suggest that he come twice a week and shoot what you've prepared between visits. That would be cheaper than having him fly up here every time you bake a cake."

"Are you trying to push my buttons?" she hissed.

"No. But I see I did just that. If you weren't so damned stubborn, your stove would already be installed."

"If I were near you, I'd poke you," she said and kicked the garbage can.

"I imagine you would. Any kind of contact would be better than none. Right?"

"Listen, *you!* Oh, all right. Would you mind installing my gas stove? And you'd better live up to your promises, too." She didn't know why she was so angry, but she was, and he'd done nothing to cause it.

"I'll be up there around four o'clock. I have to finish this chapter. And don't worry, I'm not in the habit of letting people down, and I certainly have never disappointed a woman. Bye."

"What did you say?"

He'd hung up.

Chapter 3

A smart man would leave that woman alone, Brock cautioned himself, puzzled as he was by her behavior. But he pushed the notion aside, thinking that he'd deal with it later. He'd known a lot of women, but none had affected him as she did. He sensed that she was fragile, even wounded, and he had an unusual desire to protect her. That worried him, although not enough to make him stay away from her. He put on a CD and got down to work.

A few minutes before four o'clock, satisfied with what he had written, he picked up his toolbox, called Jack, got in his SUV and drove to Allison's cabin. To his amazement, Jack jumped out of the car and headed for Allison's front door wagging his tail. When Allison opened the door, the dog dashed past her to Dudley, greeting the child as if they had been separated for years.

"Hi," he said to Allison. "My dog seems to be taken with Dudley."

"Dudley has a way about him," Allison replied. "He can really get next to you. Come in."

"Yeah. I suspect it's in his genes."

She didn't comment, but her embarrassment was apparent. As he walked into the house, he left plenty of space between them. After removing the old stove and moving it out to the deck, he brought the other one into the kitchen.

"That thing is heavy," she said. "Why don't you rest for a few minutes? I'll get you a cup of coffee."

He wasn't tired and didn't want coffee, but she wanted to do something for him, so he accepted. "Thank you, Allison. Why don't you keep Dudley and Jack company while I do this? The last thing I need right now is a distraction." He shot a quick glance at her.

"Do you always say everything that comes to your mind?"

He couldn't help grinning. "Absolutely not! If I did, you'd send me out of here faster than a Thoroughbred running down the stretch. Nah. I wouldn't do that."

She didn't move and lowered her voice so that it was barely audible. "Why are you trying me, Brock?"

He peeled the label off the stove and set the appliance down within an inch of her foot. "I'm accustomed to working alone, Allison," he said, ignoring her attitude. "This won't take too long. We can talk after I finish."

She folded her arms at her waist, gazed at him for a minute and walked out of the kitchen. If he seemed an enigma to her, he was not in a mood to explain himself. Hearing her footsteps as she walked around the house, he dropped the wrench on the floor, got up and went to the door leading from the kitchen to the living/dining room just as she threw up her hands in the manner of one either exasperated or defeated. He took three steps toward her and stopped himself.

My purpose here is to install the stove and that's all I'm doing, he told himself. *Damned if I'm going to skip to her tune. No way!*

He finished the installation, turned on the oven to test it

and strolled into the living room, where he found Allison staring at the dark screen of the TV set.

"Anything wrong with your TV?" he asked her.

"Not that I know of. I haven't turned it on."

For the moment he didn't think a comment was warranted. "Do you have a couple of pieces of bread?" he asked her.

He wondered why she didn't ask why he needed it. He toasted the bread. "The oven is working," he said, holding up the bread. He handed her the oven thermometer that he'd purchased in Lake George the previous day. "I'd keep the oven on and calibrate it. If it matches this gauge, it should be all right." He walked out on the deck and called Jack. "Come on, boy."

"Can't you stay a little longer, Mr. Lightner?" Dudley asked.

"I'm sorry, Dudley. I'd like to, but I have some work to do at home."

"Thanks so much, Brock. I, uh…I know you'd be insulted if I tried to pay you, but maybe if I cook a real nice dinner one evening…I mean…would you come?"

It didn't occur to him to smile as he looked at her. "If I hadn't installed your stove, you wouldn't invite me to dinner?"

"I didn't imply that. Please don't make things difficult."

He told himself to be patient, that she had every right to take her time with him as any smart woman would do. "That's the way you made it sound. Look!" He slapped his right fist into his left palm several times. "The problem with us would be easily solved if we were alone. I don't want to push you, but I think you know what I mean. I'll be glad to have dinner here with you any time you ask me." He lowered his voice. "And if Dudley wasn't staring at me, you know what I'd do right now." He hunkered in front of the boy, hugged him, picked up Jack's leash and headed out the door.

"Mommie, if I can't play with Jack, what about the guitar? You said you'd get me a guitar teacher. I finished my lessons and I don't have anything to do."

"I haven't had time, honey, because I have to finish this book," she said.

Brock turned around. "Does he have a guitar?"

She nodded. "My sister gave him a guitar that she'd used during her fling with folk singing. He sees people playing the guitar on TV and he wants to learn, but I haven't had time to find a teacher for him and I don't want him to strum. I want him to learn music."

Did he want to do it? Brock thought. Before he could decide, Dudley said, "Can you help Mommie find a teacher for me, Mr. Lightner?"

"We'll see." He couldn't offer unless he first discussed it with Allison. "I'll call you," he said, looking at her, "and let you know whether I can help." He winked at her and left. Now if he'd only remembered her phone number correctly!

She hated wishy-washy people and Brock Lightner probably thought of her as precisely that. If anybody had asked whether she'd kiss him the way she had earlier that day, she would have denied it. She'd never kissed a man that way, had never wanted to. But she had wanted a lot more from Brock than a kiss and she'd foolishly let him know it.

Aware that the telephone was ringing, she went to look at the caller ID screen, saw that the caller was Brock and lifted the receiver.

"Hello, Brock."

"Hi. I didn't want to say this in Dudley's presence, because I wanted you to have the option of saying no. I play the piano and the guitar, both of which I began studying when I was about Dudley's age. I can teach him to play the guitar, provided he wants to learn, but if you'd rather I didn't, I won't hold it against you. So feel free to turn me down and find someone else to teach him. Before you answer, I want you to know that I won't accept one penny for it."

"You don't leave me an option, Brock. If you aren't his teacher and if Dudley knows you play the guitar, he'd want to know why you didn't teach him. He'd learn well with you, because he trusts you and cares for you. But I couldn't let you do it free of charge."

"Are you talking to Mr. Lightner, Mommie? Did he say he'd find me a teacher? Mommie, can I please speak with Mr. Lightner?"

"No, darling. I'm speaking with him now."

"I'd teach him at home," Brock said, "so you needn't worry about him. Think about it before you say no."

"All right. I will. And thank you for offering to help."

She hung up feeling uneasy. She'd seen nothing of Brock that would make her suspicious of him. She'd become paranoid about Lawrence and his threats of revenge, but she'd die if he stole Dudley from her and took him outside the United States to a country where women had little legal status. The man had the cunningness of a fox and nothing was beyond him. But somehow she couldn't accept that Brock would be working with a man like Lawrence Sawyer.

"If he agrees to teach Dudley here while I'm at home, what can go wrong?" she asked herself. What indeed, other than that Dudley would develop an even stronger attachment to him. She had to risk it. Any teacher would have an influence on her child, and Brock's influence had already eased some of her problems with the boy. Still…

She dialed her sister's number. "I'm in a dreadful dilemma," she told Ellen after they greeted each other.

"Oh. Mr. Wonderful getting to you already?"

"Mr. Wonderful, as you call him, got to me the minute I saw him. The problem is that he plays the guitar and offered to give Dudley lessons. But I'm not sure I want Dudley to become even more attached to Brock Lightner. He's already nuts about the man and his dog. But I'm not convinced that this perfect Adonis isn't up here at my ex's behest, although he hasn't given me a single reason to believe that. In fact, it's just the opposite. But I know how devious my ex-husband can be and I don't know what to do."

"I gather he hasn't made a move on you."

Allison rested her left elbow on the table. "He made a move, but he didn't have much choice. I was there and I wasn't going anywhere."

"I'm going up there and having a look at that specimen. I didn't know you could even feel that kind of attraction. You'd better find out something about that man, 'cause from where I sit, you can forget about not going to bed with him."

"Don't joke, Ellen. I admit he's stirred feelings in me, but when push comes to shove, Dudley is first with me. I'm not going to do anything that will make me lose him."

"Hmm. Apart from sex, what do you think of the guy?" Ellen asked her.

"So far, all he's done has made me think he's a wonderful man. You know how Dudley can be. Well, Brock disciplined him about disobeying me a couple of times, but he did it in a gentle manner. Dudley has stopped misbehaving. He's also become more considerate and helpful because Brock told him that boys are supposed to help their mothers."

"Wait a minute. You said you weren't going to have anything to do with that man. When did that change?"

"Long story, but you can imagine with some of Dudley's antics."

"My advice is go with your gut, sis. You can't afford to be so paranoid that you ruin Dudley's life and yours, too. The boy needs to be with people and if there aren't any his age, being with a good role model will do a lot for him. Nobody can make me believe that you'd fall for another man like Lawrence."

"No, I don't think he's a bad guy and I haven't fallen for him."

"I'm not the one who needs convincing. If the man helps Dudley learn to play the guitar at your place, what are you worried about?"

"You're right. Thanks. I should call him. Bye." She hung up, dialed Brock's number and got a busy signal.

Brock knew that he could easily spare a couple of hours a week teaching Dudley to play the guitar. But Allison wouldn't let the boy out of her sight and that meant being closer to her than he needed to be. He could still smell her scent two hours after he left her. She was starved for love and affection and she wanted him. But he couldn't understand her reluctance and he definitely did not welcome it. Something was wrong and until he knew what it was, he'd tread carefully. As he thought about his relationship with Allison, the phone rang. He hoped he'd hear her voice.

"Lightner here."

"Lightner *here*. How's it going, man?" his older brother, Jason, said.

"Hey! What's up, brother?"

"Plenty. I need a favor. I know you've retired from private investigating, but I need you as I never did before. I have a client who's innocent and unless you help me, she's going to have to pay a hefty price."

"You're so sure she's innocent?"

"Absolutely. After practicing law for twelve years, I know when a client is lying and when she's telling the truth."

"I told Mom that I'd quit and I was going back to practicing law. What's the problem?"

"My client's married and she spurned the attention of a man on her staff, told him that he was harassing her and threatened to tell his wife if he didn't stop it. Afraid that she might tell his wife, the man charged *her*—his boss—with sexual harassment. I need some background info on the man."

He loved his brother, his closest friend and confidant, but he didn't like going back on his word to his mother. "Tell you what. You explain it to Mom, call me back and tell me what she says. I'm not in the habit of lying to her."

Seconds after he hung up, the phone rang and he saw

Allison's number on the caller ID screen. "Hi, Brock. I asked Dudley if he'd like you to be his guitar teacher and he's so excited that he's practically orbiting the earth. I'd appreciate it if you could give him lessons here."

He thought for a minute. "We can try that, Allison. But if your presence creates a problem…" He let the thought hang and added, "When I go to your place to teach Dudley, I'll leave Jack at home. Does that guitar have all six strings?"

"I'm sure because we've never taken it out of the case since my sister, Ellen, gave it to him."

"Good. If from four to five on Thursday afternoons is good for you, we'll start." He'd forgotten about his promise to Jason. "I'll let you know when I can start." She thanked him but seemed reluctant to end the conversation.

Brock prided himself in being cautious, but he hadn't had much experience with what he was feeling and he doubted that just being cautious would solve his problem. And another thing, he had to tell Allison that he'd probably be away from Indian Lake for a week or two, but he didn't want his announcement to appear more important than it was. In any case, he had to wait until he heard from Jason.

The phone rang but it wasn't Jason who called him. He should have known he'd hear from Darlene Lightner. "Hi, Mom," he said when he answered, having seen her name on his caller ID screen. "Don't tell me. I know you've just spoken to Jason. I think I might help him, provided I can."

"Of course you should help your brother. But I told him that the next time he needs a private investigator, he should find someone else. How's your book coming along?"

"It's coming along. I'm only now getting into it. The problem is what to exclude."

"If I were writing it, I'd start with the first case you took and why you took it. It isn't often that a lawyer decides to work as a P.I. The rest I'd treat like an autobiography. But I'm not writing it."

He sat down and got comfortable. His mother—a university professor—had taught English composition and writing for years and he could have discussed with her his plans for the book. But he didn't want his mother to help him with his work.

"Thanks, Mom. I'll keep that in mind and thanks for understanding that I want to help Jason if I can. I don't plan to resume work as a private detective, so not to worry."

"Thank the Lord. That's dangerous work. When are you coming back this way, son?"

"I should be in Washington day after tomorrow to start work on Jason's case. I'll be staying with Jason, so I'll drop by from time to time." He knew that pleased her. "How's Dad?"

"Your father's fine and he's been on cloud nine ever since you told him you planned to practice law again. I have to get to class. Bye for now."

He said goodbye and hung up. Neither of his parents had approved of his work as a private investigator, but neither had interfered. He was glad that a single opportunity evolved into a career that in eight years had made him a wealthy man. And thanks to the experience, he'd be a better lawyer. He remained seated, thinking how best to tell Allison he'd be away for a short while. Normally, it wouldn't be a problem, but he'd just agreed to teach Dudley the guitar and he had to postpone the first lesson. He lifted his right shoulder in a quick shrug. The way she reacted would tell him a lot about her.

Allison grabbed Dudley, sat him down and told him, "Mr. Lightner offered to teach you how to play the guitar. You are not going to strum like those kids you see on television. The guitar is a musical instrument, and—"

"It's okay, Mommie. I'll learn whatever Mr. Lightner teaches me. How often is he going to give me lessons? Every day?"

She felt a little ashamed about her attitude. Even if he only learned to strum, he'd be able to entertain himself. "He to work, Dudley, so he can only teach you once a week. Besides, that's the way most music teachers teach their students, once a week."

"Okay. If that's what Mr. Lightner says. When is he coming?"

The phone rang, saving her an answer, at least for the moment. "Hello, Brock."

"It's a nice day, Allison, too nice to stay inside. Would you like to walk along Adirondack Lake for a while before twilight? Dudley might like to get out of the house, and Jack needs some exercise."

"These cinnamon rolls need to bake for another half hour. After that I'm free."

Half an hour later, he knocked on her front door. When she opened it, Jack—behaving as if he were home—dashed inside to find Dudley.

"Here," he said. "I brought you this walking stick. They're useful for climbing that little hill and for discouraging small animals. Ready?"

She wished she could accept what she saw in his eyes. The warmth, sweetness and tender caring—expressions she'd never once seen in her ex-husband's face—were for her. How had she made such a gargantuan mistake with Lawrence Sawyer?

Dudley ran into the living room, followed by Jack. "You're going to teach me the guitar, Mr. Lightner? You want to see my guitar?"

He didn't shift his gaze from her face. "I'll have a look at it when we get back."

Dudley stepped close and looked up at Brock. "Where're we going?"

"We're going to walk around the lake before twilight sets in."

Brock reached for her hand and without thinking, she clasped his tightly. His slightly narrowed eyes told her that she'd surprised him. She let it roll off her. Hadn't he surprised a few times?

r relief, they didn't encounter any wild animals as around the lake at the edge of the woods, but the wildlife began their eerie conversations and fish could be heard jumping in the lake. She felt a lot safer when they reached her house.

"Would you stop in for a while?" she asked Brock.

"Yes. I promised Dudley I'd check out his guitar and I'm eager to sample your cinnamon rolls. I love those things."

"Dudley, get the guitar for Mr. Lightner while I make some coffee."

In the kitchen, she whispered, "Lord, please don't let me make a mistake with this man. I need him, but I don't know whether he's for good or evil." She made fresh coffee and put a plate of cinnamon rolls on a tray along with coffee cups, sugar, cream and a glass of lemonade for Dudley.

"This is a fine guitar," Brock said when she returned to the living room. "It has a great tone." He played a few bars of "The Girl from Ipanema."

"Am I going to learn to play like that, Mr. Lightner?"

He patted Dudley's shoulder. "If you practice and study, you'll play better than that." She regarded her son's eyes, his expressions of awe and happiness and thought about how much she owed Brock. She looked steadily then at the man who was digging a place for himself inside her heart and knew with certainty that he was a part of her destiny. She reached toward him, but he must have read her mind and pointed to the tray.

"Are you planning to give me some of those rolls before they get cold?"

Embarrassed that she'd forgotten her son's presence, she pushed the tray toward Brock. "Help yourself."

He bit into the roll and closed his eyes. "I could eat every one you cooked if you didn't have to photograph them. By the way, when do you want the photographer?"

"Monday will be fine. For the first run, I'm baking things that can be photographed after they're days old."

He seemed in deep thought for a minute before he said, "Will you and Dudley go out to dinner with me tomorrow evening? For the boy's sake, we can eat around seven, if you like. If we go down to North Creek, we should be back by nine-thirty."

"I'd love to," she said.

"I'm going, too?" Dudley asked when Brock told him. "I always had to stay with a sitter when Mommie went somewhere."

"Not this time," Brock said.

She wanted to hug him, but she didn't dare. His eyes told her that he wanted the same and more. Holding Jack's leash, he walked to the door. She stepped outside before him, closed the door behind him and, sheltered by the darkness, he pulled her into his arms and she parted her lips for his kiss. With his tongue deep in her mouth, he leaned against the house, gripped her buttocks with both hands and sent frissons of heat plowing through her. She'd never wanted anything or anyone as she wanted the feel of him deep inside of her at the minute. As if he knew how she longed for him, he loosened his grip on her, caressed and hugged her with such gentleness that she blinked back tears.

Maybe she shouldn't ask questions but should just "take the money and run." Her common sense told her she'd be a fool to pass up her first chance at genuine lovemaking. Because if Brock Lightner wasn't a tender and considerate lover, surely no man could be.

She fussed for an hour the next afternoon about what to wear and when Dudley asked if he could wear his white pants, she readily agreed because that gave her an excuse to wear a pale green, sleeveless sheath of cotton voile. And when she opened the door to Brock and saw that he wore a beige linen suit and a tie, she gave silent thanks for Dudley's ~~vanity~~. The boy loved clothes and, for once, he'd steered her ~~correctly~~.

~~Mommie~~, can I wear my jacket? Mr. Lightner's wearing

She said nothing, but went into the boy's room, got the jacket that matched his pants and handed it to him.

"You look lovely," Brock said and handed her two day lilies that he'd picked from his garden. She thanked him and put the lilies in a vase with water. This Brock Lightner was far and away a different man from the one who walked around in T-shirt, sneakers and Bermuda shorts. She'd thought him handsome and the personification of sexiness, but the man before her had a commanding presence with which she was unfamiliar. He was a man who knew who he was.

"Where's Jack?" Dudley wanted to know.

"He's taking care of the house. Jack doesn't go to restaurants."

She stared up at him. "There are certainly no flies on you, Brock. You look…" She thought it best to leave it unsaid. "Let's go."

He drove them to a restaurant just past North Creek that she knew hosted weddings and other important celebrations. Their reservation was for a small, intimate dining room in which four other tables were occupied. As they ate, she noticed that Dudley copied Brock's every move and it occurred to her that she may not be able to reverse the relationship even if she wanted to. Dudley had accepted Brock as a part of his life and she realized that her son needed the man.

"I'd better tell you now that I'll be away for a week or two and I'll start Dudley's guitar lessons when I get back."

"Where are you going?" she blurted out and immediately wished she hadn't.

"My brother lives and works in Washington, D.C., and he asked me to come down and help him with a problem he's having. Jason's my closest friend as well as my brother and it didn't occur to me to turn him down. Ross Hopkins, the photographer, will call you tomorrow and make an appointment to start photographing your recipes. I can assure you that he is completely trustworthy in every respect. If he wasn't, I wouldn't recommend him to you. I'll call you from Washington. What's the matter?"

"This is... I don't know. Knowing you're close by has made this a different place for me. Are you sure you're coming back?"

"As sure as I am of my name. If Ross has to stay overnight, he'll get lodging down at Glen Falls."

"What's the matter, Mommie? Don't you like the dessert?"

"I do, honey. I'm fine."

"Oh. I thought you were going to cry," Dudley said, his voice plaintive.

Brock reached across the table and took the boy's hand. "I'll be away for a week or so, Dudley, so you be good and obey your mother. When I get back, we'll start your guitar lessons. I want you to promise me that you won't sneak out and you'll do as your mother tells you. Understand?"

"Yes, sir. I always behave now. Don't I, Mommie?"

"Yes, you do and I'm proud of you."

On the drive home, she didn't feel much like talking. Her thoughts lingered on Brock's having invited her to dinner in order to say he'd be away for a week or two. Why? He could have told her on the phone. *I shouldn't be mean-spirited about it,* she thought. *He didn't have to tell me at all.*

"I want to come in," he said when he parked in front of her cabin.

She sensed his purpose and had a mind to ask him what he'd do if Dudley wasn't there. However, the years she'd spent controlling her emotions and behavior served her then and she kept the thought to herself. He opened the front passenger door, helped her from the SUV and held her close for a second before unfastening Dudley's car seat and taking him out of the vehicle. Walking between them, he began to whistle a tune that wasn't familiar to her. It didn't matter, though, for she sensed his contentment.

Once inside the house, he lifted Dudley, hugged him. "I'd like you to go to your room, because I need to talk with your mother. Remember your promise."

"Yes, sir. I'll remember. Thanks for taking me out."

When the boy was out of earshot, he said, "I'd give anything to spend the night in your arms, Allison, but our time will come."

"Do you have a woman in Washington or any other place? I need to know."

"No, I don't, and please don't start second-guessing me. Are you telling me that you care whether there's another woman in my life?"

"Don't put me on the spot, Brock. You aren't forthcoming about your feelings, so—"

As quick as lightning, his whole demeanor changed and like a predatory animal claiming his territory, he gripped her shoulders, locked her body to his and stared into her eyes. She didn't know or care what he'd do next. Tension gathered within her and her heart fluttered madly. His fingers sent fury ripples spiraling down her arms and tremors shook her.

"Do something," she moaned, when his gaze became feral-like and his stance possessive. "Stop torturing me, Brock."

"I've never known a woman like you and I've never wanted one as badly as I want you," he said, lifted her to fit his body and plunged his tongue into her mouth. She wrapped her legs around him, encasing him between her thighs, and undulated wildly. Out of her mind with desire, she didn't give a thought to her actions. Enveloped in his aura, tasting and smelling his heat, she could stand no more of it and slumped in his arms.

"Can't you admit that you want me as I want you?" he whispered to her. "Can't you trust me enough to tell me what you feel? If we can't accept this much, we can't have a relationship, and without that, we'll never know each other. Allison, sweetheart, unless we trust each other, we'll never have more than this and I'm beginning to suspect that it won't be enough for me. If I ever sink into your body, everything will change for both of us. Can you handle that?"

"I don't know. I have so many issues that you aren't aware

of. I'm not sophisticated about a lot of things, Brock. You'd be surprised at what I've learned from you. Just…come back."

His kiss fell softly on her lips. "You can count on it. I'll think about what you said and when I return, we'll talk and we'll deal with this. I'll be in touch."

She locked the door behind him and stood there until she could no longer hear the motor of his SUV. "I wish I knew where this was leading," she said aloud as she headed for Dudley's room.

She found the boy sitting on the side of his bed with one shoe on and the other one off. She knelt and pulled off his other shoe and both his socks. "Why didn't you go to bed?" she asked him.

"I was waiting for you to come and read something to me. Is he really coming back? I wish he wouldn't go."

She sat down and took the forlorn child into her arms. "He's coming back, because he said he would."

"Did he take Jack with him?"

She tried to sound cheerful. "Of course, honey. He wouldn't leave Jack alone with no one to care for him. Come, I'll read you a story about a brave Native American boy."

Normally, Dudley slept before she finished reading, but when she stopped reading, he hugged her and said, "You sure Mr. Lightner is coming back, Mommie?" She told him that she was. "I love you, Mommie." He put his head on the pillow and was soon fast asleep.

"I know," she said softly. "The thought comforts me, too."

At three-thirty the next afternoon, Brock drove the SUV into the driveway of his brother's house on Woodley Road off Connecticut Avenue in Washington, D.C., and felt in his pockets for the door keys. Family members carried the keys to each other's homes. He found the key, rang the front doorbell and entered the house. He didn't welcome the silence that proclaimed his brother's absence. Few things could warm him quicker or lighten his mood faster that his older brother's broad grin and the laughter that seemed to spring from the pit of him. When Jason was at home and not in bed, music could always be heard. They shared a love for music. Brock went into the kitchen, found the makings of a ham sandwich, opened a bottle of ginger ale, and quelled his hunger.

He'd said he'd call her, but he hadn't counted on the driving need to hear her voice and see her smile. After forcing himself to finish eating and to dissipate his eagerness to talk with her, he went up to the guest room, unpacked and hung up his clothes. Suddenly, he laughed aloud. *Why am I fooling myself? I'm nuts about that woman, and I can hardly wait to hear that soft, mellow voice of hers.* He dialed her number and waited while the phone rang.

Chapter 4

Brock paced the floor while the telephone rang and rang. Where could she and Dudley be? After nearly thirty rings, he hung up, walked to the window and looked down on the park. What could be wrong? Unless she needed something urgently, she only went to market early in the morning. He walked back to the telephone and snapped his finger. She didn't recognize his brother's phone number. Maybe that's why she didn't answer the telephone. He opened his cell phone and dialed her number.

"Hello. Where are you?"

He released a long breath in relief. "Allison. I dialed you a minute ago on my brother's house phone, and when you didn't answer, I thought something might have happened to you or to Dudley. As you've now guessed, I'm in my brother's house. I got here half an hour ago."

"I…uh…I don't answer the phone, Brock, unless I recognize the number or the caller's name on my caller ID screen."

"That occurred to me. And it means I'd better give you

Ross's cell-phone number." He could think of several things he wanted to say to her, but none seemed appropriate. In his mind's eye, he pictured her sitting cross-kneed in a chair beside the kitchen door with that mesmerizing smile on her face. Lord, he could love that woman!

"Maybe we can go fishing or boating when I get back. The Adirondack region is one of the country's most beautiful areas. Do you ski?" She said she did but that Dudley didn't.

"He'd learn in twenty minutes. At that age, children aren't afraid and they learn easily. It's like swimming."

"I don't have skis," she said, "but I suppose we could rent some."

They weren't saying anything important and he hated small talk. "Do you miss me?" he asked her, getting down to cases.

"You just left."

"I'm not in the mood to fence with you, woman. I haven't been away from you any longer than you've been away from me and I miss you. Now would you please answer my question?"

The sound of her laughter warmed his heart. "Behave yourself. Of course, I missed you. I missed you even before you left me."

"Now that's what I like to hear. May I speak with Dudley?"

Her hesitancy didn't surprise him, for he had concluded that the mystery about her had more to do with Dudley than with her. "I miss him, too," he said, making it more difficult for her to refuse.

"Wait a minute," she said.

"Mr. Lightner? Where are you now, Mr. Lightner?"

"I'm in Washington, Dudley."

"Are you going to see the president?"

"No, I'm not. It's difficult to get permission to visit the president, because he's so busy."

"Oh. Can you come back soon?"

"As soon as I can. All right?"

"All right. Bye."

After he hung up, it occurred to him that by asking to speak with Dudley, he'd made something of a statement. He thought about that for a few minutes, shrugged, kicked off his shoes, turned on the TV and waited for his brother to come home.

Over dinner that evening, he listened to Jason's description of his client's accuser and knew he might have his work cut out for him. Head of a division of a major insurance company, the woman—Jason's client—had repeatedly rejected the advances of Phil Miner, her male deputy. When she promised him that she would tell his wife if he ever hit on her again, he took preemptive measures and indicted Jason's client for sexual harassment.

"Hmm. Sounds like a first-class moral gentleman. Know anybody who works with those two?"

"You bet," Jason said, "and it's one of the reasons why I'm positive that my client is innocent."

"Tell me what you know and don't breathe it to anyone, including your client, that I'm on this case. I'll give you a report in a couple of days."

Camouflaged with a beard and a pair of black-rimmed glasses, he knocked on Phil Miner's office door in the Midlife Insurance Company. As a part of his modus operandi, Brock always made it a point, when possible, to meet and observe his subject. Pretending to need a large amount of life insurance on short notice, Brock judged from the man's attitude, demeanor and selling tactics that integrity was not his strong point. Satisfied that the hard work he'd probably have to invest in the case would pay dividends. he collected the information that he needed and developed a plan. After setting up office in the building that housed the insurance company, he made friends with the janitor, and with the janitor's help and a few one-hundred-dollar bills, had several powerful voice recorders installed in the company offices.

At the end of the week, he collected his trophies, took them to Jason's house and played the tapes. He had listened for two hours when a woman's voice identified Miner, swore at him and threatened to report him if he didn't keep his hands to himself. She then said, "Everybody knows you are the one who chased Helen. She couldn't stand you. And you're suing her because you want her job."

"Nobody will believe you, just like nobody believes her. Either you play with me or look for another job." Brock marked the tape, went to his room and began to pack.

"Let's eat dinner with Mom and Dad tonight," he told Jason. "I've seen them twice, but I think I ought to go over tonight because I'm leaving early tomorrow. You've got more than enough there to win your case."

"I'm in your debt, brother. How'd you get this recording?"

"What you don't know won't hurt you. I have my methods and I didn't break the law. At least I don't think there's a law that covers it exactly."

A grin spread over Jason's face. "Damned if I'll look a gift horse in the mouth. Better not tell Mom. She thinks a person should starve rather than forfeit his integrity."

"Tell me about it."

"What's the rush to get back to the Adirondacks?" Brock's father asked him at dinner that evening.

"I left my work to come down here. I've been up there two months and three measly chapters that can hardly be called a first draft are all I have to show for it. This year will be up faster than you can say 'blink.'"

"I don't suppose you'd find any pretty girls up there in that hinterland," Darlene said, although he knew it was a serious question.

He stopped eating and looked at her. "Mom, my cabin's in the woods." At least it hadn't been necessary to lie.

The next morning, as Brock stood beside his SUV preparing to leave for Indian Lake, Jason asked, "What's her name?"

Stunned, Brock's eyes widened. "What on earth gives you… Her name is Allison and she hit me like a ton of bricks.

But don't be too concerned. I'm not sure that it's going anywhere. I'll call you."

"Wait a minute, Brock. Not so fast. I can see that you think a lot of her, so what's holding you back? This doesn't seem like the guy who walks in, surveys the place, sees what he wants and goes for it. Let's go back in the house. I'll make some coffee." Why hadn't he remembered that he'd never been able to keep a personal secret from Jason because his brother knew him as well as he knew himself? He shrugged. Maybe it would help to talk with his brother about it.

Jason made a pot of coffee, filled two mugs with it and sat down at the kitchen table. "Mom may not have noticed how you finessed her question, but I did, and whenever you do that, I know you're covering something. Are you in love with her?"

"I don't think so, but any way I look at it, this thing is pretty heady. I've never known a woman like her. I also feel as if I don't know her. She's hiding something. She has a five-year-old boy and for some reason, when we first met she tried to prevent my knowing his name. Why is a beautiful, thirty-year-old divorced woman with a five-year-old kid living in a log cabin in the woods back of the Adirondack Lake? I think she's on the lam and I don't believe she's a criminal."

"You're right. It's strange. Unless there's a first-class school there, the poor kid is missing plenty. Where did she live before she moved to Indian Lake?"

"She lived here or in the suburbs. She teaches Dudley at home and writes cookbooks for a living. She drives an Audi, man, and those things cost money."

"Hmm. You bet they do. What's her last name?"

"Sawyer."

"That rings a bell. I wonder if she's the same woman who was party to a famous divorce case here in the District about two years ago? The man was Lawrence Sawyer and he was depicted in the trial as powerful and unscrupulous. If I remember, she got full custody. Maybe she's hiding from her ex-husband. What do you think of the kid?"

"He's lovable and he's taken a shine to Jack and to me."

"Well, if you care for her, get her to open up to you. How does she shape up in other ways?"

"She's obviously well-educated and has very good manners. As a person, she suits me. It's all the stuff I haven't been able to fathom that's been bothering me."

"You can handle it." He winked. "I'll pay you a visit and check her out."

"I'd love some fishing company," Brock said. "Think about it. I'd better be going."

"Drive carefully and call me when you get home."

After speaking with Brock, Allison paced the floor, rubbing her arms and shaking her head. Was she falling in love with the man? She didn't know anyone who knew him, not a family member or a friend, and it wasn't wise. But her heart and her hormones obviously didn't operate on wisdom and logic. When she'd heard his voice, her heart had thudded loudly enough for her to hear it. He'd left her only a few hours earlier and she'd welcomed his call and the sound of his voice as if she hadn't seen him for years.

"I'm not going blindly to my destruction," she vowed aloud and called her lawyer in Washington.

"Do you know a man named Brock Lightner?" she asked him. "He's in Washington on business and I think he's from around there."

"Good to hear from you, Allison," the lawyer, a close family friend, said. "The name Lightner is associated with a prominent lawyer here in the District of Columbia. I don't know if he's the one you want, but I'll be glad to check it."

No help there, but if he was a lawyer, couldn't he be a member of the team that represented Lawrence? Maybe he was and maybe he wasn't. But she was taking no chances. She'd had enough unwanted surprises for a lifetime. She packed what she'd need for Dudley and herself in an emergency, put it into the trunk of her Audi and hung her second set of car keys on a nail beside the front door. If she had to make a run for it, she could.

Brock stopped once for the twenty minutes that it took to get gas, a hot dog and a cup of coffee. He ate as he drove. He didn't ask himself why he drove above the speed limit and why he didn't stop and rest although his shoulders ached from the tension created by the long drive in frequently heavy traffic. When he turned off Route 28, he drove into Allison's driveway. She opened the door as he knocked and he had her in his arms.

"Yes," he said, grinning with the relief he felt. Suddenly, he stepped back and regarded her. "What's the matter, Allison? That felt like a blast of Canadian air in the dead of winter."

"Nothing's the matter. Come on in."

He stepped inside, but didn't go farther. He'd practically risked his life getting back to her and she treated him with the kind of nonchalance reserved for enemies. "Where's Dudley?"

"Mr. Lightner?" The sound of Dudley charging through the house to greet him made up in some measure for Allison's cool reception. "Mr. Lightner. You did come back. I was scared you wouldn't," Dudley said and launched himself into Brock's arms.

He hugged the boy, taking from him warmth he needed from Allison, but which she had denied him. "I'll always do what I tell you I'll do, Dudley, unless it isn't humanly possible."

"When will we start my guitar lessons?"

"Thursday at three o'clock." He didn't look at Allison when he said it. If she had a different agenda, too bad.

"Gee, I'm sure glad you came back, Mr. Lightner. Did you bring Jack?"

"Yes. I have to go now." He looked at Allison, censoring

her with his gaze. "I haven't been home yet and I want to check out my place before it gets dark."

She had the grace to appear chastened, but he didn't let it affect him. She had some explaining to do. He hugged and kissed Dudley, said, "I'll see you later," without looking at Allison and left. He couldn't help laughing when he got into his SUV and Jack ignored him, showing his displeasure at not having been allowed to go inside the house.

He found his house as he had left it, fed Jack and looked around in his kitchen for something edible. A frozen dinner warmed in the microwave oven would have to suffice. He'd had a notion to take Allison and Dudley out to dinner that evening, but what the heck. It wasn't his first disappointment. He opened a bottle of pilsner, went out on his deck and sat down to enjoy the evening breeze. His cell phone rang.

"Hi, Jason. What's up?" he said, having recognized his brother's phone number.

"I checked out that divorce case. Man, it was a humdinger. She sued him for denial of her conjugal rights and for severe child abuse. She got full custody and he's supposed to pay child support, but he can only see the boy with her permission. I sure hope she doesn't punish you for that jerk's behavior."

"Something was wrong with that guy. It's left her cautious and maybe scared. If she got full custody, I'll bet he threatened to take the child."

"Maybe. I didn't follow the trial, but it seems he's a very rich man, so he had to have been guilty as sin to lose that case. Tread carefully, Brock."

"You bet. Thanks."

Well, well. He suspected that he had his work cut out for him. So he'd better make up his mind as to how far he was willing to go with her and the first step would be to find what cooled her off in so short a time. He knew she wanted him and that nothing had changed that...or had it? He dialed Ross's number.

"Say, man, how'd you get on with Allison? Done any layouts yet?"

"Yeah. I'm pleased with what we've done, a bunch of petits fours, cinnamon rolls and things like that. Thursday, I'm supposed to photograph chocolate candy. Now I can get really interested."

"In that case, I'll see you Thursday. I promised Dudley I'd give him guitar lessons."

"You're his patron saint. That kid talked about you nonstop. He said he loves you and Jack. Do you know who Jack is?"

"Jack's my dog. See you Thursday."

Brock hung up thinking that he hadn't learned anything important, but if Ross was the reason for Allison's coolness, he'd know it Thursday.

He talked to Dudley on the phone several times before Thursday arrived, because the boy had evidently asked his mother to teach him how to call Brock. He welcomed the child's calls and he did not ask him whether Allison knew that he had contacted him. He focused on his work and tried not to think of her, but that was becoming an increasingly difficult task. Thursday finally arrived. He wrote a chapter that morning, ate lunch, read the chapter that afternoon and tore it up. After tuning his guitar and doing some finger exercises, he drove to Allison's cabin.

When Allison opened the door, Dudley dashed out to greet him. He lifted the boy, hugged him and set him on his feet. "How are you, Allison?" he said, walked past her into the house and looked around.

"Say, man, how's it going?" Ross said, walking toward Brock. "I was hoping you'd get here before I left." They embraced as they'd done for years upon greeting each other and he turned to see Allison watching them.

"I didn't realize you two knew each other so well," she said.

"We've known each other since kindergarten," Ross said.

"We're even frat brothers. If you want to know something about this man, I'm the one to ask."

"I'll bet," she said drily.

"Come back here, Brock, and take a look at these chocolate candies," Ross said.

Brock followed him to the kitchen. "The real thing or the photographs?" he asked as they walked.

"The real thing," Allison said, indicating that she followed them. "Would you like some of these?" she asked Brock. He gazed at her, uncertain as to what his expression communicated.

"You may sample all of them, but I think these are the best." She offered him a chocolate truffle.

"Excuse me," Ross said.

"Where's he gone?" Allison asked, turning toward the living room and appearing to be befuddled.

"Ross isn't crazy and as he said, he knows me. You're willing to give me candy, but when I came here Tuesday afternoon, you had nothing sweet to offer. I'm not sure I want any of these."

Her eyes flashed the fire of her anger. "Then I shouldn't have saved them for you."

His hands shot out and grabbed her shoulders, but the minute he touched her, his grip softened. He stared down at her, longing to bring her body close to his, to hold her and love her. But he shoved his feelings aside. "I raced back here to see you, not even bothering to go home before I stopped here. And what did I get for my foolishness but a shower of ice from you. Give me one reason why you were justified in rejecting me. If you can't do it this minute, I don't ever want to hear anything you've got to say."

He released her and stepped away. "You've got until three o'clock. That's when Dudley gets my full attention."

"You're ordering me to—"

He interrupted her. "I'm not ordering you to do a damn thing. It's up to you."

When she folded her arms, laid her head to the side and looked at him, he braced himself for the abrupt termination of their relationship. But she surprised him. "Is it you or your brother who's a lawyer in Washington, D.C.?"

His eyebrows shot up. "My brother is a lawyer of some standing there. I have a law degree, but I won't begin private law practice until after I finish this book." When he'd practiced briefly before becoming a private investigator, he'd worked at a law firm, but he wasn't his own boss.

That seemed to disappoint her, but she perked up. "What does your father do?"

"I can't see how that's relevant to what goes on between you and me," he said, "but since you seem to think it is, both of my parents are physicians. Mother's a professor, and my dad is an oncologist. They have separate offices. I have only one sibling. Anything else?" When she didn't respond immediately, he said, "Dudley's waiting for me. Maybe Ross would like some of your truffles."

She gaped at him. "Ross? What do you mean?"

He walked away and left her standing there.

"Mr. Lightner, it's three o'clock." He looked down at Dudley, saw the hope and, yes, the exhilaration in the child's eyes, sparkling eyes not unlike those of a sailor who was beginning a new and uncharted voyage. He hunkered down in front of the boy. "We're going to learn a little at a time, but in the end, you will play the guitar better than I. All right?"

Dudley looped his arms around Brock's neck. "Yes, sir, it's all right."

"First, I have to tune your guitar. Where is it?" As the boy ran off to get the instrument, Ross walked into the room, and Brock decided to bite the bullet. He looked at his friend. "Did anything develop between you and Allison?"

"Good heavens, no. I got the impression that she was yours, so I didn't even think about it, much less act on it. Nothing here, buddy."

"I didn't think so, Ross, but I had to be sure."

He took Dudley into his room and tuned the guitar. He had

never given anyone guitar lessons and hadn't thought he would like it, but the child was so eager to learn. He worked so hard at doing what he asked him to do that he didn't sense the passing of time.

"It's five-thirty, Brock," Allison said. "You may teach him for as long as you like, but I thought it only fair to let you know how late it is."

"Mommie, you ought to let him teach you. It's fun."

"I wish I had time, honey," she said to Dudley.

"We'd better stop now," he told Dudley. "If I give you too much, you won't remember all of it. I want you to practice at least one hour every day. And next Thursday, I'll see how much progress you've made."

Dudley looked up at him with a plaintive expression. "How long does it take next Thursday to come, Mr. Lightner?"

"Not long. So you must practice." He turned to Allison. "Same time next Thursday."

"How did it go? Do you think he has any talent?"

"If our session today is evidence, I'd have to say he does." He could see her relax as her breathing deepened. "I'm glad. He wants to play so badly. Uh…Brock, he'll be extremely unhappy if he doesn't see you again until Thursday."

He wanted to say, What about you? But he didn't. She'd already made that clear to him. "He calls me."

"He *what?*"

"You mean you didn't give him my number?"

"Of course I didn't. I'd never encourage him to interrupt you when you're working. When did this happen?"

He bunched his shoulders in a careless shrug. "Several times since I was here last."

"I taped your number to the refrigerator, but I didn't dream that he'd read your name, figure it was your number and call you. I'm sorry about that."

"He's almost six, you've taught him to count and to read. He made good use of it, so don't be sorry. Be proud of him. I am."

"I have to be going," he said. A few more minutes and he'd

have her in his arms. He didn't believe in patching up relationships. Either you repaired them or you discarded them and he was in a mood to do the latter. He called Dudley. "You had a good lesson today. Don't forget to practice and keep your guitar in its case when you aren't using it."

"Yes, sir. Otherwise, it will be out of tune."

He hugged the child and headed for the door. He could see Allison standing in the door between the kitchen and the living/dining room, but he looked straight ahead and left without saying anything more.

Allison went back into the kitchen, put the chocolate truffles in a glass jar, closed it and sat down. She didn't believe that Brock would do anything to hurt Dudley and her heart told her that he cared about her, but if she was wrong, she would lose her child.

"I won't cry. I refuse to," she whispered, wiping a tear.

"I see you gave Brock all the truffles," Ross said to her, when he walked into the kitchen.

She shoved the jar of candy to him. "He didn't want any."

"You're joking. I've placed the layout for the first four chapters on the deck. Would you like to have a look?"

She thought her heart would break. Why didn't he leave? When words wouldn't come and she couldn't force herself to get up, she shook her head as if denying something. He opened the jar of truffles, took a few pieces and looked hard at her.

"This isn't my business, Allison, but if Brock Lightner turned down homemade truffles, something is drastically wrong. Did you do something that displeased him?"

"Evidently I did. I…I wouldn't intentionally hurt him, but…well, what's the use?"

"You're miserable," Ross said, "and so is Brock. Look, Allison. I've known Brock for thirty of his thirty-four years, and I can tell you he's straight. He's an honorable man. But no matter how he feels about you, if you aren't straight with him, he'll walk. Talk with him. Can't you see that he loves your son and don't you know what that means?"

"I don't know why he's in my life, Ross, but all he's done is make things easier and more pleasant for me and for Dudley. I know Dudley loves him, and—"

He interrupted her. "Are you trying to deny that Brock loves your child? He does and that means he has some deep feelings for you, too. Don't screw up, Allison. Brock Lightner is worth a woman's love."

Worth it or not, she thought with alarm, he certainly had hers. To Ross, she said, "I don't know how to touch him without seeming like a phony. He gave me a chance to make it right."

"And you didn't take it? Why?"

"With him staring down at me like a judge penitent, I'd never felt so intimidated. I couldn't think. I couldn't articulate my feelings."

"I definitely believe that. If you get on the wrong side of Brock, he can really mess up your mind. Call him and don't put it off. I'll see you tomorrow."

Minutes after Ross left, Allison's sister phoned her. "Hi, Ellen."

"What are you so down about?" Ellen asked.

"I'm not down. I'm frustrated and if I'm smart, I won't talk about it."

"Allison, what do you know about this guy who's causing you to feel something deeply other than motherly love for the first time in five years. I want to meet him."

"His house is half a mile from mine, but he spends 24/7 in my head. I don't want to talk about him."

"Well, you know what happened before when nobody could get your head out of the sand. You wound up marrying that gosh-awful Lawrence. Dad liked him because he didn't keep you out late and he'd nurse a finger of cognac for hours. But I couldn't stand the sight of him."

"Lawrence is history and I'm trying to keep it that way. I

love you, Ellen, but I have something important to do right now. Bye."

She hung up and dialed Brock's number. "Hello."

He knew it was she and he was not going to make it easy for her.

A second passed and she wondered if he'd say more or if he'd hang up. "Brock, I know you know this is Allison. I'm hurting, Brock. I don't want you to slip out of my life. I—"

"Why not? Surely, you don't think I've primed myself to be your pal."

"When you were away, I conjured up all kinds of stupid ideas. I…I need you."

"Really? Do you remember your response when I let you know that I needed *you?* I had convinced myself that you cared and I don't want to remember your reaction when you opened your door and I put my arms around you."

"I was scared, Brock. My lawyer told me to be wary, that my ex-husband would use any means to get revenge against me."

"What did that have to do with me? And if you're wary of everybody, I didn't notice your being particularly vigilant around Ross."

"You told me I should trust him."

"But nobody told you that you should trust me. Right? Look, I have to finish this scene. I'm going to Rutland for a couple of days. I'll have to think this over."

The sun had nearly set when she walked out on the deck that joined the back of her cabin and looked into space, musing over the conversation she'd just had with Brock. If she ran forever, she wouldn't outrun Lawrence Sawyer's reach, and how many friendships would she destroy in the process? She hadn't taken time to know Arnold Parker in Nashville, Tennessee, because she had been so certain that he was on her ex-husband's payroll. Yet as she looked back, the man had some admirable traits and a gentleness that seemed to come natural to many Southern men. But she had dismissed him with little thought for his feelings, thinking only of herself and her child. And there were others. But she couldn't dismiss Brock Lightner, for he took possession of her the first time she looked into his face.

Allison laid back her shoulders, went inside and opened Dudley's room door. She thought her heart would break at the sight of her child bending over a book of guitar scales and practicing the lesson that Brock gave him. She closed the door, went to the bathroom and splashed cold water on her face. The ball was in Brock's court.

Brock closed his computer, packed his notes in his brief-case, put a shirt and a few personal items in an overnight bag, called Jack and locked the house. A few minutes later, he was on his way to Rutland, Vermont, where he was more likely to find good library resources than down in Lake George. From the time he reached puberty until he left home to go to Yale University, his father had preached to him at least twice a week the folly of letting his libido rule his life.

As he drove through the night, he thought of those lectures and wondered if he should work on getting Allison Sawyer out of his system and his life. But as he tossed the pros and cons of it around in his mind, he inevitably concluded that he'd spend the rest of his life wondering how it could have been with her. Emotionally and intellectually, she was his type and he'd never had such a strong physical attraction to any other woman. Add to that her personality, which he had just begun to decipher, and which tantalized him, and…. He slowed down when he realized that he was driving at eighty miles an hour, drove into a truck stop and parked. Should he give it a chance? As long as she was alive, he'd want her. After deciding to listen to what she had to say, he put on a Duke Ellington CD and continued to Rutland.

The next afternoon, leaving the Rutland Free Library, he passed a Children's Village and remembered that Dudley would have his sixth birthday the coming Saturday. When he went inside, an aluminum puppy, a robot, caught his eye and he bought it and had it gift wrapped.

But as he sat in his room at the Hampton Inn, trying to concentrate on his writing, it hit him forcibly that he loved the child and that his feelings for Dudley were not contingent upon his relationship with Allison. He telephoned the boat leasing company and tentatively reserved a cruiser for the following weekend. He and Jason rented a cruiser from that company at least twice each summer that Brock had stayed in Indian Lake. At the end of the next weekend, he'd know for certain where he and Allison stood with each other. She said she needed him, but if she refused to spend the weekend with him, he'd write *finis* to her chapter in his life.

As he entered Hampton Inn's lobby, his cell phone rang and he recognized Allison's house phone number. "Hello."

"Mr. Lightner, my mommie burned her finger and it hurts."

He sat in the nearest lounge chair. "What happened, Dudley? Is she all right?"

"She was baking cookies and I think it hurts a lot."

"Dudley, I'm not at home. Remember I told you that I carry my cell phone everywhere I go? Well, I'm in Rutland, Vermont, more than two hours from you. Let me speak with her."

"She doesn't know I called you."

"I told her that you call me sometimes. Did she say you shouldn't call me?"

"No, sir."

"Then she doesn't mind. Let me speak with her, please."

After what seemed like ages but could only have been a couple of seconds, he heard her voice. "Hi, Brock. I'm sorry Dudley disturbed you."

"He didn't disturb me. What happened to your finger?"

"It's my right thumb and it's pretty miserable. I put some baking soda on it, but it's still burning."

"I'm sorry about that and I'm glad Dudley called me. I'm in Rutland, but I'll be back there in about two and a half hours.

If you don't smile when you open the door, that will be my cue to keep moving. Let me speak with Dudley."

"Is Mommie's finger going to be all right, Mr. Lightner?"

"Yes, but it may take a while. Thanks for calling me. I'll see you in about two and a half hours. Bye for now."

He hung up and headed for his room. He had intended to work there that night and return to Indian Lake the following morning, but he wanted to see that finger and to be certain that she didn't need a doctor. Burns could easily become infected. When he checked out, he asked the desk clerk for the address of the nearest florist, went there and bought two aloe vera plants, one for Allison and one for himself. If she'd had one and had applied the liquid from inside one of its leaves to the burn, chances are the pain would have receded almost immediately.

Two hours and eighteen minutes later, he knocked on her door.

Chapter 5

"Does it still hurt, Mommie?" Dudley asked her.

She hugged him and attempted to allay his fears. "Just a little and I'm sure it will soon go away."

"Don't worry, Mommie. Mr. Lightner is coming and he'll fix it. I love Mr. Lightner, Mommie."

She stroked her son's back with her right hand while she protected her left thumb. "I know you do, son." She didn't dare tell Dudley that she also loved Brock, but why couldn't she make herself tell the child that Brock loved him? She thought about it for a minute and decided that it would be prudent to allow Brock to tell Dudley how he felt about him, and especially because she didn't know what fate had in store for her and Brock.

She glanced at herself as she passed the mirror and gaped. "Am I crazy?" Hurriedly, she freshened up, brushed her teeth and changed into white short shorts and a yellow-and-white striped cotton shirt, the tail of which almost covered her shorts. She stuck her feet into a pair of white Keds, took another look at herself and combed her hair down. She wasn't going for broke, but she wasn't going to pass up the opportunity to get his hormones racing either.

She had never heard Brock's dog bark and she wasn't certain that it was Jack, so she ran to the kitchen window, saw the SUV and raced to the front door only to discover that Dudley beat her to it.

"That's Jack and Mr. Lightner, Mommie," he said with an eagerness that she rarely saw on her child's face. "Open the door, Mommie."

"There is no point in coyness," her mind told her and she slipped the chain and opened the door precisely when Brock's fist moved toward it.

When she looked up and saw him standing there, she felt more like crying for joy than smiling, but she forced the smile and, immediately, tears trickled down through her maze of artificial happiness. Neither she nor Brock noticed that Jack ducked past them and ran to greet Dudley.

"Can you ever forgive me?" she asked him in a voice that trembled.

"Yes, I can. But first, I want to look at your finger and put some of this on it. Let's go into the kitchen." He explained to her about the plant and its healing properties. "I want you to keep this on the kitchen window, and whenever you or Dudley has a burn, squeeze some of this juice on it. If doctors use it, you should, too." He broke off one of the fleshy, lance-shaped leaves and squeezed its juice over the burn on her thumb.

"Is that going to make it better, Mr. Lightner?" He glanced down and saw that Dudley watched him, his face the picture of concentration. "Can me and Mommie keep the plant?"

"May Mommie and I keep the plant?" Brock repeated what Dudley said. "Yes, and it should stay on this windowsill. According to the florist, you water it when the soil is dry."

Dudley hugged Brock's thighs. "I will, won't I, Mommie? Thanks, Mr. Lightner," he said and walked with Jack back to his room.

"Did you eat dinner?" Allison asked Brock, although she wasn't certain whether he wanted to eat at her house.

"I haven't had time. Would you like us to go out?"

"I have enough for you, Brock. That is if you don't mind eating here with us."

He dragged a chair from the table, sat down and pulled her to him with a little more strength than he'd intended and she landed on his lap. When she attempted to move, he stilled her.

"Stay here, unless you're not comfortable." She eased her arm around his shoulder and relaxed because she was precisely where she wanted to be. "If it won't bother your thumb, we'll eat here. I'll clean the kitchen."

"I cooked dinner before I burned my thumb. Say, the burning stopped."

"Good. I expected that it would. Now talk to me, Allison. If you want us to be more than casual acquaintances, I have to know exactly where I stand. I don't play games with people's feelings. I realize that my attraction to you is not merely physical, that it goes deeper, but I am not a masochist. If you don't care for me, I'll leave right now and I won't look back. But if you do care and if you're straight with me, I'll be here for you."

"I'm ashamed to tell you what I let myself think."

"Let's start with the fact that you had an unhappy marriage, sued for divorce and gained total custody of Dudley. Does that have anything to do with your relationship with me?"

She tried not to stiffen because she wanted him to know that she believed in him. "When I publicly accused Lawrence of vicious child abuse and of…" How could she tell a man that her husband slept in the bed with her for two years and didn't make love to her?

"What else? I need to know."

"He…forced me to share his bed, but he pretended I wasn't there and he did that for two years until I filed for separation, took Dudley and left him. He didn't want children and my pregnancy turned him off.

"When he lost that case, he told me that he'd get Dudley if he had to die trying. Considering how mean he is, I have every right to believe him. My lawyer told me to be wary of every man who sought my friendship and that was still fresh in my mind when I opened the door to you that afternoon.

"I didn't believe it. I didn't want to believe it, but after I fled Washington, D.C., to escape Lawrence, I lived briefly in four states, covering my tracks so to speak, before settling here in Indian Lake. When Lawrence makes a move, he won't come in person, he'll send one of his henchmen to trick me."

"I see. And you thought I could have been one." She wanted to level with him, so she decided to risk telling him the truth. "How do you feel now?" he asked her. "Look at me."

She gazed into his face and, struck by his pained expression, she hugged him. "I don't believe you would do anything to hurt me or Dudley and I know you're honorable. Lawrence Sawyer could never buy your integrity."

He blew out a long breath. "Thank God. Right now, I couldn't be trusted in the same room with that man."

Suddenly his lips brushed her throat and his arms tightened around her. She cradled his head to her breast, stroked his hair and caressed his face.

"Keep that up and I won't want any supper," he said.

"If it weren't for Dudley, I wouldn't either," she replied.

And when he looked up at her to determine whether she was serious, she leaned forward and pressed her lips to his. His tongue rimmed the seam of her lips and she opened her mouth and took him in. She thought he would devour her and his fingers stroked her bare thighs as she sucked his tongue deeper into her mouth. When she tried to twist in his lap and face him, she felt his heat and the pressure of his erection and nearly screamed in frustration. Frantic for more of him, she led his hand into her shirt. He released her right breast and with a groan that excited her unbearably, he sucked its nipple into his mouth, greedily, as if he'd been starved for days. When she felt the evidence of her own arousal, she cradled his head with her arm.

"I...uh...I forgot where we are. I'm sorry, because I didn't intend for it to get this far here in the kitchen."

"You needn't have worried," he said. "I was listening for the sound of Dudley's steps."

"I wish I could say the same," she said, annoyed with herself for having taken such a risk.

Brock moved her from his lap. "Show me where the food is and I'll heat it up while you set the table."

She stared at him. "Is this a man thing or is there something wrong with me? A minute ago, you had me in an emotional tsunami and I assume something was going on with you, too. But less than a minute later, you're standing here acting as if all you did was lean against one of those trees out back."

He stuck his hands in his back pants pockets, looked first into the distance and then at her. "Why do you think I gave you the job of setting the table? I've seen your porcelain and crystal and I'm in no shape to handle it."

"And you think I am?"

His wink, wicked and charismatic, made her want to hug him, but she controlled the urge.

When she'd set the table, he took her hand. "I want to take you and Dudley on a cruiser up Lake Champlain next weekend. It will be a wonderful birthday present for him. I'll have the food catered and we'll swim, fish, hike and have a good time. Jack loves it when I take him on a cruise and Dudley will, too. We'll leave here late Friday and come back late Sunday. The boat will have two staterooms. What do you say?"

"You're full of surprises. I'd love it. Wow! If you're not careful, I'll kiss you." A frown clouded her face and from his own worried expression, she supposed he thought she was about to change her answer. So she hastened to tell him that she'd have to work doubly hard in order to meet her editor's deadline.

"Layla—she's my editor—does not have a sense of humor about deadlines. She said three months and she doesn't mean thirty seconds longer. As things are now, I should meet the deadline with ease. Ross had done product layouts before and he has wonderful ideas. I'm going to attribute photography and layout to him on the book's cover. It's not in our contract, but I know it's because of you that he's adding these extras."

"How do you know it isn't because of you?" Her glare didn't make him flinch; he merely shrugged.

"If he was interested, he'd have made a move. It's been my experience that men don't hide their interest in a woman. Besides, we talked about you and he seems to think you wear wings."

"I know he's a good guy. I don't think you should mention our excursion to Dudley," he said, changing the subject. "Excuse me. I'd better find out why they're so quiet."

He returned a minute later wearing an expression of awe. "I think he's trying to teach Jack how to play a guitar and Jack was trying to learn."

"You're joking!"

"Go see for yourself. The food will be warm in a few more minutes. Should I run up to the liquor store and get some wine?"

"I have some that should be all right." She went to Dudley's room, opened the door and saw Dudley's arms around the German shepherd as he placed the dog's paws on the guitar strings. "We're going to eat in a couple of minutes, Dudley, so please wash your hands."

"All right, Mommie, but I think Jack was just learning that chord."

"Chord!" she shrieked. "You're supposed to be learning notes."

"I know, Mommie, but Jack can't learn notes, so I'm teaching him a chord."

She rushed back to Brock, but with his hands up and palms out, he stopped her. "Dudley is only five and he lives in a child's world of imagination. He knows Jack can't play a guitar, but he wants to share his happiness with his friend."

"Yeah. I should have had another child, but Lawrence didn't even want this one."

"It's best not to dwell on the past, especially if it was painful. Think about how much we're going to enjoy this weekend."

Feeling vulnerable and exposed, she looked up at him with a question in her eyes. "We are, aren't we?"

He rushed to her and wrapped her in his arms. "Don't doubt us, Allison. If you do, we're finished before we begin. In relationships, trust is a two-way thing. I'm trusting you with my emotions just as you're trusting me not to exploit yours." He placed a quick kiss on her lips and left her standing there.

"Dudley," she heard Brock say, "didn't your mother tell you to wash your hands and get ready to eat supper?"

"Yes, sir, but we were having so much fun that I forgot."

"You must always obey her. You understand?"

"Yes, sir. I'm sorry. I want to, but I forgot."

"Wash your hands and tell her you're sorry."

"Yes, sir. I love you, Mr. Lightner."

Unshed tears glistened in her eyes when Brock hunkered beside the child, put his arms around him and said, "I love you, too, son."

By the time Brock got home at ten o'clock that night, he was too tired and too sleepy—thanks to three glasses of red wine—to contemplate all that had happened during the past seven or eight hours. He remembered to telephone the boat leasing company and confirm the reservation, took a shower and crawled into bed. His last thought before falling asleep awakened him at six-thirty the next morning and he sat up abruptly.

In his mind, he'd made a commitment to Allison Sawyer. He jumped up and strode from one end of his bedroom to the other and back. How had that sneaked up on him? He slipped on a pair of shorts, walked out on his deck and inhaled deeply the morning air. Was he certain of his feelings for her? And if he was, so what? She came with baggage. A lot of it. He ran his hands through his hair, punishing his scalp. *One step at a time,* his mind counseled. He went back inside, made a pot of coffee, warmed a doughnut in the microwave and sat down to the first leg of his breakfast. Later he'd eat something nourishing, but right then, he had to think. Half an hour later, after consuming three cups of coffee, he laughed at himself. Thinking couldn't help his problem. Only Allison could do that.

That Friday night, beneath a halo of clear and perfect moonlight, Brock parked his SUV in the garage provided by the Upstate Boat Leasing Company, helped a sleeping Dudley from the car and went into the waiting room. A porter would unload his trunk and carry the luggage to the cruiser.

"Is everything in order?" he asked the manager.

"You bet, Mr. Lightner, and if you need anything else, call me and one of our speedboats will deliver it."

He thanked the manager. If he and Jason were going alone to fish, he would have steered the boat himself and he wouldn't have hired a cook/maid, but he was entertaining a woman for whom he cared and who, he was learning, had been deprived of tenderness and loving.

"This way," he said to Allison and headed for the gangplank. As he walked beside the speechless woman, he suspected that when the cruiser docked there Sunday night, he'd be a different man and she'd be a different woman. He put her suitcases in the master galley, Dudley in the smaller one and his belongings in the captain's office, which contained a sofa that opened into a bed.

Their captain shook hands with Brock. "You're right on time, sir. My wife said supper's ready."

"Please ask her to give us half an hour to freshen up."

"Yes, sir."

Brock showered and changed into white pants and a sky-blue collared T-shirt, went to the bar and poured two glasses of white Burgundy wine. When Allison floated into the lounge wearing long, red wide-bottom pants, a matching halter top and with her hair below her shoulders and silver hoops in her ears, he gulped the remainder of the wine in his glass and stood.

"If I didn't know better, I'd think you planned to seduce me. I've never seen you look like this," he blurted out and immediately wished that he hadn't.

She laid her head to the side in the manner of one making an unspoken dare and said, "Maybe that's because you haven't seen me with enough self-confidence to look this way."

His whistle split the air. "I'm not about to complain. Are you going to wake up Dudley?"

"He's sound asleep, so I won't wake him. He ate supper just before we left, so he'll sleep until I wake him in the morning. Where's Jack?"

"Probably sleeping beside Dudley's bed." He handed her a glass of wine, noticed that her fingers shook and said, "Maybe we ought to take that to the table."

"You hired a cook?" she asked him, flabbergasted, when the captain's wife appeared with the first course.

"Surely you didn't think I'd want you to spend the weekend cooking and keeping house." After she said grace, he sampled the soup and said, "Excellent. I need all the help I can get."

"What do you mean by that?"

"I'm trying my best to seduce you, woman. Haven't you figured that out yet?"

She laughed, because she couldn't help it and decided to needle him a bit. "Really? I wish you luck."

"What?"

"Worry not. Didn't I say I wished you luck?"

"Yeah, but in a tone of voice that said the idea's laughable."

She finished her soup, picked up her napkin and dabbed at the corners of her mouth, leaned back and grinned at him. "In my mind's eye, I can still see those fantastic legs of yours as you walked around in a pair of Bermuda shorts. I thought, My Lord! Is there any more where that comes from? You don't even have ugly knees. I'll bet you're a lot of fun when you…uh…decide to be."

She told herself not to laugh at the sight of his gaping mouth. "You fill up that T-shirt nicely, too. Hmm. These little crab cakes are fantastic. Wonder what we're having next."

He didn't answer and she didn't care, for she could see that his breathing had become shorter. *Better not excite him to the point where he decides that I'm not going to finish this great meal.*

The cook served a rack of lamb with roast potatoes and braised endives. When Brock still didn't speak, she asked him, "Are you annoyed with me? Surely you don't mind if I take a good look now and then and like what I see, do you?"

"This food is delicious and I'm enjoying it, Allison, but if you continue this line of talk, I guarantee you won't eat dessert."

She glanced at him and then said, "What do you mean? What will I be doing that I can't have dessert?"

"Have you ever tried moving one hundred and ninety-six pounds?" he asked her.

She stopped eating and gave the impression of deep thought. "No, I haven't and I can't think of a reason why I would want to. By the way, how many pounds do you pack?"

"One hundred and ninety-six and food is fast becoming the least important thing on my mind."

"Well, not mine. This is one of the best meals I've had in years." The cook removed their plates and Allison said to her, "That was delicious. What are we having for dessert?"

"Crème caramel."

"Wonderful," Allison said, looking directly at Brock. "That's my absolute favorite."

"Why did I know you'd say that? Go ahead and have fun. Nothing like a sumptuous meal to whet my...uh...appetite. Don't think I'm going to let you addle me."

She reached beneath the table and rubbed his knee. "How could I possibly think that? Everything about you says you're a man who can take care of...uh...whatever's given to him."

When he squinted at her, she wondered if he was about to

tell her off, but he smiled and said, "I'm glad you noticed and I hope you're prepared for a sample of it."

Nearly gleeful, she said, "What do you mean by that?"

She wasn't certain whether his glare was friendly or hostile, but she didn't intend to let it bother her. He'd be hers before he slept and the thought fired her up to the extent that she laughed aloud.

"I wish I knew what's going on with you," he said.

"Come now," she said, looking at him from beneath lowered lashes. "I thought you told me you were thirty-four. You should have figured that out thirty years ago." She knew she'd gotten to him when he stood abruptly and started toward her.

"Would you like coffee now or later?" the cook said as she placed the elegant dessert in front of them. She glanced up at Brock, who had walked back to his chair. "Oh, did you want something else, Mr. Lightner?"

"Nothing, thank you. We'll have the coffee in the lounge."

"Hmm. This is delicious," Allison said. "Where were you headed when the cook came in a minute ago?"

"I was going to cool you off temporarily, but that can wait. If anybody had suggested to me that you were this fresh, I wouldn't have believed them."

"Well, if *anybody* had dreamy eyes and a kissable mouth, he'd know what you know."

He flung his napkin on the table and a second later lifted her from the chair. "Dreamy eyes and a kissable mouth, huh?"

She rimmed her lips with the tip of her tongue as she gazed into his eyes. "Yeah. And sweet as sugar."

"You witch!" he said, parted his lips and she sucked his tongue into her mouth. But immediately he broke the kiss. "She'll be out here in a second with the coffee. Let's go into the lounge and you behave yourself."

"Wouldn't think of it. Watching you steam is so much fun."

"Is it now? Let me know when you get serious."

"I've been serious ever since we've been here. It's the first time in my life that I've just let myself go and I think I like me when I'm frivolous."

With her hand in his, they walked into the lounge. "Would you like a liqueur?" he asked her. "Because I don't have to drive, I'm going to have some cognac."

She wasn't used to drinking liqueurs after dinner or any other time; her ex husband reserved that pleasure for himself. "I'll have something light, Drambuie or Grand Marnier." She noticed that his eyebrow shot up before he smiled in what she knew was approval. Her common sense told her that Brock didn't want a drink but was killing time until the cook brought the coffee and left them alone.

He poured the drinks, put them on the table in front of her, sat down and slid his arm across her shoulder. But the minute she snuggled up to him, the captain walked in with the coffee.

"Will there be anything else tonight, sir?"

"Thank you, Ryan. And thank your wife for a great meal. Good night."

"Breakfast can be served anytime after seven. Good night, ma'am. Good night, sir."

Brock lifted his glass, clicked hers and said, "Now, let's see what's behind that smart mouth of yours?"

Her nerves began rearranging themselves in her body and, to avoid responding to him, she started sipping the liqueur.

"Well?" he said, his voice low but insistent. He put his glass on the table and turned to her.

"I don't know what you're talking about," she said.

"Kiss me."

He had never been so bold. Did he mean it? She gazed into his eyes, exposed and not trying to hide her vulnerability. His fingers, warm, strong and masculine, worked their magic on her bare back and arms, sending tremors through her and firing her wherever he touched.

She knew she was out of her league and that he would expect more than she knew how to give. Her lips trembled when she said, "I'm not sophisticated, Brock. I only look as if I am. You…you can teach me what every woman longs to know and feel because it's never been mine."

She tensed when he sucked in his breath, but he tightened his hold on her and whispered, "Do you want me to teach you?"

"Yes. Oh, yes. I do. I do."

He stood, held out his hand and she took it. She must have walked with him to her room, but she didn't remember getting there. She became aware that he closed the door behind them and when his hand caressed her back, she could feel herself tremble.

"Don't be afraid, sweetheart," he said. "This can only be a pleasure for both of us." He turned her to face him. "Do you trust me?" She nodded, because she didn't trust herself to speak. "I want you to remember that you're precious to me. If you like something, let me know it, and if you don't, tell me at once."

She knew her eyes widened as she said, "You mean you'd stop?"

"Look here, Allison. The purpose of this is to deepen what we feel for each other, and to do that, we give each other pleasure. You're damn right I'd stop. Do you want me?"

"I told you I did."

His laughter lightened the air, but his hands on her body were strong and firm. He gazed into her eyes, eyes that were no longer laughing, but which darkened to obsidian. Everything about him seemed to change, as he widened his stance. She watched him wet his lips with the tip of his tongue and heat plowed through her directly to her groin. His aura enveloped her, his heat seemed to jump out to her and the man in him seemed suddenly to possess her.

"Come here to me," he said, lifted her and fastened her to his body. He covered her lips with his own and, when she opened to him, he thrust his tongue into her with a hoarse groan, exciting her and heating her blood. She held him to her, caressing his head and their tongues dueled until she sucked it deep into her mouth. Hot and getting hotter, she rocked against him and when she felt the evidence of his erection, she untied the halter of her jumpsuit and let her breasts spring free. He rewarded her by sucking one of her nipples into his mouth and nourishing himself until, crazed with desire, she gripped his buttocks and rubbed her body against him.

He lowered her feet to the floor. "May I take this off you?" he asked of the jumpsuit. She unzipped the pants at the side and he slid them to the floor. He stepped back and looked at her.

"Don't. You're so beautiful. Exquisite," he said as he threw back the covers, lifted her and put her on the bed.

"Are you on the pill?" he asked, and when she said that she wasn't, he told her that he'd take care of it.

With only the tiniest bikini panties shielding her from his hot gaze, she crossed her knees in modesty. But she forgot the modesty as he shed his clothes. Seeing him nude, she licked her lips, spread her legs and opened her arms to him in a gesture as old as Eve.

He stumbled into her arms, gathered her to him and seared her lips, eyes, ears, forehead and cheeks with feathery kisses. She wanted his mouth on her breasts, but he kissed her throat instead.

"Kiss me," she pleaded.

"I am kissing you," he said, nibbling on her shoulders.

"But I want you to kiss my breasts," she said.

"I will. You said you trusted me."

"I do. You know I do, but I—"

"Shh. We've just started." He kissed the inside of her arm.

Hot and impatient, she reached down and attempted to caress his penis, but he moved away from her. When she tried it again, he took both of her hands and held them over her head. Then he sucked a nipple into his mouth and she let out a keening cry. He stopped.

"You like that, don't you?"

"Yes, you know I do. I want it some more."

But she was learning that he charted his own course. What was he...? His lips and tongue teased her navel and worshipped her belly. His tongue made trails on the inside of her thighs, stopping an inch from her swollen vagina and she thought she'd lose her mind.

"Please, I can't stand this. Get in me. Get in me."

"Don't worry, I will as soon as you're ready."

"I'm ready. I've been ready an hour."

He rubbed her pubic hair. "I'll know when you're ready. Shh. I need you to give yourself to me, Allison. Stop fighting me and relax." His hands gripped her knees, slid them over his shoulder and not knowing what to expect, she tensed. He parted her folds and thrust his tongue into her as screams tore out of her. He kissed, licked and sucked until a strange kind of heat claimed the bottom of her feet and seemed to work its way up her body.

"Brock, please. Honey, get into me. I need it. Something is happening to me."

"All right. Now, I want you to follow my lead. It's important."

"I will. Just get in me."

He raised her knees. "Take me in, love," he said, guiding her hand to his penis. Looking into her face with the most beautiful smile she'd ever seen, he pushed slowly into her. "It'll be all right in a minute," he said and bent to her breast. The minute he began to move, the clinching began.

"Am I in the right place?" he asked her.

"I don't know, but I've never felt anything like this."

"Look at me, sweetheart. We're making love to each other. Are you comfortable?" She stared into the dark desire of his mesmerizing eyes and thought she'd lose consciousness. Desperate for fulfillment, she flung her body up to him.

"I want to burst. This thing… Oh, Brock, it's… Honey, I can't stand this. It won't come out."

"It will, sweetheart. Trust me. It will." He drove harder, unleashing his power until she felt as if he dropped her into a deep canyon.

"Oh, Lord. Brock, I must be dying." But he hurled her up to the stratosphere and she felt herself erupt around him as she moaned his name.

"That's right. Give it to me. I'm right with you, baby," he said and gave her the essence of himself.

Minutes later, after covering her face with kisses, he gazed into her face. "I knew it would be like this. How do you feel?"

"I'm happy, but in time I'll be angry about having been cheated. Thank you for making it so beautiful for me."

"It was just as beautiful for me. With the chemistry between us as it is, how could we miss? We're a firecracker and a lighted torch."

Looking down into her beautiful, peaceful face, the face of a happy, sated woman, he wondered if he'd ever truly made love before, if all those other times had been mere physical release with pleasant company. Still locked inside of her, he gathered her up to him and kissed her eyes, her chin and then her lips. She had him poleaxed and no other woman could lay claim to that.

"So that was your first orgasm?" he asked her.

"Uh-huh." She shifted her hips beneath him as she stared into his eyes with the expression of a woman besotted.

"What are you doing?" he asked, feeling like a peacock among a flock of peahens and wearing a grin that reflected it. She undulated again in a haphazard fashion. "Hey!" he said. "What do you want? Tell me."

"Can we… I mean, how long before we can do that again? I want some more," she told him, her tone just short of strident.

He kissed her then with all the emotion, the tenderness that welled up in him. Knowing that he'd satisfied his woman, his lover, made his soul sing. "All you have to do is let me know that you want me," he said as he grew hard and strong within her. This time, he wrapped her long legs around his hips and took her on a fast ride to the stratosphere.

He wanted to awaken the next morning with Allison in his arms, but how could he explain it to Dudley? Shortly before sunrise, he eased out of her arms, tucked the cover around her sleeping frame and went quietly to his own bed. Not long thereafter, he felt Jack's paws on his legs. He patted the dog on the head, turned over and was about to go to sleep when he remembered that he wasn't at home, that Jack was probably hungry and wanted to be fed. He threw on a robe and went to the galley where the cook had begun to prepare breakfast and asked for the remainder of the previous night's rack of lamb. He fed Jack on deck and went back to the galley.

"Any coffee, yet?" he asked the cook. "If it's ready, I'd like to have two mugs full."

She prepared a tray, and he took it to Allison's room and knocked gently. When she didn't answer, he went in, sat on the side of the bed and put a cup close enough for her to smell the coffee's aroma.

"Dudley, what have you been doing, honey?"

"This isn't Dudley. It's your man and I brought you some coffee."

She braced herself on her left elbow and looked at him. "Gosh. Oh, my goodness. Brock." A mild yawn eased out of her and she looked at the coffee. "Hmm. I could get used to you."

He put the cup down and brushed her lips with his. "I got used to you last night, sweetheart, and I don't think it's going to leave me anytime soon."

"I should hope not."

If she thought he was joking, she was in for a surprise. He'd wanted her from the minute he saw her, but the feeling wasn't near as compelling as the need he experienced when he looked down into her face after she rocked him senseless.

Chapter 6

After drinking the coffee Brock brought her, Allison crawled out of bed and collected her thoughts sufficiently to remember that she had a child, that she wasn't home and that she'd best check on him. About to brush her teeth, she gazed at herself in the mirror, the same yet different and, as she squeezed out the toothpaste, it occurred to her that the previous night had been what her wedding night should have been and that she should forgive Lawrence and move on. She had only herself to blame for that debacle; Lawrence was the same man he'd been when they courted. The problem was that she hadn't known what to expect and, in spite of her suspicions, had accepted his crumbs.

Feeling like a teenager in love for the first time, she finished her ablutions, dressed in white shorts and yellow T-shirt, went in search for Dudley and found him on deck with Jack, Brock and the captain.

"I'm hungry, Mommie, and we're waiting for you so we can eat."

"Sorry to keep you all waiting," she said and hugged Dudley, but didn't look at Brock. She couldn't.

"I take it your wife is a Southerner," Allison said later to the captain after consuming a breakfast of orange juice, grits, sage sausage, scrambled eggs and buttermilk biscuits.

"Yes, ma'am. She comes from South Carolina and she loves to eat Southern cooking, but she can cook any kind of food."

"I've enjoyed her meals," Allison told him. She glanced at Brock and nearly wilted from the heat of his gaze.

"We're going to dock in about an hour," Brock told her. "That'll give us a chance to swim and fish. The cook will pack us a picnic lunch. Did you happen to bring any long pants?"

Her eyebrows shot up? "Uh…yes. Why?"

"Fishing is different from lolling on a beach. I'm concerned about protecting those beautiful legs of yours from sand flies, mosquitoes, poison ivy and…" He couldn't help grinning at her stricken expression. "I could go on."

"All right. I'll put on a pair of jeans."

"Mr. Lightner, do I need to put on long pants, too?"

"Your jeans are fine."

Dudley's lip poked out. "But you're wearing white pants. I want to wear my white pants, too."

Brock patted the boy on his shoulder. "Your jeans are all right, Dudley. Come into the office so I can show you on the map where we are and how far we are from Indian Lake."

"Yes, sir. We won't get lost, will we?"

"No, indeed. Both the captain and I know how to take a boat home."

Allison's eyebrows shot up. "You can steer a boat?" she asked Brock.

"You don't think I'd put myself, you and Dudley at the mercy of a guy I'd never seen before and with no proof that he could captain a private cruiser up this lake, do you? A big commercial cruiser with a thousand passengers is a different story. You bet I could take it straight back to Westport."

It wasn't the first time he thought he saw an expression of admiration in her eyes. Oh, yes. It was there and more. He reached past Dudley, gripped her right arm, leaned down and put a quick kiss on her lips. "Sometimes, I feel like grabbing you and running away with you," he heard himself say. She flinched and he wondered if he'd said the wrong thing.

Feeling wicked, he winked at her. "I should think it's common for a man to want to take his woman off to his lair and keep her there, wouldn't you?"

She winked right back at him. "Being a woman, I imagine that would be exciting. Sexy, too. But if you try that with me, please be sure to make prior arrangements for Dudley and Jack."

Lord, how he wanted her! "You are one fresh woman. Go put on those long pants, before I follow you and change our plans."

"You'd need my permission for that," she said.

He imagined that his eyes mirrored the surge of his libido when he said, "And you're saying I won't get it?"

"Because we're not prepared to test this, I'll just go change."

He took a step toward her, eager to see her response when she thought he was about to bring it to a head, stopped inches away and let a grin float over his face. "Who's not prepared to test it? Speak for yourself. All I have to do is put a guitar into Dudley's hand and tell the captain not to dock, and we'd see which one of us is best at playing dirty pool. Do I tell Ryan to stop or not?" he asked her, rubbing his finger down the bridge of her nose.

For an answer, she walked past him, bumping him, and then turned and whacked his bottom with the palm of her hand. "If you don't behave, you may wake up in *my* lair. Be back in a couple of minutes."

He turned and watched the inviting, seductive sway of her hips as she walked and he knew that with every passing second, she drew him deeper into her cocoon. Realizing that he didn't mind shocked him. *I can't have my cake and eat it, too. I want her and I don't want any other man near her. That means I have to stick around.*

He glanced up, saw that Ryan observed the two of them and decided to find Dudley and Jack. Ryan flicked his cap back and said, "I've lived a long time, sir, and I know the real thing when I see it. Looks to me like you do, too."

"Thank you, Ryan. If you know that much, you also know that recognition is merely the first step."

"You're sure right about that," the man said, put his cap on and disappeared into the galley.

Half an hour later, after paying the toll, the cruiser docked at Port Kent. Brock walked with Allison and Dudley until they reached the pier extending out into the lake. He rented aluminum folding chairs, put a life jacket on Dudley, baited their hooks and sat down with them to wait for the fish to bite.

"What if they don't bite, Mr. Lightner?"

"It's been known to happen, Dudley," he said. "When it does, we sit and enjoy the moments of peace and quiet."

Allison's line jerked and she reeled in a striped bass. "I'm satisfied," she said, gazing in wonder at the big fish.

"Are you so easily pleased?" he asked her.

"I came to fish and I got one. So I feel successful. Whenever I achieve a goal, I give thanks and don't quibble about what else is out there for me."

"I'm quibbling," Dudley said. "Suppose we have to go back and I don't have a fish."

"Not to worry, son," he said, stroking the boy's shoulder. "I've fished a lot of times and come up with nothing."

"Are you still talking about animals that live in water and have scales or—"

He interrupted her. "Both. I've struck out with both."

"Mr. Lightner. Mommie. Something's jerking my line."

He put an arm around the excited child, gripped his line and helped him reel in a ten- or twelve-inch pike. "Can we go back now? I want to show this to the captain," Dudley said.

"No, we're going to eat lunch and then we'll go down to the beach."

After their lunch, Brock rolled out a pallet in the shade.

"We can have a nap here," he said, and when Dudley lay down beside him and put his head on Brock's shoulder, he looked up at Allison, saw her wistful expression and stretched out his other arm to her. She rested her head on his chest, threw an arm across his body and closed her eyes.

"I could hold you like this forever," he whispered to her, "but with your body pressing against me like this, I think you'd better move."

She sat up and stared down at him, but he nodded toward Dudley. She leaned down and pressed her lips to his. "You don't want him to know?"

"I don't mind if he knows how we feel about each other, but I don't think he should grow up too fast, and in another minute I'd have been ready for…for anything."

She lay down again, put her head on his shoulder, but made certain that her breasts didn't touch him. Nearly an hour later, a cool wind woke him. He looked around, saw the dark clouds and roused Allison and Dudley.

"We'd better get back to the boat. I think we're in for a storm."

"But, Mr. Lightner, I wanted to swim."

"You will, but storms on these lakes are very dangerous, so we'd better get back to the boat."

"Yes, sir."

Moving quickly, Brock gathered their belongings, put Dudley on his shoulders and got them back to the cruiser.

Ryan greeted them. "Looks like it's going to be a bad one."

"Yeah, and I hope it doesn't last long," Brock said, putting Dudley on his feet.

"We can play checkers," Dudley said, looking up at Brock. "I play with Mommie lots of times."

They had played checkers for nearly an hour when Dudley said, "It's not raining. The sun's shining. Can we go swimming, Mr. Lightner? I want to go swimming."

"Another time," Allison said. "I don't want to go back out there right now."

"But me and Mr. Lightner can go." He turned to Brock. "Can't we, Mr. Lightner? I never swim."

"Mr. Lightner and I," Allison said.

"See what Jack's doing in the lounge," Brock said to the boy. He turned to Allison. "Do you trust me to take him to the beach and swim along with him?" He needed to know that she had banished her fear that he might have ties to her ex-husband and that she believed in him without reservation. She looked up at him, wide-eyed and the picture of vulnerability.

"What is it?" he asked her.

"You're asking me if I trust you. When I opened my arms to you last night, that should have answered all of your questions concerning my thoughts and feelings about you. Anything else you want to know?"

He wanted to ask her if she loved him, but because he wasn't prepared to answer that question himself, he couldn't ask it of her. "Then he can go with me?"

"Of course," she said, "but he'll need some sunscreen."

"Don't worry. I'll take care of that. Let's go, Dudley," he called. "I'm not taking Jack," he told the boy. "Jack loves to swim in the lake, come out and wallow in the sand, and it takes me forever to get him clean. He stays here. Kiss your mother and let's go."

"Aren't you going to put on a swimsuit, Mr. Lightner?"

"I'm wearing it beneath these pants."

"Me, too," Dudley said, kissed Allison, grabbed Brock's hand and walked off without looking back at her.

Allison selected a copy of *Moby Dick* from the bookshelf in the lounge and sat down to read. She'd read that story while in high school and she had no particular love for it, but reading it would make the time pass. And although she would have preferred to sit on deck, she didn't want Brock to think that she was watching him. She opened the book and immediately words swam before her eyes and she couldn't read. She put the book on the table beside her chair and closed her eyes. Her world, indeed her life, could be divided into two segments: BB and AB, before Brock and after Brock. She hardly recognized the woman who hungered for night—a time she had once dreaded and feared—so that she could lie again in Brock Lightner's arms. Never again would she keep her mouth closed about her feelings and her needs. She rubbed her arms, unconsciously searching for his touch, stood and paced around the lounge. She looked at her watch; only half an hour had elapsed. Her breasts tingled, begging for the tug of his lips.

"Madam, it's suddenly gotten pitch-dark." Allison looked up and saw the cook standing there wringing her hands. "Didn't take but a couple of minutes. I never saw such a change. That other time was a false alarm. We get plenty of those up here, but this thing…" She walked off, shaking her head.

Allison rushed toward the deck. "Oh, my Lord. Would you look at that?" A sharp streak of lightning flashed across the eerily dark sky and shudders raced through her. The loud clap of thunder that followed made her shiver. "Where are they? If they're out there in the lake, they'll drown." She grabbed Ryan by the shoulders. "Do you have a floodlight? Anything that will show them where we are?"

"I think they're coming," Ryan said, and at that moment, she heard the sound of Brock's bang on the door. Ryan flung it open and Brock burst in with Dudley, unperturbed, in his arms.

She rushed to them with her arms open and hugged their wet bodies to her, unashamed of the tears that cascaded down her cheeks. "I was so worried that you couldn't see which way to swim, that you'd get lost out there. It got so dark so fast."

"It was fun, Mommie. You should have seen the lightning."

"I saw it," she said, ignoring the child's glee. Suddenly aware that she held the wet flesh of both the man and the boy, she stepped back and looked at them.

"Our clothes are in one of the cabanas," Brock said, explaining their near-nudity. "It happened so fast that we didn't have time to dress. We were pretty far out, so I put Dudley on my back, swam to shore as fast as I could and then ran for the boat."

"I rode on Mr. Lightner's back." He pulled on Brock's hand. "Can we show them? How you did it?"

His arm encircled the boy's shoulders. "I think they can imagine how we did it."

She watched the interchange between Brock Lightner and her son and she thought her heart would burst. Dudley's love for Brock bordered on worship. She hadn't wanted them to become close, but there was no denying their attachment to each other.

"I'd better get you dry, Dudley," she said, "before you get a cold."

His hands went to his hips. "What about me. Won't I catch a cold?"

She looked at him then, took a really good look at six feet four inches of male beauty, hidden from her eyes by less than a quarter yard of fabric. She had the presence of mind not to gape. "Hmm. And I thought you had great legs. Go put some clothes on."

"Yes, ma'am," he said with a grin spread over his face, saluted her and walked off. Already mesmerized, she didn't dare look in his direction, but with the picture of him in her mind's eye, she licked her lips. The man had a body from the gods and she couldn't wait to get to it.

She took Dudley to his room and waited while he showered. "I'm sleepy," he said later. "Do you think I can ask Mr. Lightner to read something to me? He said the captain has some books on lakes and rivers."

"I want you to take a nap and we can ask him after you wake up." She tucked him in bed, kissed him and went to the lounge.

"This storm is a dangerous one," Brock told her, "and the captain said a hurricane is headed up the coast and he expects we'll get the brunt of it sometime tonight. So we'll move out of this little lagoon as soon as this one subsides, head up to Keeseville."

"Then what?" she asked him.

He offered her a glass of ginger ale and poured one for himself. "The captain will look after the cruiser. It's my job to take care of you and Dudley and I'll do that."

Ryan walked into the lounge with a worried look. "Do you mind if we skip supper here, Mr. Lightner? The winds have died down and I think we ought to head for Keeseville right now. If you all get hungry, my wife has some snacks."

He thanked the man, took out his cell phone and dialed. "I'm calling the hotel," he told her. "Life had taught me the wisdom of having contingency plans. If the storm catches us at Keeseville, we'll spend the night in a hotel."

She'd always feared electric storms and hurricanes, but in spite of Brock's precautions and the likelihood that the cruiser would encounter difficulties, she didn't feel threatened. Looking at him, she realized that she was following her heart and that her head didn't seem to object. She hoped that she wouldn't be burned a second time, because the stakes were now far higher.

Deciding that the best way to keep his mind off possible disaster would be to give Dudley a guitar lesson, Brock took his guitar to the lounge and began to play "In Your Own Sweet Way," a piece made famous by jazz guitarist Wes Montgomery. It didn't surprise him that everyone on board soon crowded around him to watch as well as listen, for they all needed respite from the threat of the coming hurricane.

"Can you teach me to play like that?"

Brock looked down at the eager boy who sat beside his knee and smiled. "As I said, I can teach you what I know. The rest is up to you." He handed Dudley his guitar. "What have you learned?"

As if on cue, Jack positioned himself beside Dudley and the boy played scales. "How did I do, Mommie?"

"Wonderful."

"Now we have to stay in Indian Lake so Mr. Lightner can teach me the guitar."

She couldn't answer. Her gaze flew to his face and he didn't doubt that she knew she was on trial, knew that he, too, wanted to know her future plans. Was she still running from Lawrence Sawyer?

Ryan's entrance dispersed the tension. "We should be in Keeseville in about forty minutes, sir, and my boss said we should dock there, that the weather forecast gets worse by the hour."

"Then we'll do that. I've reserved rooms for all of us, Ryan, so pack what you and your wife will need for overnight. You, too, Allison."

"I thank you," Ryan said, "but the company provides only ship lodging for employees."

"I'm not leaving you on this cruiser during a hurricane. Your room and meals will be on my tab."

Shaking his head as if puzzled, Ryan thanked him and left.

"The more I see of you," Allison said, "the more I...find to...to like."

He stared at her, knowing in his heart that she was telling him he was lovable, maybe even that she loved him, but he couldn't acknowledge it, because he wasn't ready to put his own cards on the table.

They checked into the modest but comfortable hotel in Keeseville. "There's a door between your room and mine," he told her as they stood crammed into the tiny elevator. "Because I can't visit you, give some thought to dropping in on me."

She nodded and he had a feeling that he had embarrassed her. Not so, Dudley, who said, "Mommie, I want to stay with Mr. Lightner. Boys ought to stay together. Shouldn't they, Mr. Lightner?"

He hated seeing her put to the test that way, but maybe it was a good thing. "It's up to your mother," he said, hating himself for not making it easier for her, but welcoming evidence of her trust. He knew she would think of Indian Lake and that Dudley would want to spend nights with him there. He waited for her answer.

"All right, if he doesn't mind switching rooms with us. Ours has two beds, but his has only one."

"Oh, that's all right," Dudley said. "I won't keep him awake."

"Mine also has two beds," Brock said.

After dinner, as they returned to their rooms, he sensed that he was living his future and decided that he needed time to think, but the storm could be heard barreling down on them, as nearby garage doors slammed, saplings snapped and the garbage cans he saw as they approached rolled noisily around hitting posts, trees and automobiles.

"Are you scared, Mr. Lightner?" Dudley asked him.

"No. We're well protected here," Brock said.

The boy clung to his hand. "I'm not scared either." At the door, he waited until Allison gave Dudley what he would need for the night, winked at her and went on to this room wondering why having sole care of a six-year-old didn't seem strange.

"First you read something to me, then I say my prayers and then I go to sleep," Dudley said.

"Don't you plan to tell you mother good night?"

"It's okay. I can tell you good night."

He followed Dudley's instructions, decided not to sleep nude as he usually did, put on a pair of shorts and got into bed. After an hour, he decided that Dudley had gone to sleep and was about to get up, when the boy crawled into bed with him, explaining that the howling wind frightened him.

Brock laughed at himself and told his libido to go back to sleep. "Now I know why marriages with a lot of children tend to get rocky," he said silently. "Still, I'd better get used to it." Allison would have to understand.

The next morning, he decided that he'd better not knock

on her door and phoned her instead. When he didn't get an answer, he looked out of the window, saw that all was calm, even if a bit rearranged, and took Dudley down to the dining room where Allison sat with Ryan and his wife. Figuring that she wouldn't act out in the presence of other adults, he leaned down, kissed her mouth and took a seat.

"Hi, Mommie," Dudley said breezily and turned to Brock. "What can I have?"

He'd just been made a substitute mother and he'd better stop it right there. "Go over there and kiss your mother and ask her what you should eat."

Dudley bounced down from his chair and did as he was told.

Allison beckoned to the waitress. "Would you please give the boy orange juice, waffles, bacon and milk and—" she pointed to Brock "—give him coffee and a bowl of oatmeal. Thank you." She smiled a beautiful self-satisfied smile. He didn't laugh, but he could have. She would have been disappointed to know that he loved oatmeal.

"I know you're vexed with me, Allison," Brock said in lowered tones as they left the dining room, "but Dudley interrupted my plans for us last night. He woke up, crawled into bed with me, snuggled up and said he was afraid of the wind. No way could I leave him. I told my raving libido to go to sleep and tried to do the same." Aware of the small hand holding his own, he added, "He really gets to me."

"I thought I was of so little interest that you fell asleep."

"I know and that's why you ordered oatmeal for my breakfast."

"I'm sorry."

"Don't be," he said, grinning down at her. "I love oatmeal."

Ryan informed them that he'd been out to the cruiser and that it was undamaged, although some smaller boats nearby had capsized, and they soon resumed the cruise. At lunch, Brock handed Dudley a package, and said, "Happy birthday, Dudley."

The boy tore the paper from the box, opened it and saw a

robot that almost moved like a human being. After he stopped squealing, he said, "Mommie, I love Mr. Lightner. Can I be his little boy?"

"I wish it were possible," she said, "but that's not easy to fix. Let's be satisfied that he's your friend."

Brock watched her, his mood solemn. If their excursion had taught him anything, it was that he didn't know this mercurial woman who could be fresh, challenging, fun-loving, serious, stern, distant and the most passionate of lovers. He had his work cut out for him.

That night, home again after the weekend's life-changing experience, Allison settled for Brock's good-night kiss and the promise of passion in his eyes, but she hadn't cooled off from the previous night when Dudley's claims on Brock deprived her of the loving she'd looked forward to all day. "I'll get him," she vowed aloud. "There's more than one way to skin a catfish."

Brock walked into his house, fed Jack and sat down to think. He supposed he was hungry, but food held little interest. The grinding ache in him for Allison started at the pit of his belly and wound itself through his body. He wasn't used to it and he wasn't sure that he wanted the affliction of an itch that begged to be scratched by one particular woman. He went to the refrigerator on his deck, got a can of beer and sipped from it. His cell phone rang and he was inclined to ignore it until he saw his brother's phone number.

"How's the book coming?" Jason asked after greeting him.

"It's right where it was the last time we spoke. I did some research in Rutland weekend before last, but that's all."

"Really. Doesn't sound a bit like you. How's Allison?"

"Man, don't ask me."

"Is she there with you?"

"I wish the hell she was."

"I see. I was thinking of getting up there to see you Friday. Will that inconvenience you?"

"Of course not. Why should it?"

"Well, you could have had some personal plans."

"Nah. Nothing like that. I'll be glad to see you and in case you think I don't know the score, I'm sure you're looking forward to checking out Allison."

Jason's warm chuckle reached him through the wire, comforting as always. "Yeah. She's the main reason why I want to get up there. Any woman who comes between you and your work must be dynamite. See you Friday afternoon."

"Right." He hung up and called his parents. "Hi, Dad, how's everything?"

"Fine. Your mother has decided that she wants to go to Rome. I ask you, why didn't she mention it in the spring when there was time to make plans?"

He couldn't help laughing. His mother did things on the spur of the moment, his dad liked to make careful plans and they had lived in happy incompatibility for forty years.

"So you'll go next June as soon as school ends."

"Right. She's at the dressmaker. I'll tell her you called. How are things with Allison? Any progress?"

"It seems that way, Dad, but if you don't mind, I'm not ready to talk about it. Still, thanks for asking."

The cool wind announced the imminent arrival of fall and the necessity of storing up for winter's needs. Indian Lake had little or no autumn and its winter sometimes lasted until the end of April. He used oil for heating, but had installed a coal heater for emergencies when weather prevented trucks from bringing oil. He went inside and made lists of all the foodstuffs, personal and medical items he would need, and made a note to order coal, which he would store in a shed beside the house.

The next morning, Monday, he went to the hardware store and ordered a snowplow that he would attach to his SUV.

That afternoon, he telephoned Allison. "My brother will be here Friday and I'm sure he'll want to meet you. Can we all have dinner Friday night?"

"If he's driving, won't he be tired?" she asked.

"Probably, but he'll also be hungry. Where's Dudley?"

"He talked Ross to death about his experiences this past weekend, and I put him to bed so Ross can get some work done."

"I didn't realize a six-year-old took naps," Brock said.

"Maybe they don't. I've never had one before." She laughed that low, sexy laugh that he loved and that always seemed to bring out the primal animal in him.

Thinking fast, he said, "Well, if Dudley's asleep and Ross is there to babysit, why don't you get in the car and come see me for half an hour. I could use a hug."

"I... All right, but I may have flour on my nose."

"I'll kiss it off. See you."

He jumped off the front steps as she parked, opened the driver's door and lifted her out of the car.

"Taking me to your lair?" she asked, reminded of one of his comments.

"You bet I am."

Her nerves tingled and she imagined that her hair stood up. He walked up the steps without taking his gaze from her eyes, took her inside and kicked the door shut. "I can't make love to you in thirty minutes, but I can do this," he said, settled her on her feet and locked her body to his with hands that gripped her buttocks and her shoulders.

"And I can do this," she said, rubbing his pectorals through the fabric of his T-shirt.

He rimmed her lips with the tip of his tongue. "Open up and let me get inside," he said and plunged into her. It was too much and it wasn't enough. She needed to feel his driving power as he held her and loved her, forcing her to erupt all around him, clinching and squeezing, until he gave himself to her. As hungry for him as he was for her, she broke the kiss, stepped back and pummeled his shoulders with her fists.

"Take them off," she panted. "Take off my clothes. You can't leave me like this."

He pulled her shirt over her head, picked her up and carried her to his bed.

"I don't need it," she said, when she lay nude beneath him and he began kissing her eyes, cheeks and throat. "I need you in me *right now.*"

Ignoring her, his lips covered her right breast and moans spilled out of her as he pulled the nipple into his mouth and began to suckle her.

Frantic now, she reached down, found what she sought, spread her legs wider and tried to bring him to her. Holding him, she lifted her hips and he let her have him.

"Tell me you love me," he said, bringing her to the point of release and then stopping. "Tell me. I need to know it."

"Stop playing with me," she said and locked her legs across his back as the pumping and squeezing began in her vagina.

"Do you? Tell me." He quickened his strokes until it seemed as if he would fling her into the unknown. Down she went, as tremors shook her inside and out.

"Brock!" she yelled. "What are you doing to me? Oh, Brock. I love you. I love you." She thought her heart had stopped beating. With her arms flung wide, she submitted to him, giving herself completely for the first time in her life.

"Yes. Oh, yes," he said. "You're mine. You hear me! Mine!"

This time, she knew. He shook violently and then collapsed, open and exposed, vulnerable, in her arms.

"I won't ask if you got straightened out," he said, "because I felt it. You nearly wrung me out of socket. What a feeling! The trouble is that I don't want to separate from you. How *do* you feel?"

She kissed his shoulder. "Me? Totally discombobulated. Imagine living thirty years without knowing I could feel like that. You may have unleashed a tiger."

"You like it, eh?"

"Do fish love the water?"

His grin covered his face. "You're one fresh woman, but you definitely suit me," he said and pressed his lips to hers.

"I've overdone it, Brock. I told Ross I'd be back in a minute."

"Ross isn't crazy. If you told him where you were going, he didn't expect you back in one minute, not even thirty of them." He rolled off the bed. "Give me five minutes."

If anyone had told her five months earlier that she'd leave her house hell-bent on going to bed with a man, she wouldn't have believed them. But she had no intention of returning to her cabin until she satisfied herself that what she experienced with Brock on that cruiser was not a fluke. The problem was that she liked it and wanted it as often as she could get it. But how could she get it without making herself a convenience for Brock? Yes, Brock. She already knew that not every man had the requisite skills or the interest in acquiring them. All things considered, Brock had what she needed, but where did that leave her? She still had to think of Dudley.

Brock returned with two glasses and a big bottle of lemonade, sat on the edge of the bed and poured a glass for each of them. "Good though it may be, sex is enervating," he said.

"In a way, I suppose it is. You're not a man who demands what he isn't willing to give or can't give, are you?"

He rested his glass on the floor and looked hard at her. "Of course not. Where'd that come from?"

"Just checking," she said and took a long sip while he digested that remark.

"I don't get it."

"You will. Think back over words we said while we were making love. And turn your back. I'm not yet sophisticated enough to stroll around completely nude in your presence."

He got up, opened his closet and handed her a robe. "I'll think about what you said. Remember we're having dinner Friday with Jason and Dudley."

"Okay."

By the time she drove the half mile to her cabin, her body wanted her to turn around and go back to him. "No way," she said aloud, went inside and found Dudley teaching Ross what he knew about the guitar.

"He's fallen in love with Brock," Ross said. "I sure hope you two make it."

"So do I, Ross."

Chapter 7

"No wonder you love it up here," Jason said to Brock, after he stepped out of his town car. "This crisp air is like foreign matter. It's so clean and fresh I'm surprised my lungs will tolerate it. How are you?" He knelt and patted Jack, who greeted him with his tail wagging, and then handed Brock a cool box. "This is from Mom, and I think Dad put a piece of his barbecued spareribs in there."

Brock took the box inside, removed the contents and put them in the refrigerator.

"Don't you want to know what it is?" Jason asked him.

"I don't want to know, because I'd be tempted to eat it and I made other plans for the evening. We're going out to dinner with Allison and Dudley."

"That's right. I don't suppose it's easy to get a sitter out here," Jason said.

"I don't want her to get a sitter. Dudley has good manners and he's very obedient, lately at least. You'll like him."

Jason gazed at him with knowing eyes. "In other words, you like the boy a lot."

"Right. He grows on you. I've been giving him classical guitar lessons and he's trying to teach Jack how to play the guitar."

Jason's stare seemed to penetrate him. "You're joking. Doesn't he know—"

"Of course he knows, but Jack is his only playmate and he wants to share with him. What beats the hell out of me is watching this dog try to learn. You've got just enough time to shower and change."

"You wearing a suit and tie?"

"Right, because she'll dress."

It hadn't occurred to him that his brother wouldn't like Allison; she had beauty, charm, intelligence and taste, among other attributes. What man wouldn't like her? What surprised him was his nervousness about Jason's response to Dudley. He had never discussed children with his brother and didn't even know whether Jason wanted any of his own. He did know that he wouldn't let Jason's thoughts about Dudley or the fact that Allison had a child impress him.

He telephoned Allison. "Hi, sweetheart. Jason's here and we should be at your place in about half an hour or less."

"We'll be ready. By the way, Dudley wants to know what you are wearing."

He nearly laughed at that. "I'm wearing a tan suit, beige shirt and green tie."

"Thanks. I may as well press those white pants. See you later."

"Hey, woman, don't I get a kiss?" She made the sound of a kiss and hung up. "Something tells me I'm in trouble," he said to himself, raised his shoulder in a slight shrug and continued dressing.

When she opened the door, he had to suppress a whistle. What he wouldn't have given to have been alone. He stared at her in a sleeveless, dusty-rose chiffon dress that accented her luscious figure, hair hanging around her shoulders and her lipstick-free, pouting lips tempting him to kiss her. Evidently seeing that he was at a loss for words, she reached up, kissed his cheek and stepped around him.

"Hello, Jason," she said. "Come in. I've been on pins and needles ever since Brock told me I would meet you. I hope you had a pleasant drive up."

He turned around and looked at Jason, who seemed flabbergasted. "Jason, this is Allison."

"I know and I can see why you've gone bonkers. Hello, Allison. I've been looking forward to meeting you. Where's Dudley?"

"Here I am. Mr. Lightner, I don't have a tan suit and green tie, so Mommie let me wear my white suit and red tie. Is this all right?"

Brock hunkered in front of the child, who immediately hugged him. "You look perfect," Brock said and stood. "Dudley, this is my brother, Jason Lightner."

Dudley put out his hand. "Hi. Mr. Lightner and Jack are my best friends. Jack doesn't go with us to restaurants. Where do you live?"

"I live in Washington, D.C.," Jason said. "That's a long way from here."

"I know and I can find it on the map." He turned to Allison. "Mommie, what can I call Mr. Lightner's brother?" Before she could answer, he said, "I know. I'll call him Mr. Jason."

"That works for me," Jason said.

With an arm around Allison's shoulder, Brock said, "I think we'd better get started. We're going to Wells House in Pottersville. I feel like a first-class meal." He seated Allison, fastened Dudley's car seat and looked at his older brother. "It isn't often that you have a classy chauffeur like me. Try to stay awake."

"Why should I?" Jason said. "Your eyes will be on the road and your mind will be on the woman beside you."

"But you can talk to me, Mr. Jason," Dudley said, reminding them that a six-year-old can easily follow an adult conversation.

"That, I can," Jason said. "I understand you enjoy studying the guitar. Do you like your other studies?"

With their voices droning in the backseat, Brock tried to focus on getting them to Pottersville safely. But with her leg touching his and her woman's scent furling in his nostrils, concentrating on the task at hand was not easy. When he parked beside the building, he let out a long sigh of relief and reminded himself that he was Brock Lightner, a man who had survived more dangers than thrills and who knew how to keep his head straight.

The reception areas of Wells House featured American-style period furnishings as did the elegant dining room. And the place reflected its heritage. Built in 1845 and renovated many times, it had withstood the ravages of time to become a twenty-first-century local landmark building.

With his left hand splayed in Allison's back and his right one holding Dudley's hand, he walked in, turned to Allison and said, "Wait here with Jason." But Dudley continued to hold Brock's hand and went with him to the maître d'. He knew Jason would comment on that, but he didn't much care. Dudley enjoyed being with him and the feeling was mutual.

"I'm surprised to find a restaurant of this quality in a place this small," Jason said, as they ate. "This food's great. Why didn't you bring me here on one of my other visits?" he asked Brock.

"You never had any decent clothes with you. You brought that suit because you expected to meet Allison."

"What did you expect me to do? I know how to deport myself in the company of a lady. We have the same parents. Remember?"

"Last time I checked."

When the waiter asked what they'd like for dessert, Dudley looked to him. "Can I have two kinds of ice cream, Mr. Lightner?"

Maybe Brock should have said, "Ask your mother," but why should he? The boy's behavior had been perfect and he deserved the treat. He asked him what kind.

"Raspberry and chocolate, please."

Brock glanced at Allison and saw that she took no exception to his having given Dudley permission to eat ice cream, but instead, looked at the boy with motherly admiration.

"This has been a most enjoyable evening," Jason said to Allison when telling her good-night. "My brother has always had good taste." He knelt to Dudley's level. "You're a fine boy and I'm looking forward to seeing more of you."

"Thank you, sir."

Brock was damned if he let Jason and Dudley cheat him of a good-night kiss. He kissed Dudley. Then making it as light and seemingly inconsequential as possible, he said to Allison, "Kiss me so I can go home." But their kiss clung because he couldn't make himself break it, and although Jason paid no attention to it, Dudley gazed up at them with eyes wide and unmistakable puzzlement.

At home, he pulled off his jacket, threw it on a chair, got a can of beer, sat down on the living-room sofa and waited for Jason's verdict. "Get yourself something to drink, if you'd like," he said.

Jason got a bottle of pilsner, sat down and kicked off his shoes. "I can see why she threw you for a loop. She's got everything right where it belongs—looks, manners, intelligence, class. But you'd better watch it, Brock. That woman loves you and Dudley is crazy about you. On the drive to Pottersville, he talked about you as if you'd been canonized and he behaves with you as a boy behaves with his father. If you're not planning to make a family with Allison and him, they're going to shed a lot of tears."

"What about me, Jason? Do you think I don't care about them?"

"Oh, you're not immune. You love them, too, but I know you. If you make up your mind that this scene's not for you, love or no love, you'll put it behind you and get on with your life."

"I'm not callous, Jason. I've never felt for any woman what I feel for Allison and no woman I've known has suited me as she does."

"Have you told her that you love her?"

"I haven't gotten around to acknowledging that to myself."

"Then you'd better have a conversation with yourself because this is a serious relationship. Unless there's something I don't know, I say any man who that woman loves is lucky. I like her and I hope she knows how to handle you."

He had to laugh at that. "If you think I'm in the saddle this time, you're in left field. She could wrap me around her little finger."

"If she knew it was possible, you mean. That's why you haven't told her you love her. I'll bet she told you."

"She did, but at a time when I had an unfair advantage."

"I wish you luck, brother," Jason said. "Allison Sawyer wouldn't get away from me and neither would that boy."

"I hear you, brother."

After putting Dudley to bed, Allison went out on her back porch and sat down. She didn't think Brock was making a statement when he kissed her in his brother's presence; possessiveness was more like it. Besides, she knew that men shrugged off that kind of thing as male prerogative. But if Brock was having a fling, she was not and she meant to have an understanding with him. If he wasn't in it for keeps, she'd tell him to stay out of her life.

Cold chills streaked down her arms. What about Dudley? He loved Brock almost as much as he loved her and Brock's influence had changed him from a wayward, sullen child to a sweet, obedient and cooperative boy. She didn't want to resurrect the fears she'd had in the early days after meeting Brock. He'd done many things to dispel those thoughts.

The sound of angry growls made her sit up straight. Not

knowing whether an animal could scale the fence, she went into the house, locked the door and turned on the television. Shortly thereafter, the phone rang.

"This is Brock. I called a minute ago. Where were you?"

"On my porch. I heard some mean-sounding growls, so I came inside."

"I heard some around here, too. Thanks for your company tonight, Allison. You looked so beautiful. You make a man proud."

"Thank you. I...I guess I wanted you to be proud of me, Brock."

"I think Jason's taken with you, but I knew you two would get on well."

She leaned forward, propped her elbows on her knees and decided to call a spade a spade. "Did you want us to?" It was a loaded question and she suspected he knew it, but she couldn't worry about that; she was playing for high stakes.

He took his time answering. "Yes. I wanted him to like both you and Dudley. I would have been disappointed if he hadn't, but his attitude wouldn't have made a difference to me. I know what you're asking me, Allison, but I'm not quite ready to talk with you about it. Will you accept that you are precious to me, more important to me than any woman I have ever known, and that I care deeply for you?"

She could feel her blood race and her heartbeat accelerate. "All right. I accept that. For now. But considering my feelings for you, I need more."

"I know that and it's important to me. Will you have time to go fishing tomorrow?" he asked her. "I promised Jason we'd fish."

"Ross is coming day after tomorrow and I have to work. So I guess I can't."

"Okay. Let's plan to have supper someplace. What time does Dudley finish his schoolwork?"

"Around one. Do you want to take him fishing?"

"I thought he'd like to go with Jason and me. Do you mind?"

"Of course not. Come at one and I'll have hot dogs and lemonade." She told him goodbye, blew him a kiss and wondered at her willingness to allow the boy to go off without her. Fortunately, it rained all day the next day and she didn't have to put her trust in Brock to a test.

With four cakes ready for photographing, she telephoned Ross. "Hi, Ross. It rained all day yesterday and I stayed in and worked. I have four cakes ready for you, and I'll have a fifth one ready within an hour."

"Good. I have some glossies for you to look at. I should be there in little over an hour."

She placed the four cakes on the kitchen counter, finished decorating the fifth one and told herself that the great Maida Heatter, dessert cook par excellence, had nothing on her. Satisfied with her work, she decided to telephone Brock before Ross arrived.

"Mommie, who were you talking to?"

"I was talking with Mr. Lightner."

"Can I go see Mr. Lightner and Mr. Jason, Mommie? I'll be careful."

"Darling, you know it isn't safe for you to go out alone and I can't go with you right now, because Mr. Hopkins is coming to photograph the cakes."

It surprised her to see Dudley push out his bottom lip and stomp off to his room. He hadn't done that since Brock spoke to him about disobedience. She wondered at the relapse.

A few minutes later, Dudley leaned against her thighs, gave her his most charming smile and said, "Mommie, why was Mr. Lightner kissing you? Did you want him to kiss you? Did you? Huh?"

It took a minute for her to recover from the shock of his question and she decided to be honest. "He kissed me because we like each other."

His frown reflected a six-year-old's confusion and she told herself to be more circumspect about such things.

Ross photographed the cakes first uncut, then with one slice removed. "We need something extra with this," he told her. "Do you have a really elegant cake plate? I want to show a slice on a plate with a fork beside it."

"I have Bernardaud and Herend. I can't think of anything more elegant than Herend in this Chinese raspberry pattern." She hadn't used it since her divorce, but she'd kept it in case she had financial difficulty. The service for twelve and more than a dozen serving pieces should bring over fifty thousand dollars.

"I'll take that red Herend," he told her, laughing at his own joke.

She gave Ross the devil's food cake when he'd finished photographing.

"I'll get a quart of milk at the supermarket and by the time I get back to my hotel, half of this cake will be resting comfortably in my stomach," he said as he was leaving. As usual, he would continue working in his hotel room in Lake George.

With the remainder of a bright, sunny day free for writing, Allison settled down to do precisely that. After an hour, she realized that she hadn't heard Dudley practicing the guitar and, thinking that he may be pouting, she opened his room door. When she didn't see him in his room, she went out on the back porch. Alarmed, she searched the cabin, but he was not in it. In a tizzy, shaking from head to toe, she telephoned Brock.

"Dudley isn't in this house," she said, her voice high and quivering. "I don't know where he is. I've been working and I thought he was in his room. Brock, what will I do?"

"Don't worry, sweetheart. Stay right there. I'll find him."

Brave words. He didn't know where to look, but decided to check the back road leading from Allison's cabin to his, even though he didn't believe the boy could get out of his mother's back gate. He went to his SUV, searched the backseat and found what he was looking for. He let Jack smell the boy's baseball cap and hoped that the big German shepherd would get the message.

"I'd like you to stay here, Jason, in case he's headed this way."

"Is he in the habit of slipping out of the house?"

"He was, but I thought I'd made it impossible for him to get out without Allison's permission. I guarantee you this is the last time he'll do it. When I finish talking to him, he'll be a changed boy."

"Just because you're upset is no reason to get heavy-handed with that child."

He was in no mood for advice from Jason or anybody else. If anything happened to that child, he didn't think he could bear it. "If he shows up here, blow that police whistle in my top dresser drawer. See you later."

With Jack leashed, he searched the wooded area beside Route 28 and the woods bordering the Adirondack Lake until, weary and heartbroken, he sat on a log to rest. However, Jack's whimpers alerted him and, looking to his side, he saw a snake and quickly moved away. His immediate thoughts were of the possibility that Dudley may have come across one.

"Maybe I'm in the wrong area," he said to himself, but he didn't see how Dudley could have gotten to the back road. When it dawned on him that Jack hadn't picked up the boy's scent, he headed for the back road and the woods that bordered it.

"I'd better call Allison to see if he's back there."

Using his cell phone, he dialed her number. "I'm still searching, but I don't want you to be depressed. I haven't been on the back road yet and I'm heading there now. Jason is home in case Dudley goes there."

"He was mad with me. Brock, I don't know what I'd do if I lost him."

"Don't think that way. I'll find him." He took an unfamiliar path from the highway to what they referred to as the back road and immediately Jack began sniffing the bushes, but when the dog wanted to head into a thicket, Brock resisted. However, Jack whimpered and finally growled.

I'm getting nowhere, so I may as well let him lead, Brock thought and followed Jack into the woods, but when he came to a deep ravine bordered with brush and vines, he stopped. Jack whimpered loudly and began to run. Wishing he'd worn boots instead of sneakers, Brock did his best to follow the dog. Jack barked at the same time that he sighted Dudley leaning over that deep and dangerous ravine trying to reach blackberries.

"Dudley," Brock called. "Come away from there. You'll fall." The boy turned, saw Brock and nearly lost his footing. Brock grabbed the child and held him.

"You're holding me tight, Mr. Lightner."

"I've been looking for you for the past three hours, and when I found you, you were about to fall into a thirty-foot-deep ravine where no one would ever have seen you alive again. I've been out of my mind with worry and your mother is crazy with fear that something has happened to you." He put Dudley on his feet, reached down and patted Jack several times. "Good boy."

The dog greeted Dudley as if he had just found his long-lost best friend, but Brock broke up their loving exchange. He had serious words for the boy and didn't feel like witnessing a lighthearted exchange.

They followed Jack to the clearing, where Brock stopped, hunkered beside Dudley and took both of the boy's hands. "I couldn't love you more if I were your father and you were my son, but if you ever do a thing like this again, I'm through with you. What do you think is happening to your poor mother right now? Didn't you think about how she's feeling?" He gave Dudley a good shake. "Didn't you?"

"No, sir. I thought if she kissed you, she would let me go see you, but she wouldn't. I just wanted to be with you, but I got lost."

He gathered the boy into his arms. "Son, you can't do things like this. If your mother says no, it's for a reason."

"But I wanted to see you."

"Then you should have asked her to bring you to my house after she finished her work, or you could have called me and asked me to come to your house when I finished work. Do you know what it means for a person to get killed? Do you understand what happens to them?"

"You don't ever see them again."

"Right. You sleep forever and never wake up again. Your mother would no longer have you and neither would I. Now do you understand why it's dangerous for you to wander alone in this area?"

"Yes, sir."

"I have to phone your mother." He dialed Allison's number with fingers that trembled. That had been close, for nothing had stood between Dudley and that ditch but those frail blackberry bushes that he'd been leaning against.

"Dudley's with me, Allison. I'll bring him home."

He gave silent thanks as he walked along holding Dudley's hand. When they reached Brock's back gate, Jason stood there waiting for them. He slipped the latch to let them in and locked the gate behind them.

"Want to come with me to take Dudley home?" he asked his brother.

"Yeah. Where'd you find him?"

"Jack found him. He was seconds from falling into a ravine and that would have been the end of him. Let's take the chicken and dumplings that Mom sent with you. Allison won't feel like cooking. She's a wreck."

"Of course she is. I suppose you've had your talk with Dudley."

"Yeah. Let's go." He didn't remember having seen Dudley so subdued, but if he'd impressed him about the folly of his behavior, well and good.

"I'm sorry, Mommie," Dudley said when Allison opened the door. "I promised Mr. Lightner not to do that again and now he's mad with me."

"I am not mad with you, Dudley. I am disappointed and hurt that you broke your promise to me and that you disobeyed your mother."

"Why can't I go to see you, Mr. Lightner?"

"That's not the point," Brock said. "The point is that you have to obey your mother."

"Yes, sir. I'm glad you're not mad with me."

Jason sat on the floor beside Allison as she arranged and rearranged recipes and photographs of them. "I'd like to talk with you, Allison, and while Brock is giving Dudley his guitar lesson seems a good time."

She leaned back against the sofa and looked at him. "This sounds serious."

"It is serious. Stop me if I'm wrong, but I'm getting the feeling that you are trying to prevent Dudley from getting too close to Brock. That doesn't make sense to me. Brock cares deeply for you, or so it seems, and he is not a frivolous man. He loves that boy as much as he loves me, probably more. If you're trying to prevent Dudley from becoming attached to him, let me tell you that it's much too late. And why would you? Tell me."

"Brock has not committed to me and I don't know if he ever will. He's got a will of iron and I guess you know that. If we split up, Dudley's heart will be broken and I'll lose all the progress he made with Brock's guidance. Before Brock corrected him the first time, he was an unmanageable child. In a kind, gentle manner, Brock spoke with him about his behavior, the first nurturing he'd ever had from a man, and it resonated with Dudley. He tries to copy him, wants to be like him."

"I know," Jason said. "He loves Brock and idolizes him. You are being unwise to try keeping them apart. Don't you know how to get a commitment from a man who loves you?"

"He hasn't told me that he loves me."

He raised his knees and locked his finger over them. "I don't know how long you were married, but it should have been long enough to know when a man loves you."

"My ex-husband has never loved anyone, probably not even himself."

"I'm sorry. You're in love with Brock and you're proud of him."

"How do you know this?" she asked him and he wondered if he'd gone too far.

He shrugged. In for a penny, in for a pound. "I'm a lawyer. Understanding and reading people's actions correctly is the main reason why I'm successful. Let Brock know that you need him and I don't mean sex alone, although that's important. When I say need, I mean that he completes you, that when you see something beautiful, hear a lovely tune, eat good food, you need to share it with him. Let him know that you appreciate his ideas, his thoughts, even as you let him know whether you agree with him. Let him know that you'd rather walk with him than walk alone and that he's the only man who can fill your life with happiness. If you get scared at night, call him." He slapped his knees and got up. "I've talked too much, perhaps, but you think about what I've said."

She stood and faced him. "You want Brock and me to make a go of it?" she asked him with an expression of awe on her face.

"I love my brother. I want him to be happy and I believe you're the woman for him. If I had a sister, I'd want her to be like you."

Her smile radiated happiness. "That is one of the nicest, most pleasant things anyone has ever said to me. You're right. I do love Brock. I...I think he's wonderful."

"Then go for it."

"Why are you two so quiet?"

Allison gazed up at Brock, seeing in him all that her heart desired, shook her head slowly and began putting the photographs back into their individual envelopes. She hadn't stood a chance. Everything about him appealed to her. He gazed at her with those large, light brown eyes slighted shaded by long lashes that curled up a little at the end, sleepy eyes that made you want to drown in him. Suddenly his eyes darkened and narrowed. If he'd put his hands on her bare flesh, the effect would have been the same. Her breathing became shallow and she could feel her nipples tighten. She moistened her lips and leaned forward.

"How did Dudley's lesson go?" Jason asked Brock, reminding them of his presence and breaking the tension. "What's he doing?" Jason continued, as if neither he nor Allison hadn't answered Brock's question.

"I think he has innate musical ability, natural talent and he loves the guitar. I have to find some books for him." He didn't pursue his question then, but she knew he would and she hoped he buttonholed Jason first.

"Let the three of us get the cookbook organized," Brock said. "Then we can do some fishing."

"I haven't finished the baking and Ross has to take some more photographs. Until I have all of them, I can't be sure I'm showing them to the best advantage."

Brock glanced at his watch. "It's almost supper time anyway. So why don't we have a drink and I'll heat up the food."

Allison stared at Brock. "Heat it up? You mean you cooked it?"

His smile showered her with warmth and a feeling of security. "Our mother cooked it. Jason brought it and we kept it in my freezer. Do you have a couple packages of frozen veggies?"

"I have spinach and kale."

Brock rubbed his hands in a show of enthusiasm. "Give me half an hour."

Evidently having overheard the conversation, Dudley marched out of his room and headed toward the kitchen.

"I thought you were practicing," Allison said.

"I had my lesson, Mommie. I can practice tomorrow."

"I want you to—"

Jason interrupted her with a hand on her shoulder and when she looked at him, she saw in his eyes unspoken censorship. Dudley took advantage of the moment and ran to the kitchen.

"I know," she said to Jason. "I have to stop thinking that Dudley is mine and that I have to protect my property. Well, not property, but you know what I mean."

"You bet," Jason said to her. "Remember what I told you half an hour ago. In addition to that, you'll make Dudley a mama's boy and nothing is more pathetic."

Maybe she had needed to talk with someone like Jason, who didn't say what he thought she wanted to hear, but what he believed to be right. "I know you're right, Jason, but I've been fighting this demon alone so long that—"

"My point exactly, Allison. You aren't alone now. You have Brock."

She rocked back on her heels, unwilling to release to any man the control of her life that she had fought so hard to recover.

"I have to meet a man as an equal, Jason. I am never again going to accept treatment as a subordinate, not from any man or woman."

A slight frown flashed across his face, a sign that he hadn't liked what he heard. "Why should you? A modern man with sense takes his woman as his equal. Even so, you'll get from a man whatever you demand. Don't forget that."

Perhaps if she'd had a brother or if her father had survived through her teen years, she would already have known that. She patted Jason's shoulder. "Do you think Brock is really concerned about why we were quiet when he walked in here?"

Jason straightened up from his slouch against the wall. "Curious, yes. Concerned, definitely not."

Using considerable willpower, she didn't go into the kitchen because she didn't want to appear to be checking on Dudley. Instead she went to the cupboard, removed four place settings and set the table.

Later at the table, Jason said grace and she realized that he had grabbed the opportunity to let them know his views about their relationship when he added, "Lord, bless these three people with recognition of who and what they are to each other."

Her head jerked up and her gaze flew to Brock, who eyed her with a solemn expression. But suddenly his smile seemed to light up the whole room. She smiled at him and it was as if they were alone. He kissed her with his eyes and when she swayed toward him, he got up, walked around the table, leaned down and kissed her mouth. "I had to do that. You were too far from me," he said and went back to his seat.

"Mr. Lightner, why did you kiss my mommie?"

Brock looked at the boy, ran his fingers over his hair and rubbed the back of his neck as they all waited for his answer. He said, "Men like to do that when they like a woman. I like your mother."

"Oh. Mommie said you kissed her because you like each other. Can you show Mommie how to cook this?" he asked of the chicken and dumplings. "I like it."

"Dudley, I told you that my mother cooked this dish. I may be able to teach your mommie a few things, but cooking is definitely not one of them."

"Oh. Can we go fishing tomorrow, Mr. Lightner?"

"I'd like to work until around one o'clock," Brock said. "Then if it's all right with your mother, we could fish in the lagoon back of the Adirondack Lake. It's comparatively shallow and the fishing is usually very good." Brock looked at her, waiting for her reaction. She knew the explanation about where they would fish was meant for her rather than Dudley and that he wanted her to feel comfortable and not worry about the boy's safety.

"In that case, we'd have to go to the hardware store and get you a rod, but I wanted to work tomorrow."

"That shouldn't be a problem," Jason said. "I'll take him to the hardware store. You and Brock can work." He focused his intense gaze on her. "What time should I come for him?"

"About noon should be fine," she heard herself say and nearly gasped for breath.

"It isn't easy to operate on faith," Jason told her later while

Dudley and Brock cleaned the kitchen, "but you'll find that Brock is worth it."

"I know he is," she said and meant it.

Brock figured he could have cleaned the kitchen much quicker and probably more thoroughly without Dudley's help. But he believed in making the best of investment opportunities and he didn't know where the future would take him. He didn't seem inclined to put a break on his liaison with Allison, and Dudley had wedged himself deep into his heart. He loved the child and wanted a role in shaping his life, so now was as good a time as any to start. He realized that Dudley brought a meaning to his life that he didn't get from any other person, including Allison. He closed the dishwasher and looked down to reach for Dudley's hand.

"Have we finished, Mr. Lightner?"

He told the boy that they had and asked him, "What do we do now?"

"I take a shower and say my prayers, and then you read me something and I go to sleep."

Brock couldn't help laughing at the boy's slick way of getting what he wanted. An odd feeling of happiness suffused him and he enjoyed putting the child to bed. He heard Dudley's prayers, read to him a story of Native Americans—Dudley's favorite—waited until he slept and went to join Allison and Jason.

"Let's play some cutthroat," Jason said. "I haven't played since college, but I expect I remember it well enough."

Allison got a pack of cards and shuffled them, but she did it lackadaisically.

"Look, you two, maybe this isn't such a good idea," Jason said. "Brock, I think I'll take your car home, and I hope Allison won't mind driving you home."

She didn't look at either of them and he wondered about her thoughts. "I'll…uh…of course. I'll be glad to take Brock home."

Jason kissed Allison's cheek, held out his hand to Brock

for the car keys and a couple of minutes later, they heard the SUV drive off. Neither of them spoke. From across the room, they looked at each other. Her hands rubbed her sides furiously as if trying to shred her dress. The tip of her tongue bathed first her top and then her bottom lip and her eyelids seemed to droop. He stood there, spellbound by the most flagrant evidence of hot want that he'd ever seen in a woman. Suddenly she lifted a decorative pillow from the sofa and threw it at him.

"Come here," he said. "If you want me, why don't you say so?" Two long strides took him to her, and at last he had her in his arms, her hard nipples pressing against his chest and his tongue dancing in her eager mouth.

"What? What was that?" he asked at the sound of an automobile engine racing. He released her and raced to the window in time to see a gray Cadillac back up and head for the highway. "Probably some guy who'd lost his way," he said and turned back to her, but they had lost the moment.

"I'd better be going."

She said she would drive him home, but because he didn't want her to arrive at her cabin alone so late at night, he declined her offer. "It's best I drive your car and bring it back tomorrow morning." She reached up, kissed him lightly on the mouth and handed him the car keys.

By the time he reached home, he was less certain the driver who'd made a U-turn at Allison's driveway had been lost: the nearest road marker before reaching Allison's house was at least ten miles. That bore watching.

Chapter 8

Allison opened the door to Jason and steeled herself against her fear of having Dudley out of her protective reach. She forced a smile and invited him in. "Dudley's putting away his books. He's ecstatic about going with you to the hardware store. When I asked him why he was so excited, he told me that he goes every place with me and that this will be different."

"You're lucky," Jason said. "He knows he's different from you, that he'll grow up to be a man and he likes to emulate men."

"Is that why mothers have a difficult time raising their sons?"

"I'm not sure," Jason said. "But I do know that little boys need a role model in the home to nurture them into the ways of being a man. If my mother had had her way, she wouldn't have let Brock and me out of her sight, but my father refused to tolerate her excessive mothering and pampering."

"All right. I get it."

"I'm ready to go, Mr. Jason. Do I need a new life jacket?"

"Let's see the one you have?" He examined it. "Seems a bit small. You're growing and I think I'll get you another one. We'll be back shortly, Allison."

With Dudley out, she made three batches of cookie dough, cut the cookies and was preparing to bake them when the phone rang. "I'm as busy as an ant in a sugar factory," she told her sister. "I'll call you when I get these cookies in the oven." However, when she would have called Ellen, Brock arrived with her car.

He kissed her quickly on the nose, letting her know that he didn't want them to start a fire. "Would you be willing to let Jason babysit this evening, so that you and I can have dinner somewhere and see a movie? I want to know whether we can make something of our relationship, and so far, it hasn't had much of a chance."

Not sure she liked that, she narrowed her eyes. "You mean because of Dudley?"

"I always say precisely what I mean. I've never been to a movie with you, dined alone with you, seen a play, an opera, a symphony or a jazz concert with you, and I've never taken you dancing. I also haven't been swimming or hiking with you and I have no idea who your favorite poet is. Do you like to walk in the moonlight? Watch old movies? I could go on and on. We don't know each other and I want to fix that. Is it worth it to you?" He gazed intently into her eyes. "As for Dudley, he and I have a perfect understanding. You don't have to worry about us."

She laid her head to the side and gazed at him. She acknowledged Dudley's cleverness, but working out an understanding with a man of the world seemed to her beyond the boy's ability. "Mind if I know what kind of understanding you two have?"

If he were a child, she would have called him brazen, but as he stepped close enough to touch her without taking his gaze from her eyes, he was a man merely declaring his right and his position. "No, I don't mind," he said. "It's very simple. I love Dudley and he knows it. Dudley loves me and I know it. There isn't anything anyone can do that will change that."

She got that message and she was not proud of the loud gasp that escaped her. She knew he told the truth, but having it spelled out to her that way sent shivers through her. Recovering as quickly as she could, she forgot to censor her words.

"Maybe I should ask him how he does it," she said beneath her breath.

"What? What did you say?"

"I... Never mind." She attempted to move away from him, but he grasped her arms and held her there.

"He does it by being open with me, by telling me how he feels, what he wants, what bothers him and how he thinks. You have done your damnedest to prevent Dudley from forming ties with me." When her eyebrows shot up and her lower lip dropped, he said, "Oh, yes, you have. Do you think I'm crazy? Let's stop this, Allison. I need to know whether there is a chance for us to make a go of it. If we can, my role in Dudley's life is being formed now. Haven't you thought of that?"

"I haven't gotten that far and you haven't given me a reason to think that way."

"Well, start. Will you go out with me tonight?"

Maybe that was not a reason to be happy, but she was and she didn't try to suppress the smile that flooded her face. "I will if you ask me nicely."

He picked her up and twirled her around. "Jason will feed Dudley and he's a really good cook. I'll be here around five."

"Are you going to dress up?"

He tweaked her nose. "I have to wear a jacket in that restaurant and the movie theater may be cold, so bring a wrap."

"You're bossy," she said. "Kiss me."

"Okay, but don't lay it on too thick. I have to get back to work." His arms eased her to his body and his hands moved over her back and shoulders gently, as if caressing a baby. She had needed him to crush her body to him, but he opted for tenderness. His lips brushed hers and then settled on her mouth.

"What's the matter?" he asked her. "You're crying."

"I'm not. I'm…I never. You're so sweet, and I… You're making me feel so special, Brock."

He hugged her close, kissed her eyes, her cheeks, nose and hair. "You're special to me. Don't forget that." With her head on his chest, she held him as tightly as she could. Didn't he understand that she loved him?

She noticed that his breath shortened. "Careful, baby. I'm using the last fraction of my self-control. If that car engine hadn't revved up last night, we would definitely have made love. I still feel it and it wouldn't take much to make me boil over."

"Me neither. See you at five." He kissed her hard on the mouth, patted her bottom and left.

She sat in one of the living-room chairs, dropped her head into her hands and asked herself, "What do I do now? And what did he mean by 'making a go of it'?" *Remember Jason's words,* her conscience nagged. *If you don't trust him, why should he trust you?* "I'll give it a chance," she told herself, "but I'll be careful. Dudley means more to me than anyone or anything on this earth."

Remembering the feel of his soft kisses and the security she knew when he held her, she spread her arms and laughed aloud. "God must be working in my favor. Imagine me with a man like this one—handsome, kind, generous, fun and a smile to die for. All the things that Lawrence was not." She skipped to the back porch and took a few deep and invigorating breaths of fresh air. "Intelligent and sexy. And, Lord, what he can do to me in bed!" She raised her gaze to the sky. "I hope I won't be sorry, but I'm going for it."

A look at her watch told her that she had time to make two fruit pies before Ross arrived to photograph the cookies she made earlier. She mixed the dough for the crust, rolled it out and, having sweetened and seasoned the berries, dumped them onto the crust and was about to add a thickener when the doorbell rang. She froze. Then collecting her strength and determination, she grabbed an iron poker, went to the front window and peeped out. Relief flooded her when she saw her car parked in the driveway and she flung open the door.

"Mommie, I'm going to catch a lot of fish, and I can't drown because Mr. Jason bought me this." He held up a life vest. "We had hot dogs and an ice-cream sundae and we're going to have a lot of fun fishing."

"I wish I had time to go with you," she said.

"You don't have time, Mommie. You have to work. Me and Mr. Jason are going."

"Mr. Jason and I," she said, realizing that Dudley wanted to spend the time alone with his new friend.

"We're going to fish in the lagoon where it's cool and shady," Jason said to her. "The fish love it there. If the fishing's good, we'll be out there at least a couple of hours. Okay?"

"Fine," she heard herself say, "but please be back before five. Brock and I are going somewhere."

"That's my girl," Jason said, and took Dudley's hand.

"Why am I behaving like a teenager?" Allison asked herself after she took the fourth dress from her closet and, still dissatisfied, sat on the bed and knocked her fist against her thighs in exasperation. "I'm going to a movie, for heaven's sake, and ninety percent of the people there will be wearing jeans that have holes in the knees." But she was also going to dinner with Brock, a man accustomed to the company of elegant women. He hadn't said so or even implied as much, but she'd seen so many men of his apparent type among her ex-husband's friends and the women they chose to know the score. She settled on a silk suit with three-quarter-length sleeves.

When she opened the door to Brock and Jason at five o'clock, both men let out a sharp whistle. "Man, have I got a woman or have I got a woman!" Brock said, his face alight with a grin.

"Thanks." She could hardly manage that one word. Giddy with happiness, she closed her eyes, opened her arms and hugged him. "You look g-great," she said.

"You ought to live in that color. What's it called?" Jason asked her.

"Burnt orange. Thanks. It's my favorite." She made a mental note to get some winter clothing in that color.

"You think my mommie is pretty, Mr. Lightner?" She had forgotten that Dudley stood just behind her, hearing everything and remembering it all.

"She's beautiful," Brock said, gazing into her eyes. He lifted the boy, hugged him and said, "I hear you caught three bass. Tomorrow we can have a cookout at my place and fry those fish."

"Yes, sir. Uh…are you taking Mommie somewhere?" He put his arms around Brock's shoulder. "Mommie said she didn't sleep much last night. Didn't you, Mommie?"

Brock looked at her with eyes that said, "I know and I understand." Still she wished Dudley had kept that to himself.

"We'd better be going," she said, waving her right hand in an airy fashion. "We don't want to miss our supper." She kissed Dudley, hugged Jason and extended her hand to the man who had the keys to her heart.

"I chose this restaurant because you like Italian food," he said. "It's basically American, but they serve some excellent Italian dishes."

"I'll enjoy it no matter what kind of food they serve. This is exciting. My dad was so strict that I didn't date much when I was single and Lawrence was a hit with him, so that about settled it. I'm with you because it pleases me and I don't care who doesn't or wouldn't like it."

That was a mouthful if he'd ever heard one. He'd comment on it some other time, but right now, he didn't want them to talk seriously about her marriage. "We're going to see an old Jack Nicholson movie, *Five Easy Pieces*. I hope you'll like it. If you'd rather—"

She interrupted him, patting his knee. "Not to worry. Jack Nicholson is one my favorite actors."

"Mine, too. What do you think of the way Dudley took to Jason?"

"I'm not surprised. He trusted Jason because he's your brother and he discovered that he liked being with him."

"You don't understand, Allison. Jason is strict, even with me, and I'm thirty-four."

"I'm learning that my son doesn't mind discipline so long as it comes from a man."

"You're saying he's a little chauvinist?"

She relaxed against the back of the seat and folded her arms against her middle. "I don't know about that, but this is one female he'd better learn to deal with."

"I suspect he's already learned how to do that," Brock said, glancing at her from the corner of his eye.

Half an hour later, Brock parked in the parking lot beside Lakes Restaurant.

"I'm surprised to see such an elegant restaurant in this area," she said when they entered it. "How nice!"

"I'm pleased that you like it. The fish is outstanding."

Sitting across from him in that dimly lit environment, she told herself not to relax completely, but she couldn't prevent herself from doing just that. The man seemed to bring out everything in her that was soft and feminine. Trust. No matter how she tried to stave it off, she trusted him more and more every day, and each day he settled deeper and more firmly into her heart.

He interrupted her thoughts. "If you're not thinking about me right now, I'm in trouble." He lifted the fingers of her left hand and began playing with them, almost idly, it seemed.

She nearly jerked her hand from his. How was it possible that whenever he touched her she lit up like a hot coal receiving a dose of gasoline?

"Tell me you weren't thinking of another man," he said, stunning her, for it seemed like an entreaty and she saw no reason why he should consider himself at a disadvantage in their relationship.

Opting for levity, she forced a smile and said, "Brock, surely you don't believe I could sit facing you in this environment and think of another man. What kind of woman do you think I am?" She managed to look as if he had wounded her. If it worked for Dudley… She let the thought hang.

They gave identical orders to the waiter. "I can't believe we have similar tastes in food, too," she said.

With one eyebrow raised, he made a show of rubbing the back of his neck and said, "What else do we have similar taste in?"

"Movies," she replied, thinking fast. "We both like Jack Nicholson."

A grin spread over his face. "All right. I'll let you off, but that is not what you were thinking and we both know it."

They finished dinner and, thinking how nice it would be to linger with him over coffee and an aperitif, she almost wished he hadn't planned for them to see a movie. He voiced her thoughts.

"I'd love to linger here with you. In this environment, you're a hypnotic drug, but I want to see a movie with you. It's one of my boyhood fantasies."

"To see a movie?" she asked him, feeling foolish as the words passed through her lips.

"To see a movie with a woman who is really special to me. I've had plenty of movie dates."

She realized that he was serious and said nothing, merely squeezed the hand that held hers and let that suffice.

In the movie theater, he bought a bag of buttered popcorn. "I know we just ate, Allison, but this was part of my youthful fantasy."

She didn't see much of that movie. Throughout, one of his hands continuously caressed her shoulder and the other one fed her popcorn. But it didn't matter; she had already seen the movie several times.

They walked out of the theater into a quiet, clear moonlit night and she gasped. His arm immediately encircled her shoulder. "What is it?" he said, his voice carrying a sense of urgency.

She grasped his forearm. "Everything. It's so beautiful. So perfect."

"Yes. And so are you. I wish we could walk along the lake, but I don't think that would be wise."

"Why don't we go back to Lakes Restaurant and have some coffee. From where we sat in the dining room, I saw people sitting outside on a balcony."

"Good idea," he said. "The restaurant faces an…inlet, I suppose you'd call it. We could walk along there for a bit, get some coffee and dessert later and then head home."

They walked past the lobby and down the steps through a garden to a path beside the running water.

"This place was made for lovers," she said, thinking aloud.

"Yes. It was. Kiss me."

His arms encircled her and she went to him with the willingness of a bride to her husband. With one hand at his nape and the other holding the back of his head, she parted her lips and took him in. Tremors shook him and he didn't try to hide the fact.

"Don't lay it on so thick, sweetheart."

She kissed his cheek. "That's what you bring out of me. I didn't plan how I'd kiss you. It was a natural reaction."

He hugged her. "Do you think you can stay away from other men and you and I see only each other?"

Oh, the sweet communion she found in his soft words and loving arms. "That's what I've been doing," she whispered. "Haven't you?"

Laughter poured out of him. He picked her up, twirled her around, set her on her feet and pressed a kiss to her lips. "Lady, you've blinded me. I couldn't see another woman if I tried."

She stroked his cheek with the fingers of her left hand. "See that you don't try."

He smiled, took her hand and walked with her beside the

water. When she looked down at the stream, she saw their own and the moon's reflection in it. "That's supposed to be a good omen," she said.

"If it's an omen at all, let's hope it's a good one."

After having coffee and chocolate mousse on the balcony overlooking the water, they walked arm-in-arm to his SUV and headed back to Indian Lake. "Won't Jason think we're taking advantage of his kindness?" Allison asked Brock.

"Sweetheart, Jason wouldn't care if we spent the night. He's probably stretched out on the sofa sound asleep."

She didn't want to get on the wrong side of Jason, for she sensed he could be a cherished ally and that she might need one.

"What on earth?" Brock said and skidded to a stop. "Good thing I was only going sixty. Would you look at that big grizzly with two cubs?"

"What are you going to do?"

"Just hope she continues across the road and doesn't consider this car a threat. She could turn this baby over with one paw. If she comes toward us, brace yourself, because I'll be moving off in a hurry."

He could feel the tension emanating from her and sensed her fear, but he'd have to deal with that later; he had to focus his sensors on that bear. Turning off the headlights wasn't an option, because she was staring directly at him and if he had to get away, he needed those lights.

She pushed the cubs behind her. "Brace yourself, Allison," he said in an ominous tone, put the car in Drive, pressed the accelerator and shot past the animal as she started in their direction. A mile beyond the dangerous animal, he heard Allison's long breath of relief.

"Were we in real danger?"

"Absolutely. This is a two-lane road. I couldn't turn around, so I had to move past her. A female bear with her cubs is definitely not predictable and when she put those cubs be-hind her and started toward us, I knew the jig was up. Next time, if we're driving at night, we'll stick to the main highway."

Half an hour later, he parked in front of her cabin, cut the motor and put his arms around her. "I enjoyed this time with you and I want us to be together at every possible opportunity. Promise to call me whenever you need me. I want to be there for you. Do you understand?"

"Yes."

He stared into her dreamy eyes content with the knowledge that his heart belonged to her. "You told me you loved me, but that was in the heat of passion. Besides, I bribed you. Did you... I mean, could you possibly have meant it?"

"You not only held a proverbial gun on me, but you didn't tell me how you felt about me, even though you had no problem telling me that you love Dudley."

He held her in a way the moonlight let him see her eyes clearly. "I've been telling you for a long while now that I love you, not with words but in the ways that count, and I'm certain of it. Think over all that's happened between us today, beginning with this morning. I've been telling you I love you. Do you love me?"

Her eyes shone with a different light, a glow that seemed to come from inside of her, something he hadn't previously seen. "I loved you before we took that cruise. I loved you that night and I've loved you more with each passing day."

It seemed as if his chest expanded and his blood raced through his veins at breakneck speed. Staring into her eyes, he read into them what her words had failed aptly to communicate and tremors shot through him. Gathering her to him with the gentleness of a mother first holding her newborn, he kissed her eyes, cheeks and nose, smothering her face with kisses, and then rimmed the seam of her lips with the tip of his tongue. She took him in and loved him as if she couldn't get enough of him.

For the first time in his life, he knew what it was to be totally vulnerable to another human being, to need a woman as he needed air to breathe, to desire her well-being more than he wanted his own. The power of his emotions humbled him and he could only hold her to him and rock her.

The light in the living room of her house brightened and interrupted their mood. He smiled down at her. "I tell myself that we don't have to make love every time we get into a clench, but I don't really believe it." He stroked the side of her face with the pads of his fingers. "Are you my girl?"

A smile floated over her face. "Yes, if you're my guy."

"All right. It's almost midnight. I'd better take you inside, but I hate for this day to end."

"So do I. It's been…wonderful."

He opened the door with her key and they walked in with his left hand at her waist.

"I was wondering if you had decided to spend the night," Jason said.

"Did you and Dudley have any problems?" Allison asked him.

"Good gracious, no. That boy is a treasure. Smart, too. He makes you put the rubber to the road. He told me you were taking his mother to the movie so you could kiss her and wanted to know why you had to go to the movies to do it when he saw you kiss her right here."

Brock couldn't help laughing at that. "I'd like to know what answer you gave him."

Jason leaned against the back of the sofa and crossed his knees. "I told him a guy kisses his girl anytime and anyplace he gets a chance. That appeared to flummox him and he changed the subject to whether the guitar would be easier to learn if it didn't have so many strings."

Brock read the question in his brother's eyes. "We'd better be going," Brock said. "I want to work from six to ten and it goes more smoothly if I've had a few hours' sleep."

Jason stood. "Kiss her goodbye and don't take all night. I'll be in the car."

"I won't ask what you did," Jason said to Brock later as

they stood on Brock's deck. "I'll just say she's a different woman from the one who left that house at five o'clock this afternoon and you are definitely not the same man."

"You may be right about that, but trust me, we did not go to a hotel. What happened between us was more meaningful. Good night."

With rays of the rising sun flickering through the blinds, she crawled out of bed, brushed her teeth, showered and prepared to face the day.

Standing at the stove scrambling eggs, she whirled around when Dudley asked her, "Did Mr. Lightner kiss you, Mommie?" She hadn't heard him enter the kitchen. At six years old, he was becoming increasingly independent as well as inquisitive. She made it a point always to tell him the truth.

"Yes. He kissed me."

"I love Mr. Lightner," he said.

"Me, too," she replied, because that would be the next question he asked her and hoped he would drop the topic.

The phone rang and she was about to tell Dudley to answer it when she remembered why she didn't allow him to do that. She put the eggs on his plate along with toast and sausage and hurried to the phone. Seeing Layla's number, she lifted the receiver without enthusiasm.

"You're at it early this morning?" she said instead of "hello."

"It's seven-thirty up here and I'm just giving my son breakfast." The words were meant as a reprimand and she knew Layla would accept them without becoming annoyed.

"Could you e-mail me a couple of your best photos for the book's cover?" Layla asked without preliminaries. "I presume you have some by now."

"I'll speak with the photographer. Most dessert books have a chocolate cake on the cover, but I'd like something different, maybe my Cajun praline cheesecake topped with sugared pecans or my layered Southern caramel cake garnished with fresh pecan halves. We'll see."

"My goodness, you're in a great mood. Can I have it by noon today?"

"You bet." She hung up, phoned Ross, asked for his suggestion and for high-quality copy of the photos and went back to the kitchen.

"Mommie, I rinsed my plate and put it in the dishwasher. Can I have a glass of milk, please?"

Thinking that she would never get used to this cooperating Dudley, she gave silent thanks for Brock. "You may have some milk, then I want you to brush your teeth and write a paragraph."

"Can I write about Jack."

"Yes, you may…" *What was that?* She rushed to the window in time to see a gray car back out of her driveway and head to Route 28.

"Hmm. Looks as if someone is lost," she said to herself, scrambled two eggs and placed them on her plate along with sausage, grits and toast. If she got a good breakfast, she could handle the day.

"Why don't we get together and finish sorting out your photos?" Brock asked her when she spoke with him later that morning. "Jason and I can help you index the subjects. Will brother Ross be there this afternoon?"

"Ross? Say, wait. He's not your brother. I thought you said—"

He interrupted her. "A brother by a different mother. He's as close to me as Jason is."

"Come at lunchtime," she said. "We can have hamburgers or hot dogs."

"We can have both and Jason will take care of it. You only need mustard and ketchup."

"I have that. Kiss me and let me get my work done before you get here."

"Right, and I'd better do the same."

Simultaneously, they made the sound of a kiss and each said, "I love you." She didn't know she could be so happy.

Ross arrived at noon with glossy photographs of items suitable for her book's cover.

"These are exquisite," she told him, suffused with pride. "I have something to tell you. I'm asking that your name go on the book cover."

"Gosh," he said, clearly flabbergasted. "You don't have to do that."

"It's only just, Ross. You're raising the level of this product about two hundred percent."

They scanned the glossies and e-mailed the photos to Allison's editor.

Brock and Justin arrived and Dudley went out on the porch to commune with Jack while Jason broiled the hamburgers and hot dogs. After lunch, the four adults set about selecting shots for the book cover. Other that Ellen, her sister, she had never had friends, male or female, with whom to jostle, chat and exchange impersonal ideas and she marveled at her ability to hold her own with three sophisticated men.

"Man, you're about to become nationally famous," Brock said to Ross. "When I go to your house, I'll have to use the back door."

"If he pulls some 'I'm the man' stuff on you, remind him that you knew him when," Allison said.

Ross's laughter boomed like thunder and they joined him, enjoying the gaiety of the situation. "You're full of it, Brock," Ross said and looked at Allison. "Never let this guy get the jump on you. He's a master at getting ahead and staying there."

"What are you trying to do, man, ruin my reputation with the most important woman on this planet?"

"Shucks, Brock. Not even you can ruin your reputation. You remember that time you rode a hundred miles in the trunk of a guy's car, cut a hole big enough to crawl through and dislodge the front passenger seat? When the guy stopped for gas, the poor Joe came back to his car and found you sitting in the front seat. He'd been through three states trying to avoid you."

"Yeah," Jason said. "Every time I think of that I'm reminded of Somerset Maugham's tale, *The Appointment in Samarra.*"

"Right," Brock said, "or as heavy-weight champion Joe Louis said of his coming second bout with the German Max Schmeling, 'He can run, but he can't hide.'"

"Yep," Ross intoned, patting Brock on the shoulder. "You always found your man." He glanced at her. "Best private eye in this part of the good old U.S. of A."

Allison couldn't believe what she was hearing. With her arm extended to remove a picture of a lemon custard trifle, she couldn't move it. Her heartbeat accelerated and her belly seemed to have sagged to her feet. She managed to run to the bathroom, where she lost her lunch. She'd been had, damn him, but she was way ahead of him. When he was ready to make a move, she would be ready for him. Nobody was going to separate her from her child. Seducing her was one thing, but seducing a guileless child was unforgivable.

Better play it cool and act as if nothing had happened. She returned to the group, but she sat beside Ross, putting both Jason and Ross between her and Brock. The men continued to tease and laugh for the next half hour, but during that time, she didn't say one word.

"Why don't I pack Dudley and Jack into the SUV and we all run down to Glen Falls and have a good supper," Brock said. "I could taste some crab cakes and I know a great place to get them."

"I don't think so," Allison said, without guarding her tone of voice. "If you gentlemen will excuse me, I have a few things to do."

All three men stared at her and she stared right back. To press her point, she looked directly at Brock and didn't allow the tiniest bit of warmth to soften her gaze. She saw first his quizzical expression, then his pain before he shrugged his shoulders, telling her, in effect, that he didn't give a damn.

Brock went out on the deck, told Dudley goodbye, leashed an unwilling Jack and said to Jason, "If you're going with me, I'm leaving. Be seeing you, Ross." Without a word to her, he opened the door and left.

"What happened there?" Ross asked her when they were alone. "I thought you and Brock had the real thing going and I don't believe I was wrong. He's devastated. What went wrong?"

"You don't want to know, Ross. He's no more devastated than I am."

"From the sublime to the ridiculous in less that a second. Jekyll couldn't switch to Hyde that fast. No warning. I didn't say anything and I definitely didn't do anything. I didn't touch her."

"Maybe that's the problem," Jason said, groping for an explanation. "No. I'd swear she was a happy woman in love one minute an… Wait a minute. She got up and rushed to the bathroom. Hmm. Right after lunch, too, and when she got back her demeanor had changed totally. Could she be pregnant?"

"I'm not a pimply teenager, Jason. Last night, of her free will and with passion under control, that woman told me she loved me and it wasn't the first time. Moreover, I know she loves me. But from the moment we met, I've had a feeling that she's scared of something, that she's on the lam either from her ex-husband, the IRS or some other arm of the law. But I can't see how—"

"Hold it, brother. Did she know you were a private investigator?"

"I don't think so. At least I hadn't told her. She can't… Hey! Surely she doesn't think—"

Jason interrupted. "That you're a private eye on her case for someone and that you seduced her in order to get information out of her or to control her in some way. I know the thought is too painful for you to utter, but that's probably what she's thinking. You have to talk with her."

Brock parked the SUV in front of his cabin and looked at his brother. "Don't you know me better that that? If you're right, and I'm about certain that you are, she tried and sentenced me without giving me a chance to defend myself. She said she loved me, but she showed that she doesn't trust me. I don't need that kind of love."

"Don't be too hasty, Brock. She's a woman alone, a woman who had an awful marriage, and if her husband finds her, he'll kidnap the child and get him out of the country. She would never see Dudley again."

"I know all that and she's entitled to her fear, but I deserve a woman who has faith in me and who is loyal to me. Not only did she ask me to leave, but she did it in the presence of my brother and my best friend. I love her, but love will never make me a fool."

Chapter 9

Brock knew Jason would get on his case and his brother did not wait until they got home. "Did you have a reason for not telling Allison that you were a private investigator?"

He respected his brother, but right then, he didn't have much patience with the conversation and where he knew it was headed. "Look, Jason, half the women I meet seem to think that the words *private investigator* are a synonym for the word *stud*. The minute they hear that I'm a P.I., their gaze shifts from my face to my crotch. I've been sick of it for years. I don't tell any woman I'm a P.I. unless she needs to know it."

"But after you got to know Allison, you could have mentioned it."

He turned into his driveway and suddenly, as the weight of it hit him, he slumped against the back of the seat. "Yeah, I could have, but I no longer think of myself as a private investigator. Anyway, all this is history."

Jason shook his head as if in dismay. "You love her, Brock,

and she's worth a man's love, so this isn't the way to deal with it. She's scared, she's vulnerable and she is not behaving rationally. What about Dudley? If you break ties with that boy, it will destroy him. He loves you and he's given you a father's role in his life."

Brock released a long, tired sigh and opened the car door to get out. "I'm not planning to change my relationship with Dudley. What I feel for him is separate from my relationship with Allison."

"Don't fool yourself. If she doesn't trust you, she'll stand between you and her child."

"I know that, but I'll get around it. I won't let that child think he can't depend on me or that I don't love him because he can and I do. Let's warm up some frozen dinners."

Jason's eyebrows shot up. "Not this, brother. You mentioned crab cakes and I can taste them already. I'm ready for a beer. You want one?"

"Nah, man. In my present mood, beer is the last thing I need."

Knowing that his stubborn brother would live in misery rather than make the first step toward a reconciliation with Allison, Jason called her the next afternoon. "Allison, this is Jason. May I come over? I'd like to talk with you."

"All right. I'll be here all afternoon."

He drove the three miles to Sabael, bought two large "everything" pizzas, two bottles of beer and two bottles of lemonade and took them with him to Allison's house. It did not surprise him that Dudley greeted him with a question about Brock's whereabouts.

"Brock's working," he told the boy.

"I thought we'd have pizza for lunch," he told Allison and took the liberty of kissing her cheek. "We can heat it up in the oven. Whatever's left will do nicely for supper today or lunch tomorrow." He put the pizzas in the oven, turned it on and stored the drinks in the refrigerator. Aware that she hadn't objected to his taking liberties in her house, he put an arm around her shoulder and walked with her to the living room.

"Allison, your fears are unfounded. Now you're miserable and he's wounded to the core. He and I both figured out why you behaved as you did. If you had pulled all of his teeth without a painkiller, it would have been easier for him to take."

Tears gushed down her cheeks. "Jason, I've never loved anyone but Brock. I never felt for my husband an iota of what I feel for Brock or what I experienced with him. He's everything to me. But if you knew my ex and what I've been through with him these past three years, you would understand how I could think that way."

"Then you have to find a way to mend your relationship with Brock. I know him, so I know it will be far from easy. But every woman since Eve has known how to reach a man where it counts. I'm leaving tomorrow, but call me if you need me." He gave her his card. "Let's eat."

"Aren't we going to wait for Mr. Lightner?" Dudley asked when they sat down to eat.

"He couldn't join us, Dudley. He's got to finish that book."

"It's okay," Dudley said. "He sent us the pizza."

Jason and Allison looked at each other and, as if by consent, exercised the wisdom of leaving the boy with the only salve available to him.

"What are you doing?" Allison called to Dudley when he ran out of the dining room and into his bedroom. When he didn't answer, she opened his door and walked in. "All right," she said. "What's going on?"

"Nothing. I was talking with Mr. Lightner."

Her hands went to her hips. "You're not supposed to answer the phone."

"I didn't. I called him. He said he won't be seeing me much, but he'll call me at ten o'clock every morning and when I pick up the receiver, I should wait until he tells me it's him before I say anything. Mommie, doesn't Mr. Lightner love us anymore?"

What could she say to that? After thinking for a minute, she said, "Mr. Lightner and I had a misunderstanding, but that doesn't mean he doesn't love you."

"I want him to love you, too."

"Don't worry, darling. It will be all right." It wouldn't, but what else could she tell him?

"Can't he come to see me, Mommie? He told me not to sneak out and go to his house. What about my guitar lessons, Mommie?"

What a mess! Jason said she was wrong about Brock and her gut feeling said she was dead wrong, but she had so much at stake.

"The hunting season is starting, Dudley, and the hunters will be shooting all around here, so we have to be careful." She didn't know how much of that was relevant, but she had to get his mind off Brock and guitar lessons.

However, at noon the following Thursday, her phone rang. "This is Brock. If it's all right with you, Allison, I'll be there at four to give Dudley his guitar lesson."

"It's fine with me, Brock. He's expecting you. See you then." She waited, but he hung up without saying more.

What kind of man is Brock? He doesn't want to see me and he certainly doesn't want to come here. But he's made an agreement with my child and he intends to keep that. Have I made the mistake of my life? Dudley is so sad and I've never been more miserable. My disappointment in Lawrence angered me, but this is raw pain.

She went to the mailbox and got the remainder of the pictures that Ross took, put them in their respective places in the manuscript and slid the manuscript into a number six jiffy bag. After addressing the envelope to her editor, she called Dudley, "Get your sweater, we're going to the post office."

"What time will we be back? Mr. Lightner is coming at four o'clock."

"We'll be back by two-thirty. Put on your sweater. It's getting cool."

"Yes, ma'am."

After posting the manuscript to her editor, she stopped in the supermarket and bought half a gallon of ice cream. Dudley loved ice cream and maybe having some occasionally would brighten him up. She rationed it because she didn't want him to be overweight and, given the chance, Dudley would subsist on sweets alone.

She hid the ice cream in the freezer. Dudley would cry when Brock left them after the guitar classes and the ice cream would be her only means of soothing him. What should she put on? Brock knew what she wore around the house. Deciding that all was fair in love as well as war—and to her they were the same—she tried on every pair of pants she owned until she found a gray pair so tight that she dared not bend over in them, put them on and added a red, cotton knit turtleneck sweater. The combination outlined her body as well as if she were nude. She combed out her hair and put on a pair of silver hoop earrings.

If Brock noticed her curves, however, he didn't let on. When Dudley ran to Brock and hugged him fiercely even before he stooped to welcome Jack, she blinked back the tears. With Dudley in his arms, Brock's face conveyed the passion of a father greeting a beloved son after a lengthy separation. *Lord, what had she done*?

"Hello, Allison," he said, taking Dudley's hand and heading for the boy's room. He didn't wait for her greeting. His stride hadn't changed nor had the set of his shoulders, the shape of his mouth and the hypnotic power of his eyes. Yet everything had changed. She whirled around and fled into her bedroom.

"You can't do that," she heard Brock say. "I am not going against your mother's wishes, so we can't meet at the ice-cream stand. What gave you that idea?"

"I don't think you love my mommie anymore. Are you mad at her?"

"We…uh…we had a misunderstanding. I know you feel

bad because we don't have the fun together that we used to have, but remember that both of us love you just as we always did."

"But I want to be with you all the time, not just on Thursday."

"I wish it could be different, but it can't. Remember that you still have me. If you need me, call me."

From the silence that ensued, she assumed that they hugged each other. *At least Dudley had that much.* It amazed her that the child made such progress. On a simple piece, he played along with Brock, who always brought his own guitar to the teaching sessions. She remained in her room until she heard Dudley's door open and opened her room door simultaneously with Brock's knock.

"I wanted you to know that I'm leaving now."

She glanced down at Dudley, who clung to Brock's hand, effectively ruling out any move she might have made. "Thank you. I heard him play today for the first time and I was amazed."

"He's a natural. Goodbye." He strode to the door with Dudley beside him.

"You going to call me at ten?" Dudley asked him.

"Yes, of course. I will always do what I tell you I'm going to do unless something happens to make it impossible." He hugged the boy, looked up at her and said, "Don't burn your leaves. A quick shift in the wind's direction and you wouldn't have a house."

Before she could respond, he opened the door and left. She had raked the leaves into a pile near the corner of her garden and lit a match to them. It hadn't occurred to her that she may have endangered her house.

About a week later, Allison called Dudley to breakfast, but he refused to leave his room. She went to his room, determined that he was not sick and, after he declined to get up, she pulled him out of bed. Stunned, she noted that the stubborn, disobedient Dudley had returned and she didn't have to be told why. Besides, she had seen it coming.

"Why can't I go visit Mr. Lightner? He's all by himself down there. If you tell him I can go see him, he'll come and get me."

"Didn't you promise him that you would obey me? I am not going to reward you for being unruly as you were a few minutes ago."

She happened to glance out the window and saw what, to her, seemed like sleet. "It's a moot point, anyway. It's sleeting outside."

A check of the thermometer beside her kitchen window confirmed that the temperature had dropped by thirty degrees. She hadn't spent a winter in the Adirondacks and had no idea what to expect other than cold weather.

She telephoned Ellen. "Hi, sis. Would you believe it's sleeting here? We haven't even had Indian summer."

"Then you probably won't. It's sixty-eight here in Washington. How is tall, dark and handsome?"

"Oh, Lord, Ellen. Don't ask me about him. He came to give Dudley his guitar lesson and didn't say a word to me."

"Start at the beginning."

Allison did and when she finished, Ellen said, "If you did that, you deserved Lawrence Sawyer. I'd give an eyetooth for a man like Brock Lightner. One drops right into your lap and you kick him in the teeth. Don't ever tell me again that you love that man. Love doesn't allow a person to do what you did."

"You say that, Ellen, but I love him so much that I'm practically out of my mind. Not only am I miserable, but Dudley's driving me crazy."

"Next time you'll think before you do something that stupid. Let me speak with Dudley."

She called the child to the phone and went to her room. Maybe if she wrote Brock a letter. No, that didn't make sense when all she had to do was telephone him. He loved ginger snaps, biscuits and chocolate cake. She could bake something.

"I love him and I need him, but I'm not going to crawl."

Allison rushed to the ringing telephone, praying that she

would hear Brock's voice. Instead, Layla's happy soprano voice rang out with the words, "We've got a bestseller. This is a classy piece of work. Congratulations. We need to follow this up with another one real fast. What about quick breads? Can you give me something—say a hundred and fifty pages— by the end of January? Nice and clean like this one, so I don't have to let a copyeditor get her dirty little fingers on it. By golly, they'd insist on rearranging every page, crossing every I and dotting every T. What do you say?"

She couldn't make herself care. "Let me be happy over-night before I dive into another project, Layla. I'm happy that you like the book. Please be sure to put Ross Hopkins's name on the cover. His work and the time he spent on the project exceeded what I paid him for."

"I can imagine. We'll give him a contract for your next one. Call me before noon tomorrow."

The next morning, she telephoned her editor and agreed to a deal that required her to deliver the book by the end of February, provided the publisher agreed to work with Ross. She called Ellen, but her success didn't bring her the joy that it should have and would have if she could have shared it with Brock.

She went to the post office and got the box that contained Dudley's schoolbooks, went home and sat down to outline his studies. It occurred to her that the boy would need warm clothing, for he'd outgrown what he wore the previous winter. That meant drawing from Dudley's bank account, which the court established for his father's child support payments. But withdrawing it at the Indian Lake bank would be tantamount to writing Lawrence a letter that bore her return address. She phoned Ellen, gave her the information and asked her sister to withdraw it from the Ridge Bank in Washington and send it to her.

Allison finished her shopping in good time, for she had barely returned from Rutland with Dudley when she saw the first snowflakes of the season. She rushed to the supermarket, bought a supply of essentials and covered her car with tarpaulin that the locals used for that purpose.

"Mommie, can we make a snowman?"

"Maybe tomorrow if there's enough snow."

She had never made a snowman and didn't know how to begin. Brock would have enjoyed helping Dudley make a snowman and Dudley would have been deliriously happy. *How many times and in what ways would the folly of her suspicion come back to haunt her?*

"Wheeew!" Brock let out a long whistle when he woke the next morning and looked out his bedroom window. "A little warning would have been helpful." He dressed, put on a pair of boots, two cashmere sweaters and a mackinaw jacket and went outside to examine the snow. He measured seventeen inches. Not bad. He'd seen much heavier snowfalls there. After cleaning off his car, he attached the snow shovel to his SUV and removed the snow from his driveway and in front of his house.

"She'd be snowbound for the remainder of the winter and too stubborn to ask me to dig her out," he said between clenched teeth. "She knows she was wrong and that her accusation was unwarranted, but will she apologize? Not that I give a damn!" He found a red mitten, got some pieces of coal from his fireplace, a piece of red wrapping paper and a pair of scissors, put them in a plastic bag, got into his SUV and drove to Allison's house.

After removing the snow from her driveway, he hauled away most of the accumulation from the front of her house and used the remainder to make a snowman. It pained him to think of the pleasure he and Dudley would have had building a snowman, but he built one as quickly as he could, got into his SUV and went home. He took some delight in knowing that Dudley and Allison had been in their rooms at the back of the house and Allison hadn't heard the motor of his car.

However, minutes after he was back in his house, his phone rang. "Lightner." He braced himself for the sound of her soft, feminine voice and what it would do to him.

"I just saw what you did, Brock, and I don't know how to thank you. We'd have been stuck here until spring."

"I know that, Alison. Let me speak with Dudley, please."

"Brock…please!"

"It's all right, Allison. I wanted to do it," he said and waited.

"It's Brock and he wants to speak with you," he heard her say.

"Gosh, and it's not ten o'clock yet."

"Just a minute, Dudley. I do thank you from the bottom of my heart, Brock."

"You're most welcome." He wasn't going to say more because any more at that juncture would be a lie.

"Hi, Mr. Lightner. Mommie said you cleaned off the snow."

"I did. Go to the dining-room window and look in front of the house beside the driveway."

"Okay." The sound of the child's shrieks made his heart ache. He needed so badly to be with both of them, to love them and protect them. "Mr. Lightner. You made me a snowman. I asked Mommie if she and me could—"

"If she and I—"

"Yes, sir. If she and I could make a snowman. Mr. Lightner, Mommie never made a snowman. Gee, he's awesome. Thanks. I love you, Mr. Lightner."

"I love you, too, Dudley." If he only knew how much!

He hung up, walked over to his fireplace and absentmindedly stirred the coals. He had oil heat, but he installed the fireplace because he'd never lived in a home that didn't have one and to him, it spelled home, a place around which the family gathered to enjoy being together and to discuss important things. He stirred the coals with an iron poker and watched the sparks dart among each other.

"I can't go to her. If I give in on this, she will never

respect me and she'd be right. Besides, I have not forgiven her." He placed his folded arms against the mantelpiece and rested his forehead against them. "This is terrible." He ached for her.

To get his mind off Allison, he got chapter seven of his manuscript and began to read. He particularly liked that section of the story because although his clients' problems were grave, the people themselves elicited very little sympathy from him.

A rich Midwestern transportation tycoon hired him to find his wayward daughter and return her to her family. He agreed to find her, but told the man that he wouldn't carry a recalcitrant female anyplace, especially across state lines. Deciding that he didn't want the job, he quoted the man a hefty six-figure sum and the guy didn't blink. He found the teenager in a dive in Mexico City so eager to go home that she offered herself to him if he'd buy her a ticket. He pretended to agree, but instead called her father and told him to come and get her. Meanwhile, the girl used all of her imagined feminine tricks to get Brock to keep his end of the bargain so she could get the ticket, while he stalled, awaiting her father's arrival and making certain he didn't get a jail rap for having carnal knowledge of a child.

As he read it, he couldn't help laughing. The girl's father arrived, looked around at the trashy place she'd chosen over her elegant home, put her across his lap, pulled off his size twelve or thirteen shoe and gave her bottom a thorough burning. He'd hardly been able to contain himself as he'd watched that weird scene.

However, thinking how much he would love to read that passage to Allison, his mood changed to somber and he tired of it and put the manuscript away. He'd written that passage before his break with Allison, but since that day when she'd handed him the worst blow of his life, he hadn't been satisfied with anything he wrote. But he had to write and he knew he would finish the book to his satisfaction even if it took him a decade.

Recalling the minute he knew the time had come to quit working as a private investigator, he went to his laptop and wrote six pages on what it had once cost him to do his job well. He'd hunted down and interviewed a runaway wife and mother of two young children only to learn later that the woman was a victim of her husband's abusiveness. He accepted that the nature of his work always had him working with one side of a story and not always the side of truth. He'd had enough. Strangely, he wrote the passage precisely as he wanted it to read. Having accomplished that much, he got on his rented snowmobile and headed for the snowmobile trails.

Why couldn't he do anything without thinking of her? Every snowmobiler he greeted in passing consisted of a father and his sons or daughters, dads enjoying a frolic with their children. Wasn't it time he started his own family? And did he want Allison to be the mother of his children?

"There's that gray car again," Allison said aloud and told herself not to panic when the car made a U-turn and headed back down Route 28. She didn't think she was becoming paranoid and she knew that there seemed to be more silver- or gray-colored cars that any other. Still it didn't make sense that so many of them chose to make a turn at her driveway. She wished she could talk with Brock about it, but to raise that topic would be to raise a floodgate and let the debris of their discontent flow freely.

She made a batch of buttermilk biscuits, packed them in a sturdy box, took them to the supermarket and asked Mr. Wood, the manager, to let his deliveryman take them to Brock.

Mr. Wood didn't bat. an eyelash. "Glad to do it, miss. Lightner's a good neighbor. I'll send the package in a few minutes." He rejected her offer of payment and didn't let her think that he did the favor for her, but she didn't care. If she'd known the man would cooperate so readily, she would have made a chocolate cake and sent it along with the biscuits. But maybe less was more.

Jack's barking alerted Brock to the deliveryman's presence. He opened the front door and a blast of icy wind shot through him. "Well, this is a surprise, Jürgen," Brock said. "Did I lose something in the store?"

"Not that I know of, sir. The boss told me to bring this to you." He handed Brock a box. "It's mighty cold out here and they say a really big one is on the way. Folks buying up firewood like crazy and we're plum near out of kindling. You got oil heat?"

"I use both kinds of heat and I put in my supply last July. I'm set. Do you have time for a cup of coffee?"

"Thanks, but I'd better get back. I've got some things going to Sabael and North River. Stay warm."

Brock shook hands with Jürgen and eased a ten-dollar bill into the man's pocket. He knew the father of five depended on tips to make ends meet. As soon as he closed the door, he took the box to the kitchen and slit it open with his sharpest knife. The odor of warm buttermilk biscuits wafted up to his nostrils and although he welcomed the biscuits, he wondered why Marge would send him biscuits by the supermarket deliveryman. In the six years he'd known her, she had always called him and told him to come and get the biscuits.

He spread some butter on one, bit into the still-warm biscuit and focused on the bread he chewed. Delicious, but not Marge's usual biscuits. His antenna shot up and he used his cell phone to call Dick Wood.

"Say, man, thanks for letting Jürgen bring me this package. I appreciate the gesture. It doesn't have a return address. Who else should I thank?"

"No sweat, man. Miss Sawyer left it here."

He managed to hide his surprise. "Thanks a lot. I'll let her know I received it."

He rarely drank coffee in midafternoon, but those biscuits deserved the best coffee he could make. He brewed a pot of deep-roasted Colombian coffee, warmed some of the biscuits, put that, a stick of butter and a jar of raspberry preserves on a tray and carried the tray to his living room. He wasn't crazy about country music, except when Willie Nelson played and sang it; the man's music had an honesty, an integrity that made him think of old-fashioned family life. He put on Willie Nelson's *Red-Headed Stranger* CD and sat down to enjoy some of the best biscuits he'd ever tasted.

But why had she done that? Why couldn't she have gotten into her car with Dudley and brought him what she wanted him to have? He knew she cared. So why couldn't she use that opportunity to tell him she was sorry and wished she'd looked at that situation with her heart instead of some perverted logic. He shrugged. Lord, how he needed her!

He decided to take his time calling to thank her. He didn't welcome the pain of hearing her voice and of exchanging meaningless small talk with her when what he needed was the sound of her voice saying she loved and trusted him. After an hour, he admitted that it wasn't his style to repay kindness with rudeness and he telephoned her.

"Hello, Allison," he said when she answered. "This is Brock." He removed the mobile phone from its charger, walked over to the window and looked out at the barren trees and the cloudy, wintry day. "Thank you for the biscuits. They are delicious. It was very thoughtful of you."

"You're more than welcome, Brock. I…I wanted you to know that I'm…thinking of you."

"I knew that, Allison. To have things happen as they did so soon after we…after we were closer than we had ever been… Well, it was abortive to say the least and I doubt either of us will forget it. But I didn't call to discuss that and I won't. Thank you again for these wonderful biscuits. Let me speak with Dudley, please."

"He's right here. Thanks for calling me, Brock. I wasn't certain that you would."

"Surely you don't mean that. I'm not in the habit of being discourteous."

"No, you're not, but these aren't normal times, at least not with us. Here's Dudley."

He spoke with the boy long enough to realize that the break in his relationship with Allison was taking a toll on the child. "I'm going to ask my mommie to take me to see you, Mr. Lightner. Do you think she will?"

"If she has time." He didn't believe that, but Allison could correct it if she wanted to.

"I still have my snowman and he's still wearing his red hat. Mommie went out and put a broom under his arm. I love my snowman. One day I'm going to make you one."

He talked with Dudley for almost twenty minutes, mostly about nothing. They missed each other and that meaningless chatter was all they had. But damned if he'd let it drive him to do what he knew didn't make sense. Why couldn't she see what they were doing to Dudley, if not what she'd done to them?

Allison stood beside Dudley, who gazed up at her with a plaintive facial expression. She knew that she owed her son better than he was getting. He deserved friends and an opportunity to study and learn and play in the company of other children. When she sat down, he leaned against her and stared up at her in a wordless appeal. She leaned over and hugged him close.

"Can I go play with Jack, Mommie?" He hadn't reached the age of reason, but that question told her that he was almost there.

I have to show Brock that I trust him, that I know he wouldn't do anything to hurt me or Dudley, she thought to herself. "All right," she said, barely above a whisper, "you may call Mr. Lightner and ask him if you can visit him this afternoon and what time."

An expression of disbelief covered Dudley's face. "You

want me to ask him to come get me? You going to let me go to his house?"

"Yes." She tried to behave as if she'd said nothing special. "Go on and call him."

"Mommie," Dudley called a few minutes later, "Mr. Lightner wants to speak with you."

"You want to speak with me, Brock?"

"Yes. Dudley said you're going to bring him down here. Did he understand you correctly?"

"Yes, he did."

"Anytime is fine with me."

"In about an hour," she said and headed for the kitchen, where she whipped up some cinnamon buns and put them in the oven to bake. She remembered Brock's having said that cinnamon buns were his favorite. Forty-five minutes later, she took them out of the oven, cooled them for a few minutes and covered them with white icing. She put a dozen buns in a box, wrapped it and gave the box to Dudley.

"You may give this to Mr. Lightner."

Allison parked at the end of Brock's driveway, got out, unhooked Dudley's seat belt and stared openmouthed as the child jumped down from the car and sprinted toward the house. She saw Brock run to meet the boy with his arms outspread and bend down as Dudley launched himself into his arms. She stood frozen not by the temperature but by the sight of Brock and her child greeting each other as if they had been separated for years.

Brock stood, took Dudley's hand and walked to her. "There's no way you can know what this means to me. I'll bring him home in a couple of hours."

"I brought you something good, Mr. Lightner."

The smile on Brock's face radiated happiness and while he stroked the boy's shoulder, he gazed into her eyes with an expression of warmth that she hadn't seen since…. She didn't want to think about that evening.

"Have fun," she said in an attempt to downplay the importance of what she'd done. "See you later." She knew that by her action she had made it possible for Brock to initiate a discussion about why she could think him guilty of joining with her ex-husband to betray her. With the sound of Jack's barking in the distance, she headed home wondering why she had allowed Lawrence to poison her mind and why she could let herself believe that Brock could be so duplicitous.

She shook her head. "I give him too much credit. It would take an actor of Lawrence Olivier's caliber to behave with her as Brock had and not mean it." Yes, he would have to be a most talented scoundrel. Talented, maybe, but his unbending response to her unarticulated accusation proved that he was not a scoundrel. At home she parked and went inside the house. How strange to be there without Dudley.

Chapter 10

With Jack barking and wagging his tail in what Brock assumed to be dog delirium and Dudley giggling and nearly overcome with glee, he decided that he'd have to take matters in hand. Of course, he would have to deal first with Allison. She took a giant step in the right direction when she capitulated and left Dudley in his care, completely out of her sight and out of her control. But he needed to hear her say that she did not think him capable of abducting her son and delivering him to his father. If she couldn't do that, they had no future together. Still, if she could take that step, he'd make it easier for her.

"What's in the box?" he asked Dudley.

"I don't know. Mommie told me I could give it to you. I think it's something good. Gee, I like your house, Mr. Lightner. Can I see the rest of it?"

"Yes. As soon as I find out what you brought me." He opened the box and gaped at its contents. "Cinnamon buns. I'll make coffee for me and hot chocolate for you and we'll have some of these."

Dudley rushed to him and peeped into the box. "She makes those real good and I love hot chocolate. Where do you keep your guitar?"

The boy was so excited that his words seemed to tumble over each other. Suddenly, the child pulled at his hand. "Do you think Mommie will bring me to see you again?"

"Oh, she probably will," he said, trying to sound casual. "While the coffee is perking, let's look around the house."

"We had a fireplace, but I don't remember where. I like fireplaces. Do you get scared in this big house? I get scared when I hear noise at night."

"No, I don't get scared. Boys and men don't get scared easily. When you're older, you'll realize that it's best to find out what the problem is."

"I could come and stay with you," Dudley said, "but Mommie would be all by herself."

"That's right and we don't want that, do we?"

"No, sir."

He heated the milk and made the hot chocolate, poured out a cup of coffee and sat Dudley down at the table in his kitchen. "Let's see what these buns taste like," he said, removing some from the container.

"They always taste good," Dudley said, biting into his. He sipped the hot chocolate pensively, Brock thought. "Gee, Mr. Lightner, if you ask my mommie, do you think she'll let you be my dad?"

He nearly spilled his coffee on his jeans. He should have been prepared for that question or something similar to it because the boy treated him as a child would treat his father. He thought for a minute, aware that Dudley looked to him for an answer, an answer that from a six-year-old's perspective was a simple one. Dudley neither sipped his cocoa nor chewed the bun. He looked directly at Brock and waited for his answer.

To cushion the impact of the truth, he lifted Dudley from the chair and set him on his knee. "I wish I could be your father, but you already have a father, Dudley."

"I know, but he doesn't come to see me and I don't think he likes me. I was listening on the phone when Mommie told my auntie that he used to beat me. I don't think he loves me. Do you?"

"You shouldn't listen in on anyone's conversations unless they ask you to. When you do that, you deserve to hear something bad."

"That's what my mommie said."

He couldn't let the child think that he'd done something that caused his father not to love him. He tightened his arm around Dudley's shoulder. "Some people don't know how to...show love. Maybe he doesn't love himself. If that's the case, he can't love anyone else and we should pity him."

"Okay. Can we ask my mommie?"

Brock took a deep breath. How did a parent deal with a tenacious child? "I think we should wait until you're seven or eight."

"Will you ask her then?"

What could he say? His heart told him that he would want to ask her much earlier than that, but he couldn't raise the boy's hopes groundlessly. "I hope so," he said.

Dudley hugged him so tightly that he could barely breathe. "I love you, Mr. Lightner."

"I love you, too, s...Dudley." The word *son* formed so easily on his tongue, but he shouldn't tempt fate. If only it could be!

Seemingly satisfied that he would get his wish, Dudley exuded charm. "Can you play me something on your guitar?"

Brock glanced toward the ceiling, gave silent thanks that the moment's drama had receded to the background, for he didn't fool himself into thinking that it had passed. He got his guitar, acutely aware that, as if he didn't want Brock out of his sight, Dudley walked with him to his room holding his hand.

He sat on the stool that he bought for that purpose and tuned the guitar. To his amazement, Dudley sat on the floor beside him and leaned against his knee. He picked the playful theme to Joaquin Rodrigo's concerto for guitar and orchestra. When he finished, Dudley said, "Am I going to learn how to play like that?"

"If you practice, you will play much better than I."

"Gee, I'm sure going to practice all the time."

"I'd better take you home. I told your mommie that you'd be home within two hours and I always keep my word."

"I know. You told me that. Mommie will let me come back to see you, won't she?"

"Yes, I think so." He put Jack and Dudley into his SUV and drove to Allison's house.

"Did you have a good time?" she asked Dudley.

"Yes, ma'am. We had a man-to-man talk and Mr. Lightner said I can come back to see him again."

He looked down at the boy who held on to his hand. "Man-to-man? Where'd you get that expression? And how about telling your mother the truth?"

"Oh, I heard that on television."

"And the truth?"

"I asked you to ask my mommie if I can come back to see you again."

"That's better," Brock said.

"Do you have time for a…a drink or at least for a cup of coffee?" Her hopeful expression nearly made him capitulate, but he'd do that when she did the mature thing and told him she was sorry that she'd hurt him. Her hopeful, hungry expression nearly brought him to his knees. He needed her so badly, needed to lose himself in her loving warmth, but most of all, he needed her respect and to know that she believed in him without reservation. Her right hand reached for him and then fell limply to her side. Dudley moved closer to him and he knew that the child was watching the interplay between Allison and him, watched and hoped for evidence of the warmth that had existed between them.

He couldn't stand it. Why couldn't she tell him what was in her heart? He hugged Dudley, raised himself to his full height and looked at her. "Thanks for bringing Dudley to me.

I won't forget it." Minutes later, he was in his SUV heading home. Home to a big house where he would hear no human voice but his own.

She hadn't bolted the door before it began, as she had known it would. "Gee. Mommie, I like Mr. Lightner's house. It's big. He made me hot chocolate and we ate the buns, and he played the guitar for me. He said if I study I'll play better than he does. Mommie, why can't Mr. Lightner be my dad?"

That last question sent shock from her head to the bottom of her feet. She searched for an answer. "Did you ask him that question?"

Dudley nodded. "But he said it was because I already had a dad."

"That's true and a person can have only one."

His bottom lip protruded. "I don't like that."

She looked out of the window at the dark clouds and the saplings that seemed ready to break from the wind's great force. Then her gaze went back to her son, the delight of her life. "Dudley, if you are going to be a problem after your visits with Mr. Lightner, I can't let you go there anymore." That remark settled in and the little actor she knew him to be emerged at once.

"Mommie, can we go somewhere tomorrow?"

Before she could answer, her phone rang and she saw in the ID window that her caller was Jason Lightner. "Hello, Jason, how nice to hear from you."

"Have you heard from your editor about the book you turned in?"

"She loves it and wants me to do another one."

When he laughed, he sounded so much like his brother. "Glad to hear that it's a success. I hope you'll do as well with this new one. What's going on with you and Brock?"

"Nothing much. It looks as if I hurt him deeply and—"

"What do you mean, it looks as if? You know damn well that you hurt him. The man's in love with you, or he was. He refuses to talk about you or about what you said to him in the presence of his best friend and his older brother. If you haven't straightened it out, I assume it's because you don't want him."

"I love him and you know it."

"All right. If you say so, but I always thought that love seeks to heal. Be careful, Allison. When you decide to make amends, it may be too late."

She hung up with those words ringing in her ear and with tears pooling in her eyes at the memory of him staring at her with eyes that mirrored the hurt, hunger and the love that he felt for her, she wiped her face with the back of her hand.

"I'll reach out to him, if he'll let me, but he will never see me crawl. I've been there and done that and I know it'll get me nothing but pain."

Shortly after ten o'clock in the morning four days later, as she sat at the kitchen table sifting through packages of recipes, Dudley came to her and rested his head on her lap, a gesture so foreign for him that she thought he might be ill.

When she questioned him, he said, "Mr. Lightner has missed two mornings calling me."

"He's probably out of town," she said. "He'll call you when he gets back."

"But, Mommie, he tells me if he's going somewhere."

Hearing the anxiety in the child's voice, she stopped her work, put an arm around him and asked, "Why don't you call him. He said you could call him."

"I did, but he doesn't answer. Could you call him, Mommie?"

"All right, I will, but right now I have to finish checking this recipe."

He left her and she figured he'd sulk for a while. She'd just put the makings of blueberry muffins in a mixing bowl on the kitchen counter along with relevant notes on them for her next book when Dudley raced into the kitchen and yanked at her apron.

"Mommie, I hear a dog barking and whining at the front door. I know it's Jack, Mommie. Please come and open the door."

She didn't look up from her work. "What on earth would Jack be doing at our front door?"

"I don't know, Mommie, but it's Jack. I know it is." He yanked at her pants pocket. "I'm going to open the door," he said and ran toward the door. She reached it as he tried to move the chair so that he could stand on it.

"I don't like the sound of this," she said, slipped the chain and peeped out. "Jack." The dog barked louder and became more agitated. She opened the door enough to let the dog come in, but he would not stop barking and she realized that the dog was trying to tell her something. When he ran to the kitchen, looked up at her and barked louder, her antenna shot up, and she gave him a bowl of water, which he lapped up immediately. Frightened at the implication of that, she gave the dog the remainder of the spaghetti and meatballs she'd made for supper the previous evening and he plowed into it ravenously, as if he hadn't eaten in days.

"Something's wrong with Brock," she said to Dudley, whose face reflected his fear. "Put your coat on and let's go." She turned out the lights and noticed for the first time that Jack did not have a leash. Not knowing what she would face, she got a screwdriver, a hammer and a sharp kitchen knife, put Dudley and Jack in her car and headed toward Brock's house. When she turned into Brock's driveway, Jack stopped barking and she knew she would face something she would rather not see.

When she reached the house and saw the closed front door, she looked down at Jack and asked him, "How did you get out?"

Dudley followed the dog to the back of the house, saw that the kitchen window was not fully closed, ran back and called his mother. She put him through the window, told him to open the door but not to go into Brock's room. Jack followed Dudley and she had a long five-minute wait until Dudley managed to open the back door. With her heart in her mouth, she ran to Brock's bedroom.

As she walked into the room, she saw him thrashing in the

bed and took a deep breath. At least he was alive. She got a glass of water, sat on the bed beside him and raised his head enough to enable him to drink. But after a few sips, he would drink no more nor would he open his eyes. She wished she'd brought a thermometer, for she didn't feel right searching through his medicine cabinet. But having no alternative, she found aspirin and a thermometer and gave him a pill. She sat on the edge of the bed and Jack and Dudley sat on the other side of the big, king-size sleigh bed, while she put the thermometer under his arm. The reading of 103.5 alarmed her, but she didn't let on to Dudley.

She filled a pan with cold water, added some ice cubes, got a towel and sat on the edge of the bed. After dipping the towel in the ice-cold water, she wrung it out and applied it to the back of his neck, forehead and wrists. If he didn't rouse in another ten or fifteen minutes, she'd have to send for a doctor, although she had no idea where to begin the search. She washed his face in the cold water and took his temperature again.

"Thank God," she said aloud.

Dudley, who sat on the other side of the bed with Jack, asked her, "What is it, Mommie? Is he going to be all right? Is he?"

"His fever is down a little and that's a good sign. Do you think you can get me a glass of water? He needs some fluid." Dudley went to the kitchen for the water, but she noticed that Jack remained beside the bed.

She got Brock to sip a little more water and to swallow another aspirin. "Lord, if he ever fully wakes up, I'm going to tell him how sorry I am for hurting him and how much I love him," she said beneath her breath. At that point he turned over on his side facing her. She realized that he was wearing a shirt identical to the one he wore when he brought Dudley home. Had he been ill that long—four days?

After unbuttoning Brock's shirt, she found another one in his drawer, gave him a cold sponge bath from the waist up, dried him and, with Dudley's help, managed to get him into the clean shirt.

"I'd better try to get a doctor," she said to Dudley after checking her watch. "He's been sick a long time."

Dudley crawled into bed beside Brock. "Mr. Lightner, please wake up. This is Dudley. Please wake up." He kissed Brock's cheek and she told herself not to cry and put another cold towel at the back of Brock's neck.

"Hmm." He turned over and Jack sat up straighter and whimpered.

When Brock's hand reached out and stroked the dog's head, she called to him. "Brock, it's Allison. Wake up, sweetheart. Please open your eyes."

"Open your eyes and wake up, Mr. Lightner. Me and my mommie want you to wake up."

"Your mommie isn't here," Brock murmured, wrapped his arms around the pillow and seemed to sink into a deeper sleep.

"Oh, no, you don't," Allison said. "This is Allison and I want you to wake up this minute."

"Allison is at home. She doesn't want to come here, because she doesn't want me."

"I do want you."

"She said she does want you, Mr. Lightner. Please wake up."

Brock fell over on his back. "I thought I took you home."

"Mommie brought me back." Jack jumped onto the bed and licked Brock's face.

"Say, what is this? What are you doing in my bed, Jack?" He attempted to sit up and fell back onto the pillow. "What's going on here?"

Dudley flung his arms around Brock. "Are you all right now, Mr. Lightner? You're not sick anymore?"

"Sick? Who said I was—"

Allison put the glass to his lips. "Please drink this water. You must be dehydrated."

"Allison, why are you here?" She told him. "Oh, yes, I remember feeling as if I was getting the flu. I was so weak that I just crawled into bed. That's all I remember." He called

Jack and hugged him. "Good boy. You probably saved my life."

"Do you remember what day that was?" she asked him.

"I'm not sure. I'd spent the day in Glen Falls doing some research. Hmm. A couple of days after Dudley spent the afternoon with me. I was sick by the time I got home. Maybe. I don't know."

Remembering Dudley's complaint earlier in the day, she said, "Then this is the third day. I'd better make you some soup."

By the time she got to the kitchen—less than twenty feet from Brock's bedroom—her entire body shook and she grabbed the edge of the counter for support. What if Brock hadn't established a pattern of telephoning Dudley and what if she had continued to interfere with Dudley's relationship with Brock and with Jack? Her hands shook as she drank a glass of tap water and tried to concentrate on steadying herself.

"Mommie, Mr. Lightner wants some water. He said his mouth is dry."

"In a minute, honey."

"I can give it to him. Is he all right now?"

"He's going to be fine, son."

After giving him a glass of water, she opened the refrigerator and checked its contents for the makings of soup. A can of chicken stock, tomato juice and noodles produced a reasonable soup, and she took a bowl of it to Brock.

"Let me give it to him, please," Dudley begged. She handed Dudley the tray and watched his efforts to feed Brock, marveling at the man's patience as he accepted Dudley's fumbling efforts. From his position on the floor, Jack gazed up at the scene as if ready to intervene.

She thought Brock shuddered and bent over him to ask, "Are you cold?"

"I'm…uh…just not quite steady. A little weak, but I'll be my old self in no time." His gaze captured the blue plaid shirt lying at the foot of his bed. "Say, who changed my shirt?"

"Mommie and me did it, Mr. Lightner."

"Mommie and I." If she were lucky, she wouldn't get a backache from trying to move nearly two hundred pounds of dead weight.

"What can we give Jack to eat?" Dudley asked. "We gave him something at home, because he was so hungry, but it wasn't much."

"Don't worry, when Jack's hungry, he'll go to the kitchen and sit down. If there's danger, he'll bark."

"Interesting," Allison said. "At our cabin, he ran to the kitchen, sat down and barked, too."

"Dog logic," Brock said and she knew that with his sense of humor in working order, he felt better. No longer emotionally wrung out, she realized the implications of sitting beside him on his bed and made a move to get up. But he grasped her hand and restrained her.

She'd never know what would have happened between them, for at that moment, Dudley said, "Am I going to have hair on my chest, Mr. Lightner?"

That question brought home to her forcibly what a boy faced growing up without a father or another male nurturer. She looked at Brock, saw his effort to control his facial expression and sensed his compassion for the child's predicament.

"It's hard to say," Brock replied in a casual tone. "Some men do and some don't. I don't know why that is." He hadn't released her hand.

"I want hair on my chest like you," Dudley said.

Brock attempted to change the subject. "I've got a bag of chestnuts on the bottom shelf of the refrigerator and we could roast some, but I didn't bring in any coal." When Dudley asked him where he kept the coal, he told him, "It's in a shed at the back of the house, so we'll roast chestnuts another time."

"Excuse me," she said, put on her coat, went outside to get half a bucket of coal and found that a blanket of snow covered the ground and a mass of snowflakes drifted down silently without interference from wind.

"I'd better bring in a couple more half buckets," she said to herself. "This thing could go on for a while."

"What kept you?" Brock asked her. She told him and added, "Everything's white. I've never seen anything like it. It seemed to snow at an inch a minute."

"I'd better get up," Brock said.

She had no doubt that her face bore an expression of incredulity. "You're not going out of this house, mister."

He stared at her as one would if seeing a martian. "What did you say?"

"You heard me. I thought I'd lost you and when you finally responded to us, I was so happy, so overcome with emotion that I could hardly control myself. I am not going to watch you go out there and get pneumonia. So don't even think it."

He tried to sit up with the bed's headboard supporting his back and decided that the effort was too great. He didn't have the energy, but he wasn't about to let her know it. "I'd like to brush my teeth," he said.

"No problem," Allison said. "Wait a minute." She left and returned almost at once with a tray that contained a bowl of water, a glass of water, a toothbrush and toothpaste. He didn't glare at her in Dudley's presence, but he would have liked to.

She sat on the bed and said, "Okay. If you'd like, I'll go out while you do this." He folded his arms across his chest, happy that he could at least show his attitude, but Dudley spoiled his game.

"Want me to do it for you, Mr. Lightner?"

"Thanks, but I'll manage."

"Are you mad at my mommie?"

He looked at the child, whose face bore a reflection of his confusion, and stroked his cheek. "No, I'm not angry with her. I love her. I just don't understand her right now."

"It's all right," Dudley said, his face radiating a smile. "If you do what she tells you to do, everything is okay."

It was not the time for laughter, but he couldn't help it. It poured out of him until his shoulders shook. "Yeah," he said, when he could get his breath. "I know and you're right. I'll brush my teeth." Later, each time he thought of Dudley's sage advice, laughter tumbled out of him.

Later that afternoon, after consuming a ham sandwich and another bowl of soup, he got up, took a sponge bath—Allison had begged him not to take a shower, arguing that he was weak and might fall—changed his clothing and sat in the big wing chair beside the fireplace.

"Would you like me to make a fire?" Allison asked him. "The day is perfect for that."

"Do you know how?" he asked.

"Oh, yes. Until now, I've never lived in a house that didn't have an open fireplace." She made the fire and he couldn't help feeling that the woman and child who sat in front of it with him were his family. He looked down at Jack, his faithful companion for five years, lying beside his chair and thought, *Even Jack loves them.*

Allison made the fire. And as its warmth seeped through him, he told himself that it had all been for the best, that even his attack of the flu brought Allison back to him. And whether she knew it or not, before she left his house, they would find true contentment with each other.

"Can we roast the chestnuts?" Dudley asked.

"Did you say they were in the bottom of the refrigerator?" Allison asked him, already heading toward the kitchen. She cut them and put them down to roast.

The smell of the nuts roasting beside the hot coals made the occasion seem festive and he wished he were in full health, able to play his guitar and to make Allison and Dudley feel welcome in his home.

"Wha…" His eyes widened and his eyebrows shot up. Dudley crawled into his lap, put his head on Brock's shoulder and his arm across his chest. What had prompted the boy to do that? His glance at Allison told him she was equally amazed. He put both arms around the boy, leaned back and closed his eyes. What would be, would be.

About fifteen minutes later, when he had thought Dudley to be sound asleep, the boy said, "Aren't the chestnuts ready yet?"

"I thought you were asleep," he said.

"No, sir."

A smile claimed Allison's face and he didn't have to be told that she shared his frame of mind. She shelled the nuts and he didn't think he'd ever enjoyed roasted chestnuts so much.

"If I had the energy and if my arms weren't occupied," he told her, "I would have been happy to shell these for you."

"I hope you will have other opportunities," Allison said. "And before I leave here, we have to talk. I can't hold this in much longer."

He reached for her hand and held it. "I can imagine," he said, wishing he could find more encouraging words and still be truthful. He wanted to hold her as he held Dudley, but they needed a thorough cleansing before reaching that point. Yet her presence comforted him and for the first time in his memory, he wished for a life mate and children who loved him and who he loved and cherished.

Still holding Dudley close, he stood, went to the guest room and laid the sleeping child on the bed. Looking out of the window that faced the driveway, he saw at least four feet of snow and with a blanket of it dropping by the minute, Allison and Dudley would have to spend the night with him. "I ought to see about ordering some food for supper," he said to himself, went to the telephone and couldn't get a dial tone. He tried his cell phone and couldn't get a signal on it either.

"Snowbound and cut off," Allison said after he told her. "This is the most romantic thing that's ever happened to me."

"Really. Have you forgotten that you made love with me twice?"

"I have lots of faults, Brock, but I don't think lunacy is one of them. And to forget that, I'd have to be asylum-bound. I'd give anything if I hadn't behaved as if I had no faith in you, as if I thought you capable of such a heinous crime as abducting a child from his mother. I'm very sorry. If there is an excuse for me, it's that I've been obsessed with the fear of it for three-and-a-half years. I honestly don't believe you would ever harm me or Dudley. I know you love me and I know I have hurt you terribly. I'd give anything to heal that hurt and make you forget it.

"I've missed you so badly. My editor loved the book and gave me a contract for another one with a higher advance, but I couldn't be truly happy about it because I couldn't share it with you. Ross will get his own contract for this book and I don't have to pay him. I have you to thank for that."

"That's great news. It's another avenue for Ross."

Her face had a solemn, pained expression and he knew she waited for more. "What about us, Brock? During these past weeks, I've learned what it means to need someone, to need *you,* but if you can't forget what I did, please tell me now. I can't be your buddy or your casual friend."

He turned to face her. "I told you that I love you. I have never even imagined feelings for another woman such as I have for you, although I admit that I've liked and wanted others. But my feelings for you have never been duplicated. If we go on from here, Allison, this is it for me. And I don't want any more of your affection and loving unless you're satisfied now that I'm what you want and need in a man and that I can be a good, loving father for Dudley. Do you get what I'm saying?"

"Oh, yes. Yes!" Like a door blown free of its hinges, her arms flew open and she jumped up, leaned over him and pressed her lips to his forehead.

She may as well have given him a shot of vitamins. He stood, holding her in his arms and wrapped her close to him. "It seems as if I've waited years for this moment, but when I opened my eyes this afternoon and recognized you sitting beside me, I knew it would be all right, that you wouldn't be here if you didn't care."

"I love you so much that it scares me," she said.

"If I wasn't afraid I'd give you the flu, I'd kiss you breathless."

"Being in your arms is all I need right now." She kissed his cheek and they stood locked together until his libido warned him to move. Dudley might not be asleep. Besides, he couldn't start a love session that he lacked the energy to finish. So he squeezed her to him, stepped away and shook his head. First time for everything.

Her grin told him that she understood. "Because we're snowbound, I'd better check your kitchen and see what I can scrape up for a meal."

"Not to worry. That kitchen is well stocked. We wouldn't starve if the snow piled up for ten days or even two weeks," he said as she walked toward the kitchen.

"Mr. Lightner, where is my mommie?"

He looked down at the child for whom he'd just declared he wanted responsibility, hunkered in front of him and said, "She's in the kitchen cooking supper."

Dudley rubbed his eyes and seemed unsure of his surroundings. "Am I… Is she going to let me spend the night with you?"

"You're both going to spend the night with me. No one can walk in that snow and our cars won't move. So we'll simply enjoy being together."

"Okay."

Brock went to the wing chair and sat down. Immediately Dudley leaned against him.

"Will you please ask my mommie if I can go to a regular school? I want to play with other children."

"I'll ask her, but we have to accept that she does what she believes is best. All right?"

The boy yawned and rested his head on Brock's knee. "I'm glad you feel better."

Alison looked around in the kitchen. Every pot and pan was arranged by size and category. Not a single utensil, whether for cooking or eating, was out of place and glasses were arranged just as orderly. She opened the refrigerator door, saw that it was spotlessly clean and got an urge to telephone his mother to congratulate her.

"I wonder how he'd act if I got a speck of dirt on something. One of us will have to adjust. I'm not sloppy, but I'm definitely not a neat freak either." She found a tray of ground beef, defrosted it, looked into the well-stocked pantry, saw a jar of tomato sauce and numerous packages of pasta and smiled. Getting together a tasty meal would be simple. A can of artichoke hearts for a salad and a package of frozen kale for a vegetable completed the basic ingredients she needed for a wholesome meal. She got the supper started and went back to the living room, where Dudley had returned to his new favorite spot on Brock's knee.

"If anyone had told me you were a neat freak and squeaky clean, I wouldn't have believed them," she said to Brock.

"That's because you wouldn't have known that I'm lazy about housework, and that I keep things as perfect as possible, so that I won't have to spend more than half an hour at a time doing it."

"That's what you say," she murmured against his ear. "But if having everything in order is the trait that makes you the perfect lover, I'll learn to live with it."

His head jerked around. "What did you say?"

"Nothing," she replied and headed for the kitchen.

Chapter 11

"This beats a frozen-food dinner any day," Brock said of Allison's hastily prepared meal. "I can cook, and I do that sometimes, but up here mostly I defrost a frozen meal that I buy in the supermarket and I have to wash only a knife, fork and glass. If I drink beer, I don't even have to wash a glass."

"What about the meat in your freezer?" Allison asked him.

"I get tired of those unimaginative menus I get in the local supermarket. They don't include lobster or filet mignon."

"I get it," she said.

"Gee, Mommie, too bad you didn't bring him something good for dessert."

Brock got up and went to the kitchen. "Surprise! Would, say, praline ice cream make a good dessert?"

Dudley's eyes rounded. "It sure would, but you were sick and Mommie might not want you to eat it."

Allison didn't look at Brock, but she was glad that she hadn't reprimanded him about digging into that big, cold freezer. She imagined that at the appropriate time, he'd let it be known that nobody told him what to and what not to do.

Brock reached out and ran his fingers over Dudley's hair. "That's true, son, but she knows I'm old enough to know what is and what isn't good for me."

Dudley's mouth hung open for a second. Then he shrugged and ate some more spaghetti and meat sauce. She hoped the child wouldn't return to that topic, but with Dudley, you couldn't be sure. Once his mind trapped an idea or thought, he didn't release it readily.

She looked toward the window and shuddered. If Jack had waited another two or three hours to come to them for help.... She didn't let herself finish the thought.

"Mr. Lightner, do you obey your mother?"

Allison squashed a snicker and waited for Brock's reply. "When I was a child, I obeyed her even when I didn't want to and now that I'm a man, I've discovered she is very wise. So I always follow her suggestions."

"What would happen if you didn't obey her?" Dudley insisted.

"Gosh, I don't know. I haven't tested it."

"What Mr. Lightner is telling you, Dudley, is that he always obeyed his parents." She cleared the table, put the dishes and utensils in the dishwasher and returned with three servings of praline ice cream.

"Wow. This is awesome," the boy exclaimed. And then, as if he'd laid the groundwork for the results he wanted, he said, "Don't you have something to tell my mommie, Mr. Lightner?"

An expression of surprise floated over Brock's face. "I don't remember. Do I?"

"About school."

"Oh, yes." He looked skyward as if asking for heavenly guidance. "He wants to attend a school with other children, honey. I promised him I'd ask you. But if you'd rather, we can discuss it later."

She stiffened and she knew that he noticed it. "I'd rather."

"Your mother and I will talk this over later. You and I clean the kitchen now."

"I think we'd better… I mean…are you well now?" Dudley asked Brock.

"No, he isn't. I'll clean the kitchen. Thanks for offering, Brock, but I don't think you're quite there yet. Why don't you tell Dudley a story or something?"

"Can't he play me something on the guitar?"

"If he feels up to it," she said. "Why don't you ask him?"

Dudley got up and went to the window to see the snow and she leaned down and kissed Brock. "You've changed him completely."

"Maybe, but I believe he only needed a man to emulate. He's a great kid."

"Can you play me something on the guitar, Mr. Lightner?"

"I'd love to," she heard Brock say, "but I'm not quite up to it. Why don't you play something for me?"

The boy gazed up at him with widened eyes. "You're gonna let me play your guitar?"

"Why not? Yours isn't here."

Dudley ran to Brock's office and got the guitar. "I can play part of 'Greensleeves,'" he said.

"You can play all of it."

Allison hummed along while she worked in the kitchen. She liked that song, although she couldn't imagine why Brock chose to play such a simple piece right then. "I've always liked that folk song," she said, as she went back to the living room carrying more coal. "It's lovely and so… Dudley? Good heavens! I didn't dream you played that well."

"It's the only piece I learned, Mommie. As soon as I learn some Bach, Mr. Lightner is going to teach me some jazz by Wes Montgomery."

"I am really impressed. He's been studying a little less than five months."

"He's gifted. Takes to music like a fish takes to water."

Getting the boy to go to sleep proved difficult. As excited

as if it were Christmas, Dudley didn't want to release the romance of the snowy night, a roaring fireplace and the joy of being with Brock. When he began to nod, fighting sleep, Brock opened a folding cot in his office, put Dudley to bed there and read him a story.

"I think he's asleep," Brock said as he dropped himself into the chair facing the fireplace. "I never saw anybody fight sleep the way he did."

"You didn't mind?"

"I enjoyed it. That child is teaching me things about myself that I like." He didn't expect her to welcome what he had to say, but he had to say it, both for his sake and for Dudley's. He took her hand. "How long do you plan to stay up here, Allison?"

"I don't know. I haven't thought much about it. Right now, my tracks are covered and I feel safe up here."

"How do you figure that? If a man decided to break your window or to knock down your door, you could scream forever and no one would hear you. Look at what happened here. If Jack wasn't a smart dog and if I hadn't made friends with you and Dudley, I could have died here and no one would miss me. Isolation has its shortcomings. I want you to think about Dudley's future."

He held his hands up palms out. "I know. I know. That's what you think you're doing now. He's got to learn how to deal with people his age, how to negotiate with other children using society's rules. And he has to learn to share you, yes, and me with other children. You don't want him to be self-centered and selfish. He has an excellent mind and he needs a big school, libraries, museums, baseball and soccer teams."

"I know what you're saying and I know there's so much more for him, but I can't risk losing him. He's safe here."

"You think so. Even if that were the case—and I'm not so sure—what about us? Will you be content to see me only from mid-June through August, the time I usually spend here?"

"Please, Brock, you're making this very difficult for me."

"I'm asking you what about us? I want a full-time relationship with you. I want to take you home with me to Alexandria, so that you can see how I live, meet my parents and my friends."

"Maybe if I knew where Lawrence is. Oh, I don't know. I can't leave here now. I feel safe for the first time since I left him."

He couldn't live with that and he didn't plan to try. He walked the earth freely and he deserved a woman who would walk with him. Perhaps Dudley would one day conclude that the court had judged improperly in giving his mother sole custody and not guaranteeing his father visiting rights. And certainly, if Lawrence Sawyer had declared openly that he would take the boy if he got a chance, she had a right to take precautions to prevent it. But where the hell did that leave him?

"I'm not a man to have loose strings in my life. I like my affairs neatly tied, although I understand that other people may not care to march to my beat. Why can't you trust me to protect you and Dudley?"

"Can you protect him while he's in school?"

"In a private school? Yes. I'll hire a bodyguard for him, if it'll ease your mind."

"Oh, Brock. You're such a sweet man. I know you'll do all that you can."

He interrupted her. "But you don't think that will be good enough. Promise me that you'll try to see this from my point of view. I've got connections that you couldn't guess about and, if necessary, I'll call in favors. You and Dudley will be safe with me. Don't forget. Sawyer is rich. With enough money, he could trace you to Tahiti. Trust me. I know, because I've been a private investigator and, given enough time and money, I can find anybody, so long as there's no language barrier."

"Oh, Brock. I couldn't bear it if you were no longer in my life. You've given me something that… I mean it's as if I matured as a woman. With you, I mean. But I'm scared."

His left arm eased across her shoulder and he pulled her closer to him. "Sweetheart, haven't I been telling you for the past fifteen minutes that I can and will protect you and Dudley? I need to know that you have faith in me, that you believe in me."

"I do have faith in you and I love you and admire you. I don't question that. Let's not deal with this until we have to."

"If you say so, but I don't believe in sweeping refuse under the rug. I don't look forward to tonight. Knowing that you're in bed alone in my house definitely will not be conducive to a good night's sleep. But I don't think Dudley needs to know everything just yet."

"Right," she said, "and because he's sleeping in a strange place, he'll probably wake up during the night. I wouldn't like for him to find me in your bed. It would take me a week to explain it."

She probably didn't find that amusing, but he did and he didn't bother to suppress the grin that spread over his face. "I could explain it to him in one sentence. I don't swear he'd understand it fully, but I expect he can appreciate wanting to sleep with someone you love."

She gave him a look calculated to suggest the error of his ways. "I want my son to learn propriety and to be discreet."

He tweeked her nose and laughter rolled out of him. "Sweetheart, he won't learn that by what he doesn't see. He'll know it when we sit him down and talk to him in a serious fashion." When her face became clouded with a frown, he said, "All right, I can see that I'd better let up on you." He opened his arms and she walked into them and held him. With his eyes closed, he kissed her forehead and shuddered as what felt like a spiritual connection flowed from her to him.

He stepped back and gazed down at her. "I just had a strange feeling as if somehow you touched me at a different, almost non-human level."

"Funny. I had a similar feeling. Do you think we're soul mates?"

"Of course we are. Go to bed before my need for you

overcomes my concern for Dudley's mental health. Not that I think we'd damage him permanently…" He held her closer then and demon desire raised its head. "Get the hell out of here right now, baby," he said and watched her as she headed for the guest room like an unwilling child under the threat of punishment. A few hours later, when Dudley crawled into his bed saying that something shook the window in his room, Brock gave silent thanks for his foresight.

What was she going to do about Brock? She couldn't let him go, she couldn't risk losing Dudley and she knew that if she didn't show Brock that she trusted him, he'd leave her. After a sleepless night, she got up early and looked out the window. Still snowing and she estimated that at least twenty inches had fallen. She thought the trees looked like the work of an artist who covered them with white crystals and decorated the crystals with icicles of varying lengths. After staring at it for a while, she fell back onto her pillow. It was a fairyland and her life was a fairy tale that couldn't last. Brock Lightner was the perfect man for her and he would be a wonderful father for her child, but it didn't seem that she could have them both.

She padded into the kitchen, made a pot of coffee and checked the telephone. Still no dial tone. She looked out of the window and saw blackbirds huddling on the railing at the corner of the deck. Sympathy for the poor little creatures prompted her to put on her shoes and her coat, crack the back door and throw pieces of bread to the birds, who flocked to it. A search of the pantry yielded self-rising flour and powdered buttermilk. So with her fingers crossed she located shortening and eggs in the refrigerator.

"I'm eating a decent breakfast today," she said to herself, rolled up her sleeves and began making buttermilk biscuits.

With the tantalizing odor of biscuits filling the house, she defrosted sausage, measured out a cup of grits and four cups of water and told herself to be patient until Brock and Dudley got up. However, an hour passed and she could wait no longer.

So she poured a cup of coffee, added milk and a teaspoon of sugar and opened Brock's bedroom door.

"I thought you were sleeping in Mr. Lightner's office," she said to Dudley, who sat up in bed chatting with Brock.

Dudley explained his presence there and added, "Mr. Lightner didn't mind. He didn't want me to be scared."

She handed Brock the coffee. "I didn't know you had company. I don't suppose I can have a kiss now."

"Why not? Come here. I'm taking this propriety thing so far and no further."

She put the coffee on his night table, sat on the side of the bed and he pulled her into his arms. She wanted to open her mouth and take him in, but he simply held her, kissed her cheek and her lips and set her aside. Then to her amazement, he turned to Dudley.

"Don't you think a lovely woman deserves a hug and a kiss if she brings you a nice cup of coffee while you're in bed wishing for coffee?"

For a minute, Dudley seemed stumped. Then he said, "Yes, sir. I sure do. Mommie, I was thinking about hot chocolate. Did you make me some?"

Caught out, she couldn't help laughing. The child had equated himself with Brock. "You like your cocoa after you eat. Remember?"

"Oh. Excuse me."

She knew Dudley wouldn't be in the bathroom more than a few minutes, so she rolled into Brock's arms and parted her lips for his kiss. Within a second, he was inside of her, sipping, dueling, loving her and sending the heat of desire spiraling through her. She heard the bathroom door close, stifled a groan and sat up.

"I want you to go home with me, Allison. We have a precious gift, one that few people ever receive, and I'm not willing to let it go. But if we don't nourish it, we'll kill it and we'll both be miserable thinking and wondering about what might have been. Tell me you're willing to give us a chance."

"I need you as badly as you need me, Brock. We can't talk about this right now," she said as Dudley rejoined them.

"I'm getting hungry, Mommie."

"I know…" she said, almost as if her mind were half a world away. "You two get ready for breakfast. Twenty minutes," she threw over her shoulder as she headed back to the kitchen. The happiness that enveloped her almost frightened her. She wanted to hold on to it, to lock it up somewhere, because nothing so wonderful as loving a man like Brock and knowing that he loved her, too, could possibly last.

She made hot chocolate, took the biscuits out of the oven and covered them with a towel to keep them warm, fried the sausages, cooked the grits and was scrambling eggs when the two males she loved most walked into the kitchen holding hands.

"We set the table," Dudley said.

She leaned down and kissed him. "Thanks. You two sit down and I'll bring in the food."

Brock held their hands and said grace and added, "I could definitely get used to this. All of a sudden, this cabin seems like a home."

She didn't respond. She couldn't. And unaware of the drama around him, Dudley said, "Mommie, I like this better than the cereal you make me eat." He looked at Brock. "Do you like cereal, Mr. Lightner?"

"Not particularly, but I eat it because it's good for me." He winked at Dudley. "That's why I'm a big guy. I ate what my mother told me to eat."

"Okay," Dudley said, looked up at Brock and smiled his most charismatic smile. "I'm gonna eat cereal."

We can't lose this, she thought to herself. *I'll never forgive myself if I let him slip out of my life.*

As if he read her thoughts, Brock rested his fork on his plate, reached across the table and took her hand. "I want you to come home with me for Thanksgiving. I want my family to know you and Dudley. I always spend Thanksgiving with my parents and Jason, because it's a time for families, but I can't be here and there, too. Do you understand what I'm saying?"

She did and she knew it was D-day for them. She nodded and she felt as if her blood had curdled when she said, "All right, we'll go home with you for Thanksgiving."

His gaze seemed to penetrate her soul and she didn't mistake the significance of her answer. "Will you look forward to this happily as I will?" he asked her.

"If I'm with you, I'll be happy," she said. It wasn't what he wanted to hear, but she couldn't lie. She'd have some trepidation until she got back to the safety of Indian Lake.

"Then we'll drive down to Saratoga Springs and get a flight from there. It's too long a trip for Dudley this time of year. Also, Thanksgiving is less than two weeks away. We'll stay with my parents, so as soon as we can get phone connection, I'll tell them to expect us."

"Which means I'd better get some work done," she said for want of something better to say and feeling a need to hide her nervousness.

"Me, too," he replied. "You help me and when I can dig us out, I'll help you. How about it?"

"Great idea," she said. "Do you want me to proofread?"

For the next three days, as they worked together on his book, her fascination with his work and her admiration for him grew with each page she read. "When you go after something, you get it, don't you?" she asked him one afternoon.

"Absolutely. What's the point in investing my energy in something if I don't plan to succeed at it? Makes no sense."

"Is that the way you got that little nick right there?" she asked, placing her right index finger on his left cheek. "It makes you look a little dangerous."

"So I'm told. I got it from a philandering husband when I was on a P.I. job. Foolish little man. I broke his arm for it."

"He was stupid to take you on."

"He was also a coward, which is why he had a knife."

She wondered how many times he had faced serious danger as a private investigator, but she didn't voice her thoughts.

For that day and most of the next, they worked on his memoir. He wrote with the use of his laptop and she proofread the copy. With Jack as his constant companion, Dudley was content to read his books, study and enjoy the occasional attention of his mother and Brock. Their warm and loving domestic scene touched Allison so deeply that she stopped proofreading, went over to Brock, hugged him fiercely and went back to the table where she worked without having said a word to him. She had begun to experience guilt, for it occurred to her that she hadn't given up the notion of remaining in the Adirondacks. She had agreed to spend only Thanksgiving in Alexandria with Brock and his family and she suspected that Brock had other plans.

It ceased to snow the following afternoon and after sweeping a path clean on his deck, Brock got his snow thrower from beneath the deck, rolled it through the house and out the front door, where he cleaned off a path to his SUV. After removing the snow from the windows, doors and windshield of his SUV, he hooked the plow to the front of it, cleaned the section of the yard in front of the house and then his driveway.

She watched from the living-room window. "No matter how tired he is, he'll clean off my place as soon as he finishes this," she said to herself. "Three days ago he had a high fever and he doesn't seem to care that he could have one just as high this time tomorrow."

"May I have your door and car keys?" he asked her. She didn't realize he'd come inside and he startled her, but she didn't let on.

She gave him the keys. "I don't want you to think I'm trying to mother you, Brock, because I'm not. But please don't forget that two nights ago you had a very high fever."

He zipped up his leather jacket and looked down at her. "How high was it?"

"It was 103.5."

He kissed her nose and appeared thoughtful. "Yeah. That was pretty high. Not to worry. I'll be back in about forty-five minutes."

"Are we going to stay with Mr. Lightner tonight, Mommie?"

"I don't know. We'll see when he comes back." The boy stood there for a minute, then whirled around and left the dining room.

Hmm. So Dudley was planning to be a problem, but she could not let her child run her life.

Brock returned about forty-five minutes later as promised and Dudley immediately accosted him. "Am I going to stay with you tonight, Mr. Lightner?"

She looked at Brock. "Is everything there okay or was as well as you could make it?"

"The house is as you had left it."

Allison thanked him, turned around and looked at Dudley. "We'll go home as soon as Mr. Lightner can take us."

"I don't want to go home," he said and poked out his bottom lip.

"I don't want to grow old, either, but in another thirty-five years, I'll either be old or dead, so please don't even think of acting out here. We're going home and that's that."

"What's the problem?" Brock asked Dudley.

"I want to stay with you and Mommie isn't going to let me."

"I see. And you're about to turn on the attitude. Right? Let me tell you this. Your mother loves you and she needs you to be with her because she wants to care for you. That's her right and her duty and she is not going to turn that over to me or to anyone else. So you behave and appreciate the fact that you have a loving, caring mother."

"Yes, sir, but I could still stay with you if Mommie would let you be my dad."

"I thought you and I settled that."

"Yes, sir. I forgot. When are you coming to see me?"

"Every day. Now drop the attitude and tell your mother you're sorry."

"I'm sorry, Mommie," he said, ran over to her and kissed her.

She looked up at Brock. "I never used to believe magicians had special powers." To Dudley, she said, "Let's get our things together. I want us to be home before dark."

At home, she took no time in preparing a dinner of crab cakes, french fries, spinach and a green bean salad. Brock ate with them and cleaned the kitchen with Dudley's help.

"I'll see you tomorrow when I come to give Dudley his guitar lesson."

She waited for what else he would say or do before leaving her. Their relationship had changed and it was his move. Letting her know that Dudley would have to get used to their changed relationship, Brock put both arms around her, smiled down at her and said aloud, "I love you. More than any person or anything, I love you. I wasn't happy sleeping with only a wall between us, but tonight, I'll be miserable so far from you. Tell me you love me."

His lips seared her and her nipples hardened against his chest as her blood quickened and every nerve in her body quivered. "I love you. You made me a new woman and you're the only man who has the key to my heart."

His hands stroked her shoulders and her back. "I checked your phone and got a dial tone, so we're no longer isolated." He hunkered in front of Dudley, who gazed up at them. "I'm depending on you to obey your mother and to make her life as pleasant as you can. She will do the same for you." He took the child in his arms and hugged him. "I am not your dad, but I love you just as much as I would if I were your dad. Don't forget that."

"Yes, sir. I won't and I'll behave. Honest!"

"I know you will." He hugged the boy again, winked at Allison and left.

Two days and nights with Brock had afforded her a better

understanding of his personality and character. So she readily accepted his wordless departure. He dealt with temptation the way in which, as a private investigator, he'd learned to handle danger: he moved it or himself out of the way.

"Mommie, do you like it when he kisses you like that?"

She put her arms around Dudley, knowing that her face glowed with the happiness she felt. "Yes. He makes me very happy."

Several evenings later, as she put away the first photographs of her book of quick bread recipes, she walked to her living-room window to gaze out at the full moon shining against the snow and the stars so clear that she could identify the Big Dipper. As she was about to call Dudley to see the spectacle, she saw the gray Cadillac slow down and turn into her driveway, closed the blind and turned out the light and phoned Brock.

"A gray Cadillac just turned into my driveway. I've seen that car before."

"Lock your doors and windows. Put the chain on. I'll be there in five minutes."

Brock had also seen the gray car make a U-turn near Allison's driveway and he'd thought then as he did now that it was not a healthy sign. He slipped on his sneakers, put on his jacket, leashed Jack, got into the SUV and headed for Allison's cabin. Seeing the visitor knock on her door sent his blood into a wild race through his veins and as if Jack sensed his agitation, the dog released a low and ominous growl. He didn't signal the dog to remain peaceful because he didn't know what he faced.

"Looking for me, buddy?" he asked the man, who whirled around when Jack growled.

"I...uh...I must have gotten the wrong address," the man said.

Brock planted his feet wide apart in what he knew was a threatening stance. "Who're you looking for?"

"Uh, never mind. This is a mistake. Sorry." The visitor looked down at Jack, who stared up at him and pointed his tail straight out.

"Are you sure I can't help you?" Brock said, suppressing an urge to flatten the man.

"Thanks, but I don't think so."

Brock stood on the steps until the big gray car was out of sight and made up his mind right then that he was not going back home that night. If the man returned and didn't see his car, he'd make the right conclusion, especially if he was a private investigator.

He called Allison. "This is Brock. The guy's gone, at least for the time being. Open up."

She opened the door and he stepped into her house and took her into his embrace. When he looked down and saw Dudley crying, it hit him like a sledge hammer that they needed him. He lifted the boy, put an arm around Allison and said, "Where can I sleep? I'll stay here tonight because he may come back just to see if I live here, which is what he thinks now."

"Are we gonna move, Mommie?"

"I don't know, son. I'm tired of moving. We'll see."

"I'm glad you came, Mr. Lightner. I wasn't so scared until the man knocked real hard on the door. I knew it wasn't you."

"Don't be afraid, Dudley. I'll do my best to take care of you if I have the opportunity to do that. Allison, honey, what do you have around here that calms the nerves?"

"You're looking at the obvious, but I don't know how we would manage that. Would you like some pinot grigio or a pilsner? Something like that?"

He couldn't help laughing. She'd found a way to ask him if he wanted a drink without suggesting to Dudley that alcoholic drinks were good for the nerves. It didn't pay to spell a word in the hope that the boy wouldn't understand you, because television had ruined that option. "I'd love to share some white wine with you," he said, satisfied that they had successfully diverted the child's thoughts from the calming of nerves.

"When are we going to get on the plane, Mr. Lightner?"

"Tuesday afternoon. I considered going Wednesday, but the airports are too crowded the day before Thanksgiving." A thought occurred to him and he snapped his finger. "Allison, I think we should leave your car in my backyard. There's room there, and I can lock the gate. It'll be safe. I'd better tell Winifred we'll be away, so she'll hold the mail and she'll tell the sheriff to check on the place. They're very good about that."

"I hadn't thought of that," Allison said. "Besides, I didn't even know that woman's name."

"Honey, you have to be more neighborly. The managers of the post office, the drugstore, the supermarket, the sheriff and a few others I could name are the people you need in a place like this."

"I'm normally gregarious, but I stayed away from people for reasons you know well."

"Considering what happened tonight, I'd say it probably wasn't a bad idea. What time do you go to bed, Dudley?"

"Nine o'clock. Do I have to go now, Mommie?" She asked the child how he felt. "Okay. I'm not scared with Mr. Lightner here."

They sat on the side of his bed and read to him Young-Robinson's *Chicken Wing* until he fell asleep. After they closed the child's room door, Brock heard himself say, "Would you ever consider letting me adopt Dudley? He and I want that very much."

"You have discussed it with him?" she asked with a wide-eyed expression of incredulity.

"He's the one who brings it up from time to time. He wants me to ask you if I can be his father and I told him that we can't consider that until he's eight. I figured that by then my relationship with you will have been resolved. I'd never let anything drag on for two years," he added pointedly.

Allison told Brock good-night, showered, pampered her

body, put on a teddy and a matching silk robe and sat on the side of her bed doing her nails. She heard him come out of the shower and go back to the living room, where she'd made up the sofa bed for him. If he thought she'd let another night pass while he slept that near to her and not have him, he wasn't baking in a hot oven.

Stepping carefully in her bare feet, she went to his bed, looked at him sprawled out on his back with his hands behind his head and her mouth began to water. Feeling transfixed by the sight before her, she stared until heatlike lightning flashed through her veins. She dropped the silk robe on the floor, stepped out of the teddy, threw the cover off his naked body and crawled on top of him. She heard a growl just as Brock said, "Down, boy. You're not afraid he'd wake up and come out here?"

"He hasn't been asleep long enough to wake up. I need you," she said and spread herself over his hard penis.

"You're not ready," he said.

"I don't have time to get ready. I want you in me."

She parted her lips, sucked his tongue into her mouth and stifled a groan. With loving hands, she stroked him for a minute and then eased him into her. Fire caught her from the minute he entered her and within a few minutes, the pumping and squeezing started.

"Slow down, baby. If you don't, you won't enjoy it."

"I'm enjoying it. Oh, Lord, I'm enjoying it. Harder. I want it harder."

He flipped her over on her back and drove into her until she knew he could feel her gripping and clawing him. He covered her mouth to quiet her moans and she erupted around him. She knew she was dying, sinking, and then she shot up to the stratosphere, as her thighs quivered, heat seared the bottom of her feet, and her body bucked involuntarily beneath him. Ah, the glory of release. She threw wide her arms and let him have her. Immediately, he surrendered himself to her.

"I feel as if I've died and gone to heaven," he said. "I'm

not a violent man, but I pity the brother who touches you if I catch him. Baby, you're mine."

"I'd put it differently," she said, kissing his cheek. "Put your hands on another woman, and it's bye, bye, baby."

"Ah, sweetheart, I love you so much. What man who has you could want another woman? Not me."

Allison packed for the trip to Washington as if she were still Lawrence Sawyer's wife and for the first time since the early days of her marriage, she enjoyed the prospect of dressing well. They arrived in Washington shortly after noon on Tuesday and reached Reginald and Darlene Lightner's home around one-thirty. Reginald answered the door.

"Welcome, Allison. I've been looking forward to meeting you." He ignored her offer of a handshake and gave her a fatherly hug. Then the tall, stately man looked down at Dudley. "I've been looking forward to meeting you, too, young man. I've heard good things about you."

"Are you really Mr. Lightner's father? Really? Gee."

"I'm getting too old to get on my knees," Reginald said, picked up Dudley and hugged him. "Yes, I am, and my son tells me you're quite a boy."

"Mr. Lightner loves me and I love Mr. Lightner, too."

"Yes, so I heard." He put down the boy and embraced his son. "She's lovely, Brock. Thank you for bringing her and Dudley to us."

She perused the two men and knew that Reginald Lightner spoke from his heart. As she was about to ask of Brock's mother's whereabouts, Reginald said, "Your mother will be down in a few minutes. She nearly panicked when the car pulled up and she was still in the kitchen cooking. She's dressing."

Hearing footsteps on the stairs, Dudley followed the sound and ran to the bottom of the stairs. Allison was about to call him back when he said, "Are you Mr. Lightner's mother?"

"Yes, I am," she said, "and you must be Dudley. I hope you like chocolate cookies."

"Yes, ma'am. I sure do." They entered the living room holding hands. "I found your mother, Mr. Lightner. Does Mr. Jason live here?"

"He lives a few blocks away, but you'll see him this evening." Brock's arms went around the woman who gave him life. "You look great, Mom."

"So do you and I've never seen you more relaxed. You don't know how happy I am to see it." She looked toward Allison and smiled, and he walked over to Allison and put an arm around her waist.

"Mom, this is Allison Sawyer, the woman who has my heart. Allison, this is my mother, Darlene."

She had stood when Brock's mother entered the room and now she smiled at the woman who exuded warmth and friendliness and who she liked on sight.

"Welcome, Allison." She opened her arms and embraced Allison. "I've waited a long time for one of my sons to bring home a lovely woman and tell me she's special to him. I'm so glad to meet you and, of course, Dudley, who's already my friend. You're the first female Brock's brought home to me since he was eleven and I want you to feel you belong here. Brock, will you please take her things up to the guest room?"

"Dudley, Brock's room has twin beds, so I think you'll be happy sharing with him."

"Yes, ma'am. Guys should stay together."

"You couldn't have said anything that would have made him happier," Allison said. "Brock is his idol."

It amazed Allison that both she and Dudley seemed so comfortable so quickly with Brock's parents. She hoped the weekend would go as smoothly as it had started.

Chapter 12

Allison realized very soon that the nature of Brock's relationship with her and Dudley was not a surprise to Brock's parents. Still her antenna shot up when Darlene said to Brock after they finished lunch, "Are you taking them over to your town house? I'm sure they're anxious to see it."

"I'd planned to do that about now, Mom. If Jason comes before we get back, please ask him to wait. I need some information from him." He patted Dudley's shoulder. "Run upstairs, Dudley, and get your coat." He removed Allison's coat from the closet in the foyer and helped her into it.

"Can't you go with us, Mom?" Dudley said to Darlene. "Don't you want to see Mr. Lightner's town house?"

"It's not far," she said. "I've been there many times."

"Why didn't we stay at your house?" Allison asked Brock as they walked along Roost Drive.

"Because Mom and Dad wouldn't hear of it. They said you were coming to visit them and that meant you'd be a guest in their home."

After a short, four-block walk, they arrived at Brock's three-bedroom town house. "You can't see it as it really is," he said, "because the furniture is covered and the curtains and draperies are stored, but you can get an idea."

He unlocked the door, and when they walked into the great room. Dudley looked around as if in awe and said, "Won't I get lost in here, Mr. Lightner?"

He picked up the child and hugged him. "I won't let you get lost. You'll always be safe with me, Dudley."

"I know. Can you ask Mom to make some more homemade ice cream and some more crab cakes? I loved them."

"If you ask her, I'm sure she'll do it."

He gave them a tour of the house and it was clear to Allison that Brock and his parents lived well. A cathedral ceiling set off the great room, with a balcony at one end above a massive marble fireplace. The master bedroom overlooked the Potomac and had a private second-floor balcony. She looked into the bathroom and imagined herself in that Jacuzzi tub with Brock. Each bedroom had its own bath. She told herself not to think about living there because she hadn't been invited to do that.

But she heard herself saying, "I'd like to see the kitchen." He took her there and leaned against the doorjamb while she inspected it.

She nearly fainted when he said, "If you don't like it or anything else in this house, just tell me what you want and I'll change it."

She whirled around and he raced to grab her as she appeared to trip on the polished tile floor. "What did you say?" she asked, staring at him.

"You heard me, but we'll get to that later."

"I want someplace to put my guitar, Mr. Lightner. Are there any schools here?"

"Several good ones." He looked down at her then. "I'd like to go back now, because Jason may have to leave."

"Don't expect anything sensible out of me for the next

forty-eight hours, Brock. I'm not use to dealing with the kind of jolts you just gave me."

"Seems to me you should have been expecting it."

His arms eased around her. "Haven't you accepted that I love you and that we belong together?" His lips covered hers and when she opened to him, he plunged his tongue into her and she could feel him tremble.

"I love you, too," she said, "so much that it frightens me sometimes. Let's go back."

It didn't surprise Brock that Allison hadn't been able to let go of the torment she suffered in her first marriage. He figured that if the union had given her any pleasure other than her child, she would more easily have been able to release the undesirable elements of it. He hunched against the cold, put Dudley's hand in his right coat pocket and Allison's hand in his left one. At his parents' door, Jason greeted him with a warm embrace and then hugged Allison and Dudley.

"What did you want to see me about?" Jason asked Brock. He gave his brother the automobile license plate that he copied off the gray Cadillac driven by the man whose visit he'd interrupted at Allison's door a few nights earlier. "I'm out of the business now and I don't want to be tempted to investigate anybody or anything."

"D.C. plates?" Jason asked him. He nodded, because he didn't want to arouse Allison's fear, which he knew simmered just below the surface.

"Who plays the piano, Mom?" Dudley asked Darlene Lightner, as he stared with shining eyes at the keys of the baby grand.

"We all play some, but Brock and his father are a bit better at it than Jason and I."

Dudley ran to Brock. "Can you play me something on the piano?"

"Sure I can." He had long suspected that music would one day be the focal point of Dudley's life, for the child had an ear for it and what seemed like a natural ability to learn it. He pulled out the bench, sat down, flexed his fingers and let the sound of Offenbach's barcarolle fill the house. In no time, he lost himself in the music and let his fingers transport him to another world. He hadn't played since mid-June when he went to the Adirondacks and he realized how much he'd missed it.

"I'm going to learn to play like this," Dudley announced, bringing him back to himself and to the present. "Mr. Lightner is teaching me to play the guitar," he announced to those present and leaned against his thigh in a proprietary manner.

Jason called to Brock from upstairs, "Can you come up here a minute?"

Brock bounded up the stairs. "Got anything?"

"Yeah. That car is registered to Lawrence Sawyer, but that information alone won't sway a jury. You have to find out who was driving that car and I doubt it was Sawyer."

"I doubt it, too. Gosh, I didn't want to get back into this business. Thanks. I owe you one." He went to his room, closed the door and phoned the sheriff at Indian Lake. "Jeff, I'm away for the weekend, and I'd appreciate it if you'd keep an eye on Allison Sawyer's cabin and mine. If you see a gray Cadillac with D.C. license plates, check out the driver. He's up to no good."

"Sure thing, Brock. A fellow driving that car has been asking people questions about Ms. Sawyer, but you know we Yankees zip up our lips whenever we smell trouble. I'll definitely stake him out."

"This settles it," he said to himself. "She isn't safe up there in that cabin. They're going to live with me."

His father met him on the stairs and he headed back down. "I think you ought to teach Dudley to call you something other than Mr. Lightner. I realize he can't call you Dad, at least not yet."

"I'll fix that as soon as I can and I hope it won't be too long."

"I'm glad to hear it, son. Dudley is a wonderful boy and no child ever loved a father more than he loves you."

"Trust me, it is definitely mutual."

"Your mother and I haven't dreamed that we'd get as lovely a daughter as Allison. We like everything we've seen of her. She's a warm, loving and giving person, beautiful and so refined. Full of fire, too. Does she have a temper?"

"You bet she has," Brock said, with not a little pride. "Step on her toes and in a second, she'll show you how it feels. She's…all I could want."

On Thanksgiving morning, he took Dudley to his parents' basement recreation room to watch the Macy's Thanksgiving Day parade and enjoyed the child's excitement at the balloons and floats. He hadn't previously watched the entire show and he realized that a child brought all kinds of pleasure to a man's life, that seeing things through a child's eyes could be a rich experience.

"My mommie is making the dessert for dinner," Dudley reminded him. "Are we going to live with you in your big house and I can come and see Mom and your daddy?"

"That's what I'm hoping for," he said, but he knew that getting Allison to live so close to Washington might necessitate a miracle.

Darlene called them upstairs to get ready for the Thanksgiving meal, and as he and Dudley reached the first floor, the doorbell rang. "I'll get it," he called, rushed to the door and opened it.

He stared at the woman who stood there, well-dressed in a vicuna coat and holding a bouquet of multicolored calla lilies. "I'm Brock Lightner," he said. "You wouldn't be Allison's sister, would you?"

Her face bloomed into a smile. She extended her hand. "Indeed, I am and I've wanted to meet you since the day you walked into Allison's life."

He raised an eyebrow at that. "Come on in. That bears

some explaining, but I expect you won't go into that right now. Have a seat. I want you to meet my folks."

"Mr. Lightner, who was that?" Dudley called to him.

"Come say hello to your aunt." He went to the kitchen where he knew he'd find Allison and his mother preparing to put the food on the table. When he was at his parents' home, he helped his mother with the meals, but she had let him know that she wanted to learn more about Allison and that his presence would ruin any chance of that.

"Ellen's here," he told Allison. "Right now, Dudley's keeping her company. Where's Dad?"

"He's making a fire in the barbecue pit so that he and Dudley can toast marshmallows," Darlene said, taking off her apron. She patted her hair and wiped her hands.

He followed the two women to the living room and watched as Allison embraced her older sister. "Mrs. Lightner, this is my older sister, Ellen Parks. Ellen, you've already made Brock's acquaintance."

"Thanks you so much for inviting me, Mrs. Lightner, and for sharing your home with my baby sister and my nephew." She looked at Brock. "Seeing you explains a lot."

"You're going to elaborate on that?" Brock said.

Darlene spread her palms out and looked toward the ceiling. "You can't be *that* thick. Please tell your father that Ms. Parks is here."

Half an hour later, with Jason and his date, Lynnette, they sat down to a typical Thanksgiving dinner. Reginald Lightner said grace and served the turkey. Then he raised his wineglass, gave a toast and said, "I hope that by this time next year I'll have a daughter-in-law and a grandson living down the street from me." He looked at Jason. "It wouldn't hurt you to get busy. I want something to do with my time when I retire. This is one physician who is not going to practice until he's eighty."

"You're embarrassing Lynnette, Dad," Jason said.

"I am not," Reginald replied. "She needs to build a fire under you."

These two families work well together and that's more than I dared hope for. If only Allison would give up the idea that she's safe at Indian Lake. She is not, he thought, and he had to make her realize it.

After the meal, he checked the weather forecast because he did not want them to be stranded in Saratoga Springs.

"You sure you have to go back today?" Darlene asked him. "I wouldn't mind if you left Dudley with me."

"He's homeschooled," Allison said, a bit quickly, he thought, "and I have a publication deadline that's fast approaching."

Darlene released a deep sigh. "Sometime next summer, perhaps, when I'm not teaching. He's such a joy to have around."

Reginald and Dudley came inside with a platter of toasted marshmallows and they all sat around the fire in the living room to eat them. "You're welcome at our home anytime, Ellen," Reginald said. "I hope you'll feel close to us."

"Thank you, Reginald. My sister is blessed and I hope she knows it."

"She knows it," Allison said, gazing into Brock's eyes.

They flew to Saratoga Springs, reached Indian Lake by car at seven that evening. He drove directly to his house and, to his surprise and delight, Allison neither questioned nor objected. He needed to check with the sheriff before Allison went into her cabin and it was too late to call him. After he fed Jack, who seemed annoyed about having been left in Saratoga at a kennel, he made a fire in the fireplace and settled in front of it with Allison and Dudley on either side of him. They were his future and he'd soon settle it with Allison.

"Are we going to be circumspect tonight?" Allison asked Brock when Dudley was preparing for bed.

"I was going to be circumspect the other night when you stayed here, but you had other ideas," he said.

When had she gotten the courage to behave boldly with a man, to go to a man and take what she wanted? She shook her head, bemused. Maybe knowing that he loved her and wanted her made the difference.

"It doesn't make me shout, but I don't think we want to give a six-year-old an advanced course in sex, do you?"

"Of course not," she said, "but…uh…can't you think up something?"

"Honey, as hungry as I am for you right now, I think you'd better not tempt me." He went to the refrigerator and got a bottle of wine. "I take it you're not hungry because we ate in Saratoga Springs, but I bought some delicious petits fours there." He uncorked the wine, put it on the table and knelt before her.

"Will you marry me, Allison? I love you and I want to spend the remainder of my life with you. I promise to be a good husband to you and a good father to our children, beginning with Dudley. Will you be my wife?"

"I want to marry you, but I'm so afraid that Lawrence will steal Dudley from me."

"That's an excuse, baby." He told her what he knew about the owner of the gray Cadillac and its driver. "You're better off in Alexandria where I can protect you and Dudley. I'll send him to a private school and if you're not satisfied, I'll hire a bodyguard for him. I guarantee you that I love him as much as you do. We can have a wonderful life together."

She covered his hand with hers. "I know and I want to be with you always."

"Then marry me. It will be wise to leave here as soon as we can."

"I'm not marrying you because I'm scared for Dudley but because you have given me happiness such as I would not have believed possible, because you and I love each other and you love Dudley. Yes, I want to be your wife."

He stood, lifted her and wrapped her in his arms. "I'm so happy that I could fly with my own wings." His lips brushed her eyelids, her cheeks, forehead, nose and ears. "You're everything to me. Can you live in my house?"

"Can I... Are you serious? Of course. I love that house. Uh...how many children do you want?" she asked him.

"I'd like two more, but I'll take as many as I can get."

"Two more," she said, "and...uh...don't be frightened if I sleepwalk tonight."

He hugged her. "Now that you've told me what I can look forward to, I won't sleep a wink until then."

Several hours later, she kissed his closed, slumbering eyes until he opened them and smiled at her. How had she lived without him?

"When can we get married?" he asked sometime later while still buried deep within her. "And I know it's the custom for a woman to wear a color if she'd been previously married, but I haven't been and I want to see you in traditional white."

"Then that's what I'll wear."

She was not accustomed to seeing Brock in a pensive mood, and because she didn't know what to expect, she remained quiet while he frowned in silence.

After a bit, he asked her, "How many months left on your lease for the cabin?"

"I'm renting month to month."

"Wonderful. What do you think of this? You have to finish making the quick breads here and baking them in your same oven. Concentrate on baking and getting Ross to photograph the products. I'll help you with the indexing and table of contents. We leave for Alexandria at the end of this month. We can finish our books there."

"Sounds like a good plan to me, but that's a lot to do in ten days."

"I'll get a mover to do your packing. I won't pack anything but what I brought up here. If that's agreed, when can we get married?"

"Saturday before Christmas."

"What about our honeymoon?" he asked in the tone of a grumbling child.

Warm, happy and besotted, she tightened her arms around

him. "After the first of the year, you can take us to someplace warm, and after December seventeenth, we won't have to sneak out of each other's beds. That alone will be like a honeymoon."

The next morning, immediately after breakfast, Brock prepared to speak with the sheriff and to decide if Allison should return to her cabin or only work on her book there during the day. "I'm going into the village," he told her. "I want to see what information I can pick up. Someone may be watching this house. Keep the doors locked. If anyone tries to get in, pat Jack on his shoulders and snap your fingers. He'll protect you. Be back soon."

"That guy's been hanging around here just about every day," the sheriff told him. "I wouldn't be surprised if he's renting a place somewhere nearby. I can't arrest a man for asking questions, so be careful."

He didn't need to hear anything like that, but he'd deal with it. "Thanks, Jeff. I appreciate your help." He hurried back home and the relief on Allison's face when he arrived didn't comfort him. The sooner they left Indian Lake, the better.

Allison contacted Ross and agreed with him on a plan for photographing the quick breads. They worked at her cabin during the day, but before dark, Brock took Allison and Dudley home with him.

"That dude doesn't think much of his tires," Ross said one afternoon as he held a shot up to the window, checking the evenness of the color of Allison's buttermilk biscuits.

"What dude?" Brock asked, rushing to the window.

"A cat sporting a gray Cadillac. He turned at the driveway out there and took off." The doorbell rang, Brock leashed Jack and walked with the big German shepherd to the door. He got his breath back when he saw the sheriff.

"Your man drove up here, saw my car, turned around and beat it like a bat out of hell," Jeff said. "I'm surprised that he'd come down here during the day. If Ms. Sawyer wants to swear out a warrant for harassment, I can lock him up until she leaves. Because we don't know what he's up to, that may be best. I came to tell her to come to my office and make the complaint."

"Thank you. I'll drive her up there. I don't think it's a good idea for her to drive alone now."

"I'll take her, if she can leave now. She ought to be back in about twenty minutes."

"All right. Thanks, man."

Saturday morning, November thirtieth arrived and she stood with her back to the cabin as, in fleeting thoughts, she compared their move to the last four she'd made and wondered if she were jumping from the frying pan into the fire. Brock had shipped her car to Arlington and she had in her hand the landlord's receipt for the cabin returned to him in excellent condition.

"It's all behind you now," Brock said, his face shadowed with concern.

"Come on, Mommie. We're going to Alexandria. Come on." Dudley grabbed her hand. "And we're gonna stay with Mr. Lightner all the time," he said in a state of glee.

"I don't feel right shacking up with you," she told him the following morning, observing Dudley's behavior. The boy had opened the back door and gone into the garden with Jack, tossing his ball to the dog, who seemed to enjoy the sport as much as a race horse loves to run. He'd also put the dishes in the dishwasher, turned on the television in the den and behaved as if he'd lived in that house since birth. When she found him in the den, sitting on the sofa beside Brock and reading a book while Brock read the Sunday paper, she decided to say something about their cozy arrangement.

"I figured you'd have misgivings about this," he said. "So if you want to, you can stay with Mom and Dad, but we'll work here during the day."

"But I can't—"

He interrupted her. "It was Mom's idea. She said you were subject to balk. By the way, when we're married, I want to adopt Dudley. I feel as if he's mine and I want to be sure nobody can take him from me. If you agree, please tell your attorney that and in exchange, Sawyer won't have to pay child support."

"Unless he's had a religious conversion, or wants revenge—which is a definite possibility—I don't think he'd object. I'll write my lawyer now."

She packed a few things for herself and Dudley and moved with him to the home of her future parents-in-law. Staying with her sister presented too much of a risk. Besides, she'd have to share a room with Dudley and she didn't like that idea.

She sent the letter to her lawyer, but she didn't hold out too much hope that her ex-husband would agree at once to Brock's adopting Dudley. He hadn't wanted a child, didn't love him and had abused him whenever he had an excuse to do so and even when he didn't have an excuse. That her child had a bright, sunny personality continually amazed her.

She worked on the book at Brock's house each morning and in the afternoons, she shopped for her wedding gown and her trousseau.

"How can I help you?" Darlene asked her. "You're doing this in three weeks and working. I had a full year. Maybe you can find ideas for bed linens in these catalogs?"

She hadn't thought about bed linens. "Gosh, you are really precious," Allison said. "I want to be a nice-looking bride and that's about all I've been planning for."

Darlene positioned herself on the bed and Allison knew she planned to stay a while. "You'll be a beautiful bride because you're a beautiful woman. What is Dudley planning to call Brock? And he has to have a name for his grandfather. He started right with me, calling me Mom. If I were you, I'd get that straight before the wedding."

Allison leaned over and hugged her future mother-in-law. "I want him to call his grandparents what Brock calls you and I plan to do the same. Is that all right with you?"

"Lord, yes. When Brock told us about you, I prayed that we would be a close, loving family and from the minute I saw you, I knew the Lord had answered my prayers. Well, I've got to grade a stack of papers. See you later."

Ten days after moving to Alexandria, Allison ran up the stairs to Brock's den with the mail, opened a large manila envelope from her lawyer, groped her way to a chair and sat down.

"What is it?" Brock asked her. "What are you staring at?"

"It's fr-from my lawyer."

"Your lawyer? Hey, wait a minute. Open it, for Pete's sake," he said.

"I can't. I'm too nervous."

"And I'm going nuts. Here." He reached back to his desk, got a letter opener and handed it to her.

She opened the envelope, stared at the words written on the sheet of white paper, jumped up, screamed and threw her arms around Brock. "He signed the papers! Oh, my Lord. He signed the papers!" she yelled. He picked her up and swung her around. Then he laughed and laughed. Suddenly he stopped. She looked up at him and saw that tears soaked his face.

Allison wiped his tears with her fingers. "I've never loved you as much as I do this minute. Dudley will finally have a father who loves him."

Brock reread the notarized statement in its entirety, looking for any tricky phrasing. "He spells out that he will not be responsible in any way for Dudley after December nineteenth, 'including and for especially child support payments, health insurance and education or any form of upkeep.' Good. That's what I wanted to see above his signature. I'll put you and Dudley on my insurance plan today."

"I knew he didn't care, but I can't figure out why he did it so readily and especially because he harassed me with that goon in the gray Cadillac," Allison said.

"Not to worry, sweetheart. I expect it will all come to light pretty soon. Right now, I'm too happy to care about why he did it."

"How are we going to explain all this to Dudley?" she asked Brock.

"I don't think it will be difficult because it's what he wants. So why don't we get together and talk to him?"

"So after you get married, Mr. Lightner will be my father and I can call him Dad?"

"Yes and you will call Jason Uncle Jason and my father will be your grandfather."

"Oh, and you'll be my real dad?"

"Lawrence Sawyer is your real dad, but I have adopted you and that makes me your dad instead of him. I'm responsible for you and I will take care of you and your mother."

She'd never dreamed that explaining marriage to a child could be so complicated. Dudley simplified it. "Okay. The preacher will tell us that we can live together. How long do we have to wait?"

"Eleven days," Brock said and pulled in a deep breath.

When that Saturday morning arrived, she'd barely slept the previous night, but she bounced out of bed, dressed and started down the stairs. Halfway down, she met Darlene, who carried a tray of coffee and a bowl of oat cereal.

"If your mother were alive, she'd be doing this," Darlene said. "I'm a poor substitute, but I want you and Brock to be happy and I'll do my share by being as good a mother to you as I can be, starting with staying out of your business."

"And I'll try to be a good daughter to you and Dad," Allison said. She took the tray and walked with Darlene back to her room. About an hour later, Ellen arrived and Allison felt her heart settle down to a near-normal rhythm.

"Are you nervous?" Ellen asked her.

"You'd be nervous, too, if you were six hours from marrying Brock Lightner. I still can't believe it." She reached for the telephone on the second ring. "Hello. This is Allison."

"I know who it is."

Allison flopped down in the nearest chair. "I'm so glad you called. My nerves are simmering."

"Relax, sweetheart. Heck, I know it's hard. These will be the longest six hours of my life. I love you."

"I love you, too, honey. Where's Dudley?"

"Practically pacing the floor. He's driving Jack nuts. He can't wait to get into his tuxedo and he's already started calling me Dad. He said the preacher won't know unless I tell him. Here he is."

"Hurry up and get ready, Mommie. It will soon be six o'clock."

"I'll be ready, son. I'm so happy. See you later."

In Alexandria's Bethel AME Church where he was baptized and which his parents attended weekly, he stood with Jason and Dudley and watched the woman of his dreams float toward him, beautiful and elegant in white silk. Having been married, she walked in alone, although Ellen served as bridesmaid. *To hell with custom,* he thought and took the last few steps to meet her.

"You're the most beautiful being I ever saw," he whispered and took her arm. He listened intently to every word the minister said and he noticed that Allison did, too. When at last she was his wife and the minister told him to kiss his bride, his nerves failed him, but her smile reassured him, and he bent to seal their marriage with a kiss.

They hadn't planned for Dudley to walk out with them, but as if he realized that when the ceremony was over, he had a new daddy, Dudley grabbed Brock's hand and walked out along with the bride and groom.

Darlene hosted a lavish wedding reception and, to his surprise, his father gave Allison a diamond brooch that had belonged to his mother. "Welcome into our family," Reginald told Allison. "Whatever is ours is also yours."

"Hold on, there," Jason said. "Will there be anything left when I get married?"

"Of course," Reginald said. "When you finally tie the knot, you'll inherit everything, because all of your family will have been long dead."

"I love my family, Allison, but I'm ready to go home."

"Me, too. Dudley, you're staying with Mom and Dad tonight." She kissed him and her heart seemed to bloom when she realized that Dudley felt at home with his grandparents and didn't cry to go with her.

"I'm old-fashioned," Brock said when they reached home, picked her up and carried her inside. He'd left a bottle of champagne chilling and a wicker basket of cakes, fruit, cheese and crackers sat on the table beside two long-stem glasses. He poured a glass of champagne for each of them, put the glass to his lips and said, "You've made me a happy man and I'll do my best to see that you are always a happy woman." She could barely hold the glass upright, but she managed a sip.

"Could we eat these goodies later, Brock. You haven't made love to me but once in the past month."

"You can bet I know that, but I'm trying to be a gentleman."

A streak of wickedness shot through her and she winked at him. He grabbed her as she turned toward the stairs, picked her up and dashed up the steps with her.

"I'll teach you to meddle with me," he said. "It's enough that you flirted with me constantly for the past three hours. Take your medicine."

"I'm dying to get it," she said and let her hands travel from his belt buckle downward. The hot, blazing fire of desire jumped into his eyes and she backed off, less sure of herself. He pulled her close, unzipped her dress and swallowed heavily when his gaze took in her scantly clad breasts. He released the left one from the thin strip of lace and sucked it into his mouth. As bold as he, she unhooked his belt buckle, pushed her hands into his pants and began to stroke him.

"Sweetheart, stop it. Otherwise, this won't last three minutes." He put her in bed, stripped off his clothes and began to cherish her.

"You can do that next time," she told him. "I'm almost over the hill. Get in me right now." But he played and toyed with her until she wanted to jump out of her own skin. Frustrated, he flexed her knees, took his penis with both hands and brought him into her. He had never taken her on such a wild and feverish ride and bells rang in her, over her, above her and all around her as she hit the summit knowing that he was right there with her. She was a long time coming down, but when she landed, he wrapped her in his arms.

"And just think, we can do that every night," she said.

He kissed her long and lovingly. "If we do," he said, "at the end of a year, I won't weigh thirty pounds." He got up and went downstairs for the remainder of the champagne and the basket of goodies.

When he came back, she couldn't help smiling. "At last I can sleep all night long in your arms."

The next morning Brock put on his house slippers and robe and went downstairs to make coffee and get the Sunday *Washington Post.* He folded the paper and put it on a tray along with the coffee and warm scones and went back to Allison. He took a few sips of coffee and opened the paper.

"Good Lord, Allison, look at this! 'Lawrence Sawyer, CEO of Midlife Insurance, has been arrested and charged with embezzling one hundred and twenty million dollars of company funds and with making the theft look as if it's the work of the chief accountant. The indictment is the culmination of an eighteen-month investigation.'"

She sat up on the edge of the bed. "Thank goodness he is no longer my son's father."

"Yes, and thank goodness we're completely free of him."

Are they ready for their close-up?

Essence Bestselling Author

LINDA HUDSON-SMITH

Romancing THE RUNWAY

It seems as if supermodels Kennedy and Xavier have
it all—hot careers and each other. But crazed schedules,
constant media attention and unruly paparazzi threaten
their fragile new relationship. Can their searing physical
attraction and soul-deep connection be enough to
guarantee a picture-perfect ending?

*Coming the first week of March 2009
wherever books are sold.*

KIMANI™
ROMANCE

Just in time for Mother's Day comes a new miniseries about the surprise of motherhood!

SURPRISE!

Happy Mother's Day

You're Expecting...

HUDSONS *Crossing*
AlTonya Washington

Riley and Asher's bicoastal marriage is sexy and satisfying. But when living apart becomes too hard for Asher, he gives Riley an ultimatum. And Riley has an even bigger surprise in store, forcing her to decide where her heart and future really lie. Can she walk away from all she's worked for? Or can changing priorities make this couple fly even higher?

Coming the first week of March 2009 wherever books are sold.

In April 2009, look for:

NINE MONTHS WITH THOMAS by **Shirley Hailstock**
Book #2 in *Surprise: You're Expecting!*

In May 2009, look for:

LOVING SPOONFUL by **Candice Poarch**
Book #3 in *Surprise: You're Expecting!*

Welcome to Temptation Island…

Fan Favorite Author

Michelle Monkou

Only in PARADISE

For teacher Athena Crawford, the career opportunity of a
lifetime is set on an idyllic Caribbean island. But then she
and her project's administrator, Collin Winslow, start locking
horns—and sharing kisses. Can their delicate relationship
weather the storms about to break?

"*Sweet Surrender* (4 stars)…is an engaging love story."
—*Romantic Times BOOKreviews*

Coming the first week of March 2009 wherever books are sold.

KIMANI™
ROMANCE

REQUEST YOUR FREE BOOKS!

2 FREE NOVELS
PLUS 2 FREE GIFTS!

KIMANI ROMANCE™

Love's ultimate destination!

YES! Please send me 2 FREE Kimani™ Romance novels and my 2 FREE gifts (gifts are worth about $10). After receiving them, if I don't wish to receive any more books, I can return the shipping statement marked "cancel." If I don't cancel, I will receive 4 brand-new novels every month and be billed just $4.69 per book in the U.S. or $5.24 per book in Canada, plus 25¢ shipping and handling per book and applicable taxes, if any*. That's a savings of over 20% off the cover price! I understand that accepting the 2 free books and gifts places me under no obligation to buy anything. I can always return a shipment and cancel at any time. Even if I never buy another book from Kimani Press, the two free books and gifts are mine to keep forever.

168 XDN EF2D 368 XDN EF3T

Name	(PLEASE PRINT)	
Address		Apt. #
City	State/Prov.	Zip/Postal Code

Signature (if under 18, a parent or guardian must sign)

Mail to The Reader Service:
IN U.S.A.: P.O. Box 1867, Buffalo, NY 14240-1867
IN CANADA: P.O. Box 609, Fort Erie, Ontario L2A 5X3

Not valid to current subscribers of Kimani Romance books.

Want to try two free books from another line?
Call 1-800-873-8635 or visit www.morefreebooks.com.

* Terms and prices subject to change without notice. N.Y. residents add applicable sales tax. Canadian residents will be charged applicable provincial taxes and GST. Offer not valid in Quebec. This offer is limited to one order per household. All orders subject to approval. Credit or debit balances in a customer's account(s) may be offset by any other outstanding balance owed by or to the customer. Please allow 4 to 6 weeks for delivery. Offer available while quantities last.

Your Privacy: Kimani Press is committed to protecting your privacy. Our Privacy Policy is available online at www.eHarlequin.com or upon request from the Reader Service. From time to time we make our lists of customers available to reputable third parties who may have a product or service of interest to you. If you would prefer we not share your name and address, please check here. ☐

KROM08R

National bestselling author

ROCHELLE ALERS

Naughty

Parties, paparazzi, red-carpet catfights...

Wild child Breanna Parker's antics have
always been a ploy to gain attention from
her diva mother and record-producer father.
As her marriage implodes, Bree moves to
Rome. There she meets charismatic Reuben,
who becomes both her romantic and business
partner. But just as she's enjoying her
successful new life, Bree is confronted
with a devastating scandal that threatens
everything she's worked so hard for....

*Coming the first week of March 2009
wherever books are sold.*

KIMANI PRESS™

www.kimanipress.com
www.myspace.com/kimanipress   KPRA1280309

New York Times Bestselling Author

BRENDA JACKSON

invites you to continue your journey
with the always sexy and always satisfying
Madaris family novels….

FIRE AND DESIRE
January 2009

SECRET LOVE
February 2009

TRUE LOVE
March 2009

SURRENDER
April 2009

ARABESQUE®

www.kimanipress.com
www.myspace.com/kimanipress   KPBJREISSUES09